# BACK TO SCHOOL

*A Teacher series novel 1969–70*

Jack Sheffield

CORGI BOOKS

TRANSWORLD PUBLISHERS

Penguin Random House, One Embassy Gardens,
8 Viaduct Gardens, London SW11 7BW
www.penguin.co.uk

Transworld is part of the Penguin Random House group of companies
whose addresses can be found at global.penguinrandomhouse.com

First published in Great Britain in 2020 by Bantam Press
an imprint of Transworld Publishers
Corgi edition published 2021



A CIP catalogue record for this book
is available from the British Library.

ISBN
9780552177016

T

Printed a ... A.

The authorized ... Ireland,
Morr

Pen
future f
is mac

For Mary Cragg, 1945–2020.
*Gorffwys mewn heddwch fy ffrind.*

# Contents

# *Acknowledgements*

Sincere thanks to my editor, Molly Crawford, for bringing this novel to publication, supported by the excellent team at Transworld including Larry Finlay, Bill Scott-Kerr, Jo Williamson, Vivien Thompson, Katie Cregg, Richenda Todd and fellow 'Old Roundhegian' Martin Myers.

Also, thanks to my industrious literary agent, Newcastle United supporter and Britain's leading authority on eighties Airfix modelling kits Philip Patterson of Marjacq Scripts for his encouragement, good humour and deep appreciation of Yorkshire cricket.

I am also grateful to all those who assisted in the research for this novel – in particular: Helen Carr, primary school teacher and literary critic, Harrogate, Yorkshire; Margaret Corroll, retired postmistress, Stoke Hammond, Buckinghamshire; Sylvia Drummond, retired Co-op manager and expert grower of roses, Stoke Hammond, Buckinghamshire; Tony Greenan, Yorkshire's finest headteacher (now retired), Huddersfield, Yorkshire; Ian Haffenden, ex-Royal

Pioneer Corps and custodian of Sainsbury's, Alton, Hampshire; John Kirby, ex-policeman, expert calligrapher and Sunderland supporter, County Durham; Roy Linley, Lead Architect, Strategy & Technology, Unilever Global IT Innovation (now retired) and Leeds United supporter, Leeds, Yorkshire; Jacqui Rogers, Deputy Registrar, allotment holder and tap dancer, Malton, Yorkshire; and all the terrific staff at Waterstones, Alton, including the irreplaceable Simon (now retired), the excellent manager Sam and Scottish travel expert Fiona.

Not forgetting a special thank you to the dynamic events manager, Nikki Bloomer, and the wonderful team at Waterstones MK.

Finally, sincere thanks to my wife, Elisabeth, without whose help the *Teacher* series of novels would never have been written.

# Prologue

I counted them.

There were twenty-nine strangers.

We had gathered in County Hall on a warm June morning in 1969 for a so-called *pool interview* for teaching posts in the West Riding of Yorkshire.

The tiny village school where I had begun my teaching career was about to close and I needed a new job. There had been late resignations in other schools so there were posts to fill before the summer holiday commenced.

It was a time of change.

I was nearly twenty-four years old and the unknown awaited me.

Suddenly a door opened and a woman with all the charm and appearance of an East German interrogator appeared with a clipboard. 'You will be seen in alphabetical order,' she announced in a strident voice. 'If successful, you will report to Room Sixteen on the first floor for processing.' It sounded vaguely Orwellian.

Hushed conversations disturbed the motes of dust that hovered in a shaft of sunlight from a skylight window. It was a room of bleak walls, dark mahogany furniture and the engaging atmosphere of a funeral parlour.

I looked around and gave a strained smile to the attractive young woman sitting opposite. She resembled the pop singer Sandie Shaw with her long straight brown hair and centre parting. In a fashionable blue midi dress she appeared remarkably relaxed.

Miss Clipboard scanned the list of names; then she looked up. 'Miss Penelope Armitage.'

The woman who had caught my eye stood up, slung her crochet string bag over her shoulder and walked confidently into the interview room.

The interviewees never reappeared. I guessed there was another stairway to the first floor.

Finally it was my turn. The fearsome lady reappeared like an annoying cuckoo clock. 'Mr Jack Sheffield,' she shouted.

I followed her to another room and she looked me up and down. She was clearly unimpressed with my gangling six-foot-one-inch frame, unruly brown hair, wide flowery tie and flared trousers that flapped like windswept sails.

'Through there,' she instructed and pointed to a pair of imposing doors. 'The chairman is Mr Hardcastle. He's a local councillor on the Education Committee.'

I walked into a large smoke-filled room where a panel of six men in ill-fitting suits faced me from behind a huge desk.

I looked for a chair but there wasn't one so I stood there facing them.

It was reminiscent of William Yeames's painting *And When Did You Last See Your Father?* depicting the son of a Royalist being questioned by Parliamentarians during the English Civil War.

Happily, the interview was brief and to the point. I was clearly part of a production line. Their task was to make sure all the schools in the area had a full complement of teachers.

Mr Hardcastle, a balding man smoking a pipe, was looking at my letter of application: 'I see you are a sportsman, Mr Sheffield.'

'Yes, I'm keen on all sports. I play rugby for Upper Wharfedale.'

'Good team,' he said knowingly.

A man with a narrow weasel face at the end of the row stubbed out a cigarette and leaned forward. 'Norman Little needs a sporty young man in his top junior class.'

The others nodded in agreement.

A rotund man placed his cigar in one of the communal ashtrays. 'He's already got that Miss What's-'er-name.'

The chairman scanned the list of schools before him. 'You're right, Arthur, but he needs someone in the top juniors, preferably a man.'

Arthur nodded knowingly. 'Yes, for a bit o' discipline.'

The chairman scribbled on a postcard and handed it to me. 'Well done, Mr Sheffield, a successful interview. You'll do fine.' He pointed to a narrow staircase in the far corner of the room. 'Take this postcard to Room Sixteen.'

On the first floor was a long corridor leading to a large room. It was full of desks behind which clerical assistants were completing a form-filling exercise with individual teachers.

A spotty young man gestured me to sit down. 'Name and school?' he said.

'Jack Sheffield.' I passed over the postcard. 'Heather View Primary School.'

He raised his eyebrows, gave a chuckle and began to write.

It was over in a few minutes and he passed me a sealed envelope. 'All y'need t'know is in 'ere. Good luck.'

I thought he added 'You'll need it' but couldn't be sure.

When I walked outside to the car park I spotted the Sandie Shaw lookalike leaning against a rusty red Mini and reading the contents of her letter. She glanced up at me and smiled. 'So where have they put you?' she asked.

'Heather View Primary.'

She grinned. 'Hey, me too.'

This was good news. She was a striking young woman, around five feet nine inches tall, and with her high cheekbones and slim figure she looked like a model.

It was time for introductions.

'I'm Jack Sheffield.'

She seemed amused as we shook hands. 'Penny Armitage,' she said and looked down at the sheet of instructions. 'It says here we have to attend a meeting at the school on Monday, the first of September.'

'Yes, a couple of days before the start of term. So I'll see you then.'

'Heather View,' she mused. 'Sounds lovely.'

'Yes, I suppose it does.'

We couldn't have been more wrong.

Little did I know then that the year ahead would determine the teacher I was destined to be and the man I would become.

But at that moment I was happy.

I had a job and it was time to go back to school.

# Chapter One

## *First Shall Be Last*

It was early morning on Monday, 1 September 1969 when I drove my Morris Minor Traveller up a steep hill towards Heather View Church of England Primary School in West Yorkshire.

Soon I was weaving through narrow streets and crumbling terraced houses. It was an estate with cluttered back yards and graffiti-covered walls. I saw a 'SCHOOL' sign and pulled up outside a Victorian building of weathered grey stone, high arched windows and a black slate roof. It was surrounded by a tall chain-link fence and weeds were growing through the cracked concrete at its base.

The sight was depressing.

It looked like a prison.

The one saving grace was the vast moorland that stretched out behind it down into a steep valley and then on to the heather-covered Pennine Hills. To the north were the Yorkshire Dales and to the east the industrial cities of Bradford and Leeds.

A heavy chain and padlock hung from the tall metal gates. It was clear I was first to arrive so I looked for somewhere to park. A bus pulled up behind me so I moved on quickly and did two swift right turns into a narrow cobbled back street. I was aware of a red-haired woman leaning over her wooden gate and staring at me. She glowered, shook her head and hurried back inside.

I collected my leather satchel and an armful of posters, locked my car and walked back to the school where a familiar figure was standing by the gate.

'Hi, Jack, another early bird.'

It was Penny Armitage, carrying a large cardboard box. She looked great in blue flared jeans, a floral shirt and a cord waistcoat.

I smiled. 'Penny, good to see you. Do you want a hand?'

She put the box on the pavement. 'I'm fine but thanks anyway . . . just resources for my classroom.'

The local bus roared past back down the hill.

'Did you come on the bus?' I asked.

'No, my dad gave me a lift. We had a look at the school last week and he was worried my clapped-out Mini would struggle to get up here. So it's in for a service. I'm collecting it tonight so I'll be fine for the start of term.'

I nodded. 'That's good.'

In spite of the late-summer sun a cool breeze blew and I could barely imagine what it must be like in winter for this hilltop school.

Penny looked back down the street. 'So, how about you? Did you drive here?'

'Yes, I'm parked round the corner.'

She rummaged in her shoulder bag and took out a

crumpled envelope. 'I guess you got your letter from the deputy head?'

'Mrs Priestley?'

'Yes . . . and it definitely said nine o'clock.'

Suddenly a battered blue Ford Transit van appeared and pulled up with a screech of brakes. On the side was painted in bold letters:

**J. PRIESTLEY & SONS Ltd. of Long Steeton**
***Purveyors of Highest Quality Pork Sausages***

The driver, a huge balding man with a friendly face, wound down his window and waved. From the passenger seat emerged a squat lady with a head of tight brown curls, rosy cheeks and a bright-eyed smile. She hurried across the road carrying a bulky shopping bag and waving a bunch of keys.

'Hello, I'm Barbara. Sorry if I'm a few minutes late. My Jimmy had to make a delivery.' She nodded towards the large van that had driven off down the hill and grinned. 'He's a butcher.'

She put down her bag and studied us for a moment. 'So . . . you must be Penny and Jack. Welcome to Heather View.'

We shook hands and I immediately felt at ease with this engaging woman.

'Well, I hope you'll be happy here. We'll have around two hundred children on roll this term, all from the Milltown estate.' She gestured towards the rows of terraced houses. 'It's a tough place to work but I'm sure you'll be fine.'

She unlocked the gates. 'After you' – she gestured – 'and welcome to hell,' she added with a grin.

Penny looked concerned. 'Hell?'

Barbara smiled. 'That's what I was told when I first arrived but don't worry, most of the children are fine. It's just the local teenagers that cause problems from time to time, not to mention a few psycho parents.'

'What sort of problems?' I asked.

She pointed towards a broken window and sighed. 'That sort of problem. We get our fair share of vandalism.'

Penny frowned. 'What about the local police?'

Barbara was thoughtful. 'Well . . . we have a good local bobby, Phil Moxon. He's a police constable and works hard but he's up against it on this estate. You'll see him on his motorbike and he calls in to do road-safety talks. A lovely young man. Lives in our village and buys his meat from our shop.' She nodded as if this were high praise. 'He gets on well with my Jimmy.'

She unlocked the door and we walked into a large, bare entrance hall. There was a wooden table and above it a noticeboard on which was pinned a single sheet of paper. 'I put this up yesterday.'

I looked with interest at the list of my new colleagues.

*CLASS 1. Miss P. Armitage*
*CLASS 2. Mrs A. Clegg*
*CLASS 3. Mrs B. Priestley*
*CLASS 4. Mr T. Farthing*
*CLASS 5. Miss C. Brooksbank*
*CLASS 6. Mr J. Sheffield*

Next to the noticeboard was a door labelled 'Secretary' and beyond that another on which a brass plate was attached. It was inscribed: 'Mr. N. Little, Cert. Ed. Headmaster'.

'When will the head be coming in?' I asked.

There was an awkward pause. 'Norman . . . not today,' she said. I sensed a hidden meaning behind the brevity. 'Anyway, let's have a coffee and then I'll show you around.'

The staff-room was like many I had seen in the past. There was an eclectic collection of armchairs that looked like the leftovers from a jumble sale; a battered coffee table with a large glass ashtray; a sink and a worktop alongside a bookcase containing miscellaneous educational pamphlets and newsletters plus, incongruously, a packet of Flintstones Iced Biscuits.

Soon we were sipping coffee and Barbara produced a packet of chocolate digestives from her voluminous shopping bag.

She waited until we were relaxed and then looked at Penny. 'I imagine you're looking forward to your first teaching post.'

Penny nodded eagerly. 'Yes. I just hope I can settle in and remember everything I was taught at college.'

'Well, believe it or not, this was *my* first teaching post as well. I trained at Bretton Hall near Wakefield when it opened as a teacher-training college. Then Jimmy bought our butcher's shop in the next village. So I've been here for ten years.'

'I guess you must have been happy to stay here so long,' said Penny.

Barbara considered this for a moment. 'Most of the time,' she said quietly.

'What about the rest of the staff?' I asked.

'Well, Norman came a couple of years ago when Miss Tipple retired. She was lovely. So you and I, Penny, are in the infant department. The other teacher is Audrey Clegg, a really good colleague.' She looked up at me. 'Then in the juniors there's Travis.'

'Travis?' Penny and I spoke at once.

'Mr Farthing in Class Four. Bit quirky. A train buff, keeps quoting Shakespeare and loves his teaching. A fount of knowledge. You'll like him. Then, next door to you, Jack, is Connie Brooksbank. Came here four years ago from Durham.' There was a pause as if she were searching for an apt description. 'Anyway, you'll meet them all on Wednesday.'

She took a sheet of paper from her bag and pinned it on the noticeboard. 'Meanwhile, here's the playground-duty rota. I always do the first day to give everyone a bit of breathing space.'

I was puzzled. In my previous school all the teachers were always in school preparing their classrooms a week before the start of the new academic year. 'Barbara . . . what about tomorrow? I presume there will be a staff meeting.'

Barbara paused, searching for an appropriate response. 'The thing is, Jack, Norman doesn't go in for staff meetings.' She sensed our reaction. 'But don't let that stop you coming in if you wish. I'll be here.'

When we had finished our coffee Barbara gave us a brief tour of the school. There was a large hall with dining tables and chairs stacked behind a garish curtain. On each side of the hall was a corridor, each with three classrooms. Class 1 looked as though a bomb had dropped. It needed a good clean and old wooden furniture was scattered around the room.

Barbara sighed. 'Sorry, Penny, the supply teacher left it in a bit of a mess and the caretaker has a bad back.'

Penny looked disheartened.

'I'll give you a hand,' Barbara said. 'It shouldn't take long to arrange it how you would like it.'

'And I can help,' I offered.

Penny shook her head. 'Thanks, Jack, but you'll probably be busy in your room.'

'Maybe,' I said cautiously. I looked at Barbara. 'Please could we have a look at Class Six?'

'Come on,' she said. 'You'll soon gather we're not well off for resources.' She sighed. 'It's Norman who holds the purse strings.'

Meanwhile, Penny had already started to shift furniture.

'I'll be back,' I said.

She gave me a winsome smile. 'Thanks, Jack. See you later.'

Barbara and I walked across the hall and down a short corridor filled with coat pegs. 'You've got the top juniors, Jack. From here they all go to the Ridge Comprehensive. Five miles away. It's near the original Old Mill on the other side of the valley. There's a school bus from the estate. We're lucky. It's a decent school with a good ethos and a hard-working head.'

We arrived at a shabby, paint-blistered door with a cardboard number six pinned to the frame. 'Here it is. Come on in.'

I was surprised when I saw my classroom. It was clean,

fortunately, but surprisingly bare. It felt as though I was walking back into the 1950s. All the old wooden desks had sloping lids with inkwells and they were lined up in four straight rows facing the teacher's desk and the blackboard.

Barbara saw my reaction. 'Jack . . . this is how the head likes it. So don't change anything. Norman takes one lesson each week with them – handwriting.' The expression on her face spoke volumes.

Suddenly the windows began to shake. I looked up in alarm. It felt like an earthquake. Then there was the loud hoot of a train whistle. We both looked out of the window. Beyond the fence in the valley bottom appeared the magnificent sight of a steam train pulling four carriages.

'You'll get used to that,' said Barbara with a wry smile. 'It's the Keighley and Worth Valley Railway. Runs from Keighley to Oxenhope. Ask Travis, he's an enthusiast.' She looked at her wristwatch. 'Right, things to do. Let's meet up later in the staff-room for one of my Jimmy's pork pies and a mug of tea.'

'Sounds good, Barbara. Many thanks.'

She hurried off and I walked back to Penny's room. She was arranging small Formica-topped tables into groups.

'So, what do you think?' I asked.

Penny sighed and looked around the room. 'I didn't imagine my first post would be like this when I left St John's but I suppose beggars can't be choosers.'

I smiled. 'St John's in York?'

'Yes.'

'That's a coincidence. I trained there as well. Left in sixty-seven.'

Her green eyes were full of curiosity. 'What brought you here?'

'I was in a village school on the outskirts of Leeds and suddenly we were told it was closing. According to the local authority it wasn't *economically viable*.'

'So . . . do you live locally?'

'I'm renting a place – Ivy Cottage – on the High Street in Lotherswicke village, up near Skipton.'

'I know it,' said Penny. 'I was brought up round there. My mum and dad live in Askrigg.'

'So, where are you now?'

'In a flatshare in Cold Beck.'

I grinned. 'Cold Beck? Sounds a bit bleak.'

'Actually, it's really pretty, north of Skipton but tiny . . . just a hamlet.'

I looked around at the detritus of chairs, tables and cupboards. 'Would you like some help?'

'Maybe later,' she said with determined independence, 'but thanks anyway.'

At midday Barbara called us to join her in the staff-room. On the table was a pot of tea, milk and sugar and two large pork pies.

'Thanks for this, Barbara.'

She smiled. 'He's proud of his pies is my Jimmy.'

'Delicious,' said Penny as she bit into a slice.

Barbara drank her tea and stood up. 'Well, I'll leave you to it if you don't mind. I need a few things from the Corner Shop.' She pointed out of the window. 'It's only a couple of minutes away. Very handy. If you go left out of the gate to the top of the hill you can't miss it. It sells everything and there's a Post Office counter as well.' She looked at her wristwatch. 'In the meantime Jimmy will be back around four to pick me up when I'll need to lock up.'

'Thanks,' said Penny. 'My dad is collecting me before then but I should like to come in tomorrow.'

'Me too,' I said. There was a lot to do.

'That's fine,' said Barbara. 'I'll be here at nine to open up.'

She hurried out in her busy, bustling style and we watched her walk quickly across the tarmac playground.

Penny sipped her tea and sat back in her chair. 'So . . . is this what you expected?'

I paused before replying. 'Not really, but the deputy is supportive.'

She sighed and looked out of the window at the sprawling council estate with its chaotic clutter of television aerials. 'It looks to be a tough area.'

'We'll cope,' I said, trying to sound more confident than I felt.

Penny chased a few crumbs of pastry around her plate. 'I'm just glad I got the job. I was beginning to panic towards the end of my teaching course.'

Now we were on our own I found I was enjoying our relaxed conversation.

'My education tutor at St John's was Jim Fairbank,' I said. 'Did you come across him?'

Suddenly Penny's eyes were shining. 'Yes, he was my tutor on final teaching practice. I was lucky to have him. So supportive. When I left he said to me, *Teach well and you'll change lives for ever* . . . I'll never forget it.'

I smiled. 'He said the same to me.'

She put down her mug and steepled her fingers. There

was a long silence. Finally she looked at me. 'If I hadn't got a job, I was planning to go to the Isle of Wight.'

'For the festival?'

'Yes.' She pursed her lips. 'So Seb went on his own. He bought a weekend ticket for two pounds ten shillings and took off.'

'Seb?'

'My boyfriend.' She shook her head. 'I guess he's still there, spreading love and peace. I've not heard from him since.' She stared out of the window. 'Probably found someone new.'

*Boyfriend,* I thought. For a moment I felt sad. Then I saw the confusion in her eyes and tried to lift the mood. 'I heard Bob Dylan was appearing.'

Penny was suddenly animated. 'Yes, he's brilliant . . . and the Who and Joe Cocker and the Moody Blues. It was a great line-up this year.' Suddenly she got up and stretched. 'Anyway, back to reality. Time to create a painting corner near the sink.' And we returned to our classrooms.

At around two thirty, when Penny and I were standing outside in the sunshine, a Land Rover pulled up outside school and a tall, rangy, weather-beaten man got out and waved.

'Here's my dad, so see you tomorrow.' She hurried across the yard, and then paused to wave as she climbed in the car. Her father looked briefly at me before driving off.

It was then I heard the whistle of a train and I walked round the building to the back of the school and stood by the high fence to watch it steam by. It was a dramatic sight and I began to consider using it as a topic for the children in my class. History, geography, science, stories, poems and artwork . . . it was all there.

Then I heard a harsh, guttural cough. Backing on to the gable end of the school building was a dilapidated cycle shed. An old bicycle had been parked there and a man was sitting on the grass and leaning against the stone wall. His eyes were closed. He was oblivious to my presence and looked content as he took a final drag of his cigarette.

I walked over to him. 'Hello, who are you?'

He started and the cigarette dropped from his lips. His thin, pockmarked face showed anger. 'More to t'point, who the 'ell are you?'

'I'm Jack Sheffield, one of the new teachers. So, what about you?'

'Ah'm t'caretaker.' He jumped to his feet. 'Anyway . . . what y'doin' creepin' round 'ere?'

'I heard the train and came to look.'

First impressions of this scrawny little man in his filthy T-shirt were not favourable. In my last school the caretaker had been a hard-working lady with a heart of gold. Even so, I stretched out my hand in greeting. 'Pleased to meet you, Mr . . .?'

'Skinner, Eric Skinner.' He gave me a reluctant handshake and a suspicious look.

'If you're not busy now, Mr Skinner, the other new teacher, Miss Armitage, is in Class One and I'm sure she would appreciate some help. Her classroom is in a bit of a state and could do with a clean-up.'

He laughed and shook his head in disdain. 'Class One? Y'jokin'. Ah never go in there. There's allus a mess wi' paint an' suchlike. Teachers clean up themselves. An' in any case ah've gorra bad back.'

He sat down again and lit another cigarette. It was clear the conversation was over . . . for now at least.

An hour later I was taking a final look at my classroom. There was satisfaction in seeing the pinboards covered in bright posters of the universe, a human skeleton, multiplication tables and a map of Great Britain.

Then, out of the window, I saw a skinny, shaven-headed man in dirty overalls walking towards the entrance door. Barbara must have seen him first because she had hurried out to meet him. Suddenly there were raised voices and I thought I had better offer support. When I walked outside I found a heated exchange was taking place.

'It's that 'eadmaster ah want t'talk to.'

The man swayed slightly and appeared drunk. Cupped in his left hand was a cigarette. His right hand was hidden behind his back. He was unshaven and, as I approached, I smelled the stink of alcohol and sweat hanging in the air like a rancid cloud.

'He's not in today,' replied Barbara evenly. She was standing her ground bravely.

'Well, this is jus' a warnin'. Ah don't want 'im givin' my lad a 'ard time when 'e comes back t'school. Las' term 'e caned 'im f'doin' nowt.'

I stepped forward and stood alongside Barbara. 'Can I help?'

The man took a final drag of his cigarette and flicked it at our feet. He looked up at me. 'Who's this long streak o' piss?'

I looked at Barbara. 'Shall I see him off the premises?'

The man sneered, apparently undeterred by my size and physique.

Barbara frowned and gave an imperceptible shake of her head. 'I'll deal with it, Jack,' she said quietly. There was a note of caution in her voice. She turned back to our unwelcome visitor. 'Mr Speight . . . you need to go home,' she said firmly.

At that moment he held up his right hand – to my horror, he was gripping a baling hook.

It was a tool I recognized from working on a farm in my younger days when similar hooks were used to move heavy bales. He held the round wooden handle in his fist and the metal hook, about eight inches long, projected between his fingers.

He waved it in front of our faces. 'An' mebbe ah'll be back wi' this.'

I stepped in front of Barbara. 'Like Mrs Priestley said . . . you need to go home.'

He swayed and looked up at me with red-rimmed eyes. I towered over him. Finally he came to a decision. He turned and lurched back towards the school gate.

'Thanks, Jack,' said Barbara quietly. 'Though that could have been nasty.'

'Maybe,' I said. 'A violent man. He looked out of his skull.'

'He usually is. I thought he was still in Leeds prison.'

'So . . . will you ring the police?'

Barbara nodded. 'I'll do it now. They know him well.' She gave a wry smile. 'Well, Jack, you've just met your first parent . . . that was Mad Micky.'

*

It was four o'clock and I was packing my satchel when a tall, lean figure wearing a dark suit and a clerical collar walked into my classroom.

'Welcome to Heather View, Mr Sheffield. I'm Piers Witherspoon, the Chair of Governors.'

We shook hands. 'Pleased to meet you, Mr Witherspoon.'

He gave me an engaging smile. 'Please call me Piers.'

'Thanks, Piers. I'm Jack.'

I was intrigued by this new arrival. He looked around sixty with greying hair and his direct manner exuded confidence.

'I'm vicar of St Peter and All Angels. It's in the old part of Milltown in the market square. You must come to visit when you are settled. We have a small but loyal congregation.'

'Thank you, I shall, but you'll gather I'm a stranger here.'

He smiled. 'Jack, there are no strangers in my church . . . only friends who haven't met.'

I was impressed by the warmth of this gentle and articulate man.

He glanced around the classroom and gestured towards my display of posters. 'Very impressive,' he said with another beatific smile. 'Anyway, mustn't keep you. I noticed Mrs Priestley is getting ready to lock up.'

'Yes, in fact I was about to go to my car.'

'Then I shall see you out.'

At the school gate we both waved to Barbara as she climbed into her husband's van. 'Wonderful lady,' he said. 'We're lucky to have such a dedicated teacher.'

Once we reached the pavement Piers looked up and down the road. 'So . . . where did you park your car?'

I pointed across the road. 'In the back street behind these terraced houses.'

Suddenly he looked aghast. 'But it's Monday!'

'I don't understand.'

'Oh dear . . . you soon will.'

I shall never forget the sight that met my eyes. Row after row of washing lines were hung across the back alley. My car was hidden behind sheets, shirts and a variety of undergarments.

It took a long time for Piers to lift each washing line carefully as I drove beneath it. When we reached the last one the red-haired lady I had seen that morning was leaning on her gate and smiling. 'Be careful, Vicar,' she shouted. 'Ah don't want you dropping my knickers.' She hurried away chuckling to herself.

I got out of my car as I reached the junction to the main road. 'Sorry about that, Piers . . . and thanks for your help.'

'It was a pleasure, Jack,' he said with a flushed face. 'Safe journey home. I'm sure you've had a busy day.'

I looked back at the school and reflected. 'Yes, first in and last out.'

Piers nodded phlegmatically as I drove away. 'Yes indeed,' he murmured to himself. 'Matthew twenty-six, verse sixteen. "The last shall be first, and the first last: for many be called, but few chosen."'

He glanced back at the curving rows of washing lines and gave a gentle smile.

## Chapter Two

# *This Little World*

Pale shafts of autumnal sunshine lit up the distant Pennine Hills as I looked out of my bedroom window. The season was changing and in the hedgerows teardrop cobwebs shivered in the cool breeze.

On the radio the number-one record, Zager & Evans's 'In the Year 2525', was predicting the future of mankind whereas I was simply wondering about today. It was Wednesday, 3 September and my first day of teaching at Heather View beckoned.

As I drove out of Lotherswicke village wisps of wood smoke hovered above the roofs of the cottages. On the High Street small boys were throwing sticks up into the branches of a horse chestnut tree while at their feet glossy conkers were released from their spiky green shells. Beyond the grassy border outside The Weaver's Arms, chrysanthemums, amber, red and gold, were bright in the early-morning light. It was a sight that fed the spirit and satisfied the soul.

As I turned south on the A629 I pondered on what might await me. I had worked hard the previous day to prepare my classroom, create a nature table, collect exercise books and pencils from the stock cupboard and explore the meagre school library. Apart from Penny and the deputy head I had not met any of the other staff and wondered what was in store.

When I pulled into the school car park Barbara Priestley was in conversation with a short, portly lady wearing an unflattering and shapeless long brown cardigan.

'Hello, Jack. Come and meet Audrey.'

Piers Witherspoon had told me Audrey was forty years old and a regular church-goer. She had a pale oval face and gave me a hesitant smile.

'Hello, Jack,' she said. 'Welcome to Milltown. I do hope you will be happy here.'

'Thank you, Audrey. I'm sure I shall.'

Audrey frowned suddenly. 'Oh dear! I would ban those. It's teaching them bad habits.'

She gestured towards two boys who had opened a box of twenty-five sweet cigarettes and were pretending to puff away. A picture of the pop group the Monkees featured on the front of the box.

'That's Keith Lumb and Terry Duff, Jack,' said Barbara. 'They're in your class. Don't worry, they're good boys.' She turned to Audrey. 'I imagine they're simply imitating their parents, Audrey. It's understandable.'

Audrey didn't appear convinced. 'It may be *understandable* but it can lead to bad habits.'

'I'm sure you're right,' said Barbara pacifically. 'However, a new year beckons.'

'Well, I've got a lot to collect from my car,' I said, 'so see you inside.'

Barbara and Audrey walked into school while I opened the back door of my car and unloaded a large cardboard box. It contained a collection of newspaper cuttings about the recent moon landing plus an inflatable globe, a poster of the moon and a tall plastic model of Apollo 11. Six weeks ago Neil Armstrong and Buzz Aldrin had been the first men to walk on the moon. I thought it would be the perfect subject to capture the imagination of the children.

As I walked across the playground, parents of the new starters were beginning to gather. Many of them looked anxious and I could see that Penny was in for a busy morning. Suddenly a very large lady approached me. She was wearing a pinny and a headscarf that covered the multitude of rollers in her hair.

'Are you one o' t'new teachers?' she called out.

I stopped in my tracks and put down the box. It was important to make positive contact with a parent and I hoped this one wasn't carrying a baling hook. 'Yes, I'm Mr Sheffield, the new teacher in Class Six. How can I help?'

'Ah'm Betty Sweet.' She looked down adoringly at her son, who was picking his nose and then licking his finger. 'An' this is my Willy.'

'Pleased to meet you.'

'Ah need t'tell y'summat.'

'And what's that?'

' 'E teks after 'is father does my Willy.'

'I see,' I said . . . but I didn't.

' 'E's daft as a brush but 'e means well.'

'Is that Willy or his father?'

'*Both,* Mr Sheffield, so ah'll tell y'summat f'nothin'.'

'And what's that?'

'Ah don't know if ah'm comin' or goin' today.'

I was still none the wiser. It was time to bring this conversation to a brisk conclusion. 'Well, if you take Willy into Class One and speak to Miss Armitage, the other new teacher, I'm sure you can discuss it with her.'

'Fair enough, ah'll do that.' She nudged Willy, who was continuing to excavate his nostrils. 'An' y'can tell yer teacher it's y'birthday on Sat'day.'

'Don't wanna,' said Willy truculently.

'You'll do as yer told or you'll get *what-for.*'

Willy immediately acquiesced and nodded vigorously. While I could only conjecture, it was clear the little boy had a clear understanding of the meaning of *what-for.* She marched off dragging the reticent Willy behind her.

As I picked up my box and walked on, it occurred to me that in the school register he would be recorded as Sweet William, which should give Penny a smile.

When I walked into the entrance hall a short plump man in his mid-fifties was standing outside the headteacher's office. He wore a creased grey suit. The elbows were shiny and his trousers concertinaed over his suede shoes. There were stains on his tie and a beer belly stretched his shirt. First impressions were not inspiring. I put down my box of resources on the table.

He looked up at me. 'I'm Little,' he said curtly.

Since he stood only five feet four inches tall I looked down at him; I resisted the temptation to agree. An attempt at a greasy comb-over had been made on his balding pate.

'And you must be Sheffield.' He thrust out a podgy right hand.

'Pleased to meet you,' I said as we shook hands.

He looked me up and down. 'Come in,' he said abruptly, 'we need to have a word.'

The room seemed strangely bare. There were no pictures on the walls, nothing to celebrate the children's achievements, just fading magnolia and the smell of cigarette smoke. He walked behind a large mahogany desk that would have been at home in a bank manager's office with its blotting pad and a pen in a holder.

'Shut the door,' he called out as he sat down in a large leather chair. It creaked loudly under his weight. Behind him on the windowsill next to a box of matches was a packet of his favoured cigarettes, Piccadilly No. 7. Barbara had told me that, regular as clockwork, each morning he called in to the Corner Shop and bought a packet of twenty for three shillings and tenpence, largely because they came with Green Shield stamps. Apparently he was saving up for an 8-mm movie camera for which you needed to fill eight books. As you got one stamp for each sixpence spent and each book contained 1,280 stamps, I guessed it would take a long time.

He cleared his throat as I remained standing, and said, 'Just so you're clear, in this school there's a *right way* and a *wrong way*.'

'Pardon?'

He pointed a nicotine-stained finger towards the council estate. 'You need to understand right from the off that these people only understand *discipline*. We don't do mollycoddling here. If there's anything you can't deal with you send them to me.' He nodded towards the corner of the room. On the rail of a wooden chair hung a large bamboo cane. 'I only use that on the juniors. It's a slipper for the infants. Important to be fair.' He nodded as if he had dispensed the Wisdom of Solomon.

'I understand,' I said without a shred of enthusiasm.

This was very different from my last school where the children were well behaved, enjoyed their work and corporal punishment was considered a thing of the past.

'I want you to organize boys' games and keep the top juniors busy. We do the three Rs here.'

'I see,' I said dubiously.

'There's none of those high-brow Plowden recommendations here in Milltown,' he added defiantly.

The 1967 Plowden Report had recommended a move from rote learning to a more child-centred approach. It was the style of teaching I had adopted and that had been encouraged both at college and my last school.

Mr Little was becoming red in the face. 'We're not one of those arty-farty schools. So . . . any questions?'

It was clear the meeting was at an end.

'Registers?' I said simply.

'See Miss Verity.' He nodded towards the door. 'She deals with all that.'

He opened his desk drawer, took out a manila folder labelled 'Education Welfare Officer' and began to study a list of names. It was time to go.

With a heavy heart I tapped on the door of the secretary's office and walked in. Behind a tidy desk sat a slim, diminutive lady in her fifties with a short bob of ash-blonde hair.

She was wearing a crisp cream blouse, grey skirt and a knitted green cardigan.

'Good morning, I'm Jack Sheffield.'

'Ah, Mr Sheffield, do come in,' she said with a beaming smile. 'I've been looking forward to meeting you. I'm Edith Verity, the school secretary.' She stood up to shake hands and moved with the grace of a ballet dancer. 'Did you have a good journey into school?'

'Yes, thank you.'

She was sincere and engaging. 'You live in a beautiful area . . . the gateway to the Dales. I visit there often.'

'Yes, lovely countryside. I'm very fortunate.'

She looked down at her desk. 'Well, I have your registers ready. There are thirty-six children in Class Six. Twenty-two are on free dinners.'

'Thank you,' I said. 'I'm sure I shall be back to seek your advice.'

She gave me a gentle smile. 'And I shall always do my best to help . . . and please call me Edith.'

As I left I felt reassured. From past experience I knew the value of a good school secretary.

I walked back into the entrance hall where I found the other two teachers were waiting to greet me. They were a contrasting pair.

'Hello, Jack, I'm Connie.' She was almost six feet tall and gave me a level stare, her steel-grey eyes surveying me like an X-ray scanner. A twenty-six-year-old, slim, with short-cropped jet-black hair and a severe fringe, she wore a figure-hugging red blouse and a short black skirt. 'I teach next door to you.' There was a spiky confidence about her demeanour and a distinct north-east accent.

'And I'm Travis.' He smiled and we shook hands. Of average height, wiry and with fashionably long hair, he wore an oatmeal cord suit, polished brown shoes, a crumpled white shirt and what looked like an old school tie. 'I teach Class Four.' He pointed further down the corridor. An animated thirty-year-old, he looked as if he were conducting an orchestra as he spoke, with his long delicate fingers and expressive gestures. 'Let me give you a hand.' He picked up the globe and the rolled-up poster from the open box.

'I'll see you later,' said Connie. 'Call in if you need anything.'

'Thanks,' I said.

We both watched her stride purposefully towards her classroom. 'You'll get used to Connie . . . very *direct*,' muttered Travis. 'Bit of a man-eater, so take care.'

'Really?' I said with feigned surprise.

Travis nodded. 'Yes, Jack . . . you don't mess with Connie.'

By the time the bell rang to announce the beginning of another school year I had placed an exercise book and a sharp HB pencil on each desk. My registers were open with two biros, black and red, placed alongside. The children had lined up outside the classroom door full of expectation. I picked up the attendance register and walked out to meet them. They eyed me with suspicion, curiosity etched on their faces.

'When I call your name you will walk in and sit down quietly.' They stared at me in surprise and not a word was spoken. I stood by the classroom door and read out their names in alphabetical order: 'Sandra Asquith, Reggie Atha, Ronnie Atha . . .' *Clearly twins,* I thought. 'Susan Bell, Charlie Dewhirst . . .' And so it went on.

Slowly each row was filled by both boys and girls. I knew that if I had left it to them to choose a desk the boys and girls would have finished up on either side of the classroom.

After collecting the meagre amount of dinner money I introduced myself and told them I expected good behaviour. 'You need to set the standard for the younger ones to follow. Behave and you'll enjoy this year. Don't . . . and you won't.'

I had always preferred to start tough and ease off later.

Then I told them our first topic concerned space and the moon landing and I could see the interest in their eyes. Soon they were all writing in their new exercise books. I walked from one desk to another while assessing the huge range of ability and noting who would require the most help. Only a handful could write a sentence and I spent the next hour helping with spellings and sentence construction before morning assembly led by Barbara. The head made a brief appearance and told everyone to behave and work hard.

At morning break we gathered in the staff-room. Edith was serving hot drinks and explaining to me the system of staff contributions towards the purchase of tea, coffee, sugar and biscuits.

Barbara was on playground duty and the previous evening she had left her *Daily Mirror* on the staff-room table.

Norman lit up a cigarette, picked up the newspaper and flicked through the pages. The headline 'DESOLATION ROW' caught his attention and he scanned the article about the second Isle of Wight Festival.

'Load of drop-outs,' he muttered.

'What's that?' asked Audrey.

He shook his head in disgust. 'All these layabouts at this festival on the Isle of Wight. It says here "a hundred thousand hippies and weirdies left behind a huge tip of rubbish that will take two weeks to clear".'

'Weirdies?' questioned Connie. 'Seems a strange word.'

'Well, that's what it says,' said Norman, pointing to the article.

Penny looked up. 'My boyfriend went there,' she said quietly.

Suddenly the rest of us pretended to be absorbed in anything but this conversation but made sure we were listening.

'It says here they were pushing drugs,' added Norman triumphantly. 'So what sort of boyfriend have you got?'

Penny exuded calm. 'Seb is training to be a doctor.'

*This was news,* I thought.

Norman folded the paper, tossed it back on to the coffee table, stubbed out his cigarette and stood up. 'Well, he'll get plenty of practice, won't he?' He walked out and everyone visibly relaxed.

I waited.

Someone was bound to ask.

Predictably it was Connie. 'What's Seb like?' she asked bluntly.

'Annoying,' said Penny with a mischievous grin.

'Annoying?' echoed Connie.

'Yes,' said Penny, 'because he's good at simply *everything*.'

I was pondering this with a slight hint of irritation when the bell rang to dash away thoughts of what it might mean.

It was clear the children were interested in the first topic I'd chosen for them: the recent moon landing. One billion people had watched the epic moment on television when Neil Armstrong set foot on the moon. I had been at my mother's house in Leeds and she had celebrated with one of her specialities: namely, a sausage and prawn ring in her best bowl along with a few bottles of pale ale. Incongruous it might have been but it was presented in a spirit of triumphalism.

During the lunch break I had moved the children's cumbersome desks to the side of the room and arranged the chairs in a semi-circle. The children were surprised when they walked in and sat down.

I had inflated my plastic globe and pinned the poster of the moon to the front of my desk. The toy moon rocket was propped on a chair in front of the poster. On the blackboard I had written 'Apollo 11' and 'The Sea of Tranquillity'.

'Girls and boys, six weeks ago men landed on the moon. Who can tell me anything about it?'

There was excited chatter and almost every hand was raised.

Janet Stubbs was smiling. 'I know, sir.'

'Go on, Janet.'

'It were that Neil Armstrong, sir. 'E were t'first t'walk on t'moon. Ah saw it on our telly. 'E climbed down a ladder.'

'An' med a footprint,' added Reggie and Ronnie Atha simultaneously.

'Well done,' I said. 'And when he set foot on the moon Neil Armstrong said these words.' I wrote on the board: 'One small step for man, one giant leap for mankind.'

'Why can't we send a rocket to t'moon, sir?' asked Matthew Hesketh.

'Well, it's very expensive and, at present, America has the money and we haven't. This is our budget for our space programme.' I wrote '£3,000,000' on the blackboard. 'So, how much is that?'

Terry Duff was the first to raise his hand. 'Three million pounds, sir, and that's a fortune.'

'Well done, Terry,' I said, 'but wait until you see how much the budget is for NASA in America.' Slowly, I printed out '£1,300,000,000'.

There was silence.

Finally, Sandra Asquith waved her hand and said quietly, 'Ah think that's one thousand, three 'undred million, sir.'

'Excellent, Sandra.'

The little girl beamed.

I explained that our first all-British satellite, the 'Black Arrow' project, had failed.

'That's a poor do,' muttered Charlie Dewhirst and everyone nodded. It was clear they were disappointed we were lagging behind the USA.

*

When the bell rang for afternoon break I headed for the staff-room. Norman was waiting for me outside his office.

'A word,' he said with all the charm of the Grim Reaper.

'Yes?'

'I want your desks back in rows before Eric goes in to sweep the floor.'

This didn't seem the best moment for an argument. I looked down at him. 'Was there anything else?'

'No,' he said curtly. 'Just make sure it's done.'

He retreated to his office and didn't appear in the staff-room during break.

I passed Barbara, who was taking her hot drink out on to the playground, and she gave me a reassuring smile. I wondered if she had overheard the conversation with Norman.

Edith passed a cup of tea to Audrey who was looking at her *Daily Mail* while shaking her head. 'What's wrong, Audrey?' she asked.

'I need to get on with my driving lessons. It says here the driving test fee is going up from one pound fifteen shillings to three pounds five shillings next year.'

'Where are you up to?' asked Travis cautiously.

Audrey considered this for a moment. 'Well . . . we finally did a three-point turn last night.'

'How did you get on?'

'Not well. It turned out to be a seven-point turn and I mounted the kerb.'

'You'll be fine with practice,' said Edith with an encouraging smile.

'How many lessons have you had?' I asked.

There was an alarmed look from Travis, a shake of the

head from Edith and a sudden change of subject by Connie. 'How are the little ones in your class, Penny?' she asked.

Edith joined in hurriedly. 'They were certainly enjoying painting when I called in.'

'To be honest I feel run off my feet,' said Penny. 'But they seem to have settled in after a few tears this morning.'

'And that was just the parents,' said Travis, pleased with his little joke.

I noticed no one mentioned driving lessons again as we drank our tea, enjoyed a garibaldi biscuit and wandered back to our classrooms at the sound of the bell.

Connie stopped me by her classroom door. 'Best not to mention driving lessons, Jack.'

'Why is that?'

'Audrey books them eight at a time.' We looked across the hall as Audrey and Penny disappeared down the infant corridor. 'When this series is over it will be sixty-four lessons and I don't think she's got to an emergency stop yet.'

'But it must be costing her a fortune.'

'True . . . but we think she fancies the instructor.'

'Really?'

Connie studied me thoughtfully. 'Audrey has been trying to get a man for years. I think she's given up on her church group.'

'I did notice she has something of a nervous demeanour. I guess that doesn't help.'

'Very true, Jack.' There was a pause. 'I've always preferred the *direct* approach.' She gave an enigmatic smile and walked into her classroom.

*

At the end of school I joined Penny, Connie and Travis in the staff-room once more.

'So how's it gone?' asked Connie.

'Steady,' I said.

Penny grimaced. 'My day's been a bit hectic, particularly with all the new parents . . . but I've survived.'

Connie stared at me with a wry smile. 'Well, it made a change not hearing a riot in your class, Jack. You seem to have kept them busy, so well done.'

'Thanks, but I'm short of suitable resources, especially reading books.'

'Same here,' echoed Penny.

Both Connie and Travis nodded knowingly.

'You have to go to Norman if you need anything,' said Travis.

'Sadly, cap in hand – which I'm not prepared to do,' said a determined Connie.

Travis stared out of the window. '"This little world . . ."' he said quietly.

'*Little world?*' echoed Penny.

'Don't mind Travis,' said Connie. 'I'm guessing he's quoting his Shakespeare again.'

Travis gave a wry smile. '*Richard the Second*, Jack . . . Act two, scene one. "This happy breed of men, this little world".'

'Thinking of Norman, that's very apt,' said Connie, 'except nobody is happy.'

I glanced at Penny. Her expression said it all.

'Anyway,' said Connie with a grin, 'look on the bright side.'

'Bright side?' I said.

'Yes, he's away on a course tomorrow.'

It was five o'clock when we finished chatting and Penny and I walked out to the car park.

'Have you spoken to the head?'

Penny frowned. 'He had a quick word with me in my classroom. Told me he didn't want any noise and that I was responsible for keeping the classroom tidy, particularly if we're doing artwork.'

'So not exactly encouraging.'

'I asked if the caretaker could help.'

'And?'

'He said Mr Skinner has a bad back and it was up to the teachers to keep their classrooms tidy. Makes me wonder what the caretaker actually does. It's disappointing. I wasn't expecting to come to a school where the head is so different from the ones I met on teaching practice.'

'Yes, I know what you mean. Anyway . . . the rest of the staff seem fine.'

'Especially Barbara,' she said with a smile and unlocked her car.

'So, how's the Mini?'

'Much better now. My dad paid for the service.'

'Good to have a helpful dad.'

'Definitely. I'm lucky having such supportive parents. They're even helping me out with the rent until I get on my feet.' She threw her shoulder bag on to the passenger seat and sighed. 'In fact I'm broke until we get paid at the end of the month.'

I took a deep breath. 'Maybe we can have a meal together at the weekend . . . my treat.'

There was a pause. I could see she wasn't sure.

'That is until Seb gets back,' I added hastily.

'That's kind, Jack, but my flatmate makes lovely meals so I won't starve.'

'Well, the offer's there,' I said.

She climbed into her car, wound down the window and looked up at me. 'How about you come to me? Friday night and bring a bottle. My flatmate is called Sue. Teaches maths in Skipton. You'll like her.'

Her cheeks were flushed as she drove off.

I guessed mine were too.

## Chapter Three

# *The Problem-Solving Post Office*

The idea struck me as I parked my car.

Heather View was surrounded by squat terraced houses, crumbling roads and ugly metal fences. There was no grass and there were no trees. When I looked at the school playground it was bare and featureless, just a rectangle of tarmac. A few children had arrived early, turned out of their homes by parents who worked at the local factories. A group of girls were huddled outside the boiler-house doors while a gang of boys were dominating the big spaces and kicking a leather football.

They were using coats for goalposts.

I paused and took in the scene. It was Wednesday morning, the first day of October, and on the other side of the valley the distant hills were shrouded in a blanket of mist. At the school gate the children arriving were spectres in a grey world.

When I had left Lotherswicke village the hedgerows were rich with wild fruit and robins were claiming their territory.

Fallen leaves, gold and amber, lay like scattered souls by the roadside. It had been a perfect early-autumn scene and the contrast here on the Milltown council estate was stark.

As I walked into school I decided to grasp the nettle. I tapped on Norman's door and walked in. 'Excuse me, Mr Little, may I have a quick word?'

I had soon gathered there was no thought of first-name terms in private conversation.

He looked up sharply, clearly not pleased at being disturbed. 'What is it?' he asked gruffly.

'I'd like to plant a tree in the school grounds.'

'What?'

'It would be a valuable experience for the children.'

He looked at me as if I had just arrived from another planet. 'Have you ever looked at our playground? If you haven't noticed it's all crushed grit, tarmac and concrete.'

'I've thought of that. I can get the tools.'

He put down his pen, realizing I was serious. 'What about County Hall? You'd need permission.'

'I don't see that as a problem. We would be improving the school and when the local adviser calls in for his termly visit he will probably be impressed.'

This struck a chord. I could see him thinking there would be some reflected kudos here. 'Well, I'm not keen but I suppose you could ask Miss Verity to ring the Grounds Maintenance team.'

'Thanks,' I said and hurried out before he changed his mind.

It was morning break when I called in to the secretary's office. Edith was busy winding the handle of her Roneo spirit duplicator and producing letters advertising the forthcoming Harvest Festival at St Peter's.

'Good news, Jack,' she said. 'I rang County Hall. It took a while but my friend Pauline works there. She said there's no underground pipework in that area so they've no objection.'

'Excellent, Edith. Many thanks.'

She was enthused. 'I'm so excited. No one has ever planted a tree here before.'

'I'll confirm with Mr Little and then I'll see about getting a tree.'

She smiled. 'Good luck, Jack.'

I received a reluctant agreement from the headteacher when I spoke to him at lunchtime. 'The office said yes,' he muttered, 'but they've no money for it . . . and for that matter neither have we. It's a stupid idea. Waste of time and effort.'

I gritted my teeth and tried to remain positive. 'I'll see what I can do.'

Just before the bell for afternoon school, the caretaker, Eric Skinner, approached me in the school hall.

'Ah've just 'eard t'news,' he said gruffly.

'What's that, Mr Skinner?'

' 'Bout this tree idea. Ah'm not 'appy 'bout you messin' up t'playground.'

I was beginning to understand why Connie called him 'Idle Eric'.

'An' jus' so y'know . . . sweepin' up leaves isn't part o' my job.'

'Well, let's see how things develop. My job is to educate

these children and I'll always do my best for them just as I imagine you will want to do the same.'

I left him to work this one out as I returned to my classroom for afternoon school. The children were excited when I raised the subject.

'So, what do you think?' I asked.

'Nearest trees are in Fairy Wood, sir, near t'big school,' said Terry Duff.

Hands were shooting up around the room. It seemed everyone had an opinion. 'An' there's some next to t'railway,' said Keith Lumb.

'But y'can't go near there,' warned Janet Stubbs. 'Too dangerous.'

'Me an' Reggie like climbing trees, sir,' said an eager Ronnie Atha.

'That's right, sir,' echoed Reggie, 'an' we climb 'igh ones an' shout like Tarzan.'

'That's what I used to do when I was young,' I said with a smile.

I had since learned that the two boys had been named after the infamous Kray twins who had been given life sentences for murder earlier in the year. Apparently Mrs Atha was a huge fan of the gangster duo, which was slightly disconcerting.

In the staff-room at afternoon break I was keen to share the news of my tree-planting idea. Penny was on duty but everyone else was there except for Norman, who had left early to attend another course. Word had it that, on occasions, it turned out to be a *golf* course.

There was a hum of conversation.

Travis was busy encouraging Audrey to rent a black-and-white television set. 'They've changed the law, Audrey, so it's easier to rent a more up-to-date set. There's no forty-two-week advance payment needed now on televisions made before the start of this year.'

I wondered how Travis knew all these obscure facts. He was always a source of information.

Audrey was enthusiastic. 'I'm certainly interested because my picture is so poor.' She gave a dreamy sigh. 'And Patrick Macnee is on tonight at eight o'clock.'

It was well known that Patrick Macnee as John Steed in *The Avengers* was Audrey's heart-throb.

Meanwhile Barbara and Connie were having a heated debate about the Prime Minister. Harold Wilson was urging pay restraint.

'He'll struggle,' muttered Connie.

'And Ted Heath will benefit,' said Barbara.

The two women were both staunch socialists.

I decided to speak up. 'Can I make a quick announcement, everybody?'

The hubbub ceased. Edith smiled. She knew what was coming.

'On Friday I'll be digging a hole in the playground.'

There were surprised looks. 'For Norman, I hope,' said Connie.

Audrey pursed her lips in disapproval. 'Now then, Connie.'

'"Words without thoughts never to heaven go,"' recited Travis. '*Hamlet*, act three.'

Connie ignored the reprimand. 'Go on, Jack.'

'My class will be planting a tree.'

'Hey, that's terrific,' said Connie. 'Can we help?'

'Well done, Jack,' said Travis. 'Great idea. If you need any tools let me know.'

'So . . . what did Norman say?' asked Barbara, ever the cautionary voice.

Edith chipped in: 'I spoke to County Hall. They agreed and Mr Little said go ahead . . . but, sadly, we've no funds for it.'

'No surprise there then,' said Travis.

'I know someone at the garden centre who might help,' said Connie. 'Let me check it out and I'll get back to you.'

I was pleased with the positive response – I knew I had been a bit hasty in announcing my plans but had been confident that a way forward would reveal itself. There was excited chatter. Audrey launched into a list of her favourite trees while thoughts of Patrick Macnee and Harold Wilson were forgotten.

At 3.45 p.m. the bell went for the end of school. The children in my class were excited about the prospect of their own tree and walked out chatting happily.

Connie called in to my classroom. 'Jack, I've just spoken to a guy called Barry Wiggins at the Pollock Garden Centre near Skipton. He'll help with the tree if we call in tomorrow after school.'

'That's terrific. Many thanks.'

'We'll go in our cars. You can follow me,' Connie said, decisive as always.

'Fine. Let's do it.'

She gave me that searching look once again. 'And I was

thinking . . . maybe we could have a drink afterwards. There's a good pub next to the garden centre.'

This was unexpected. 'Sounds good,' I said with a smile. Life was full of surprises.

It was Thursday morning break and I looked around me at my colleagues. The usual banter ebbed and flowed in the staff-room. Penny was enthusing about the Beatles' latest album, *Abbey Road*, while Edith was expressing concern about the demise of the ten-shilling note, soon to be replaced by a seven-sided coin.

Connie came to sit next to me. 'OK for tonight?'

'Yes, looking forward to it.'

I wasn't aware that Penny had forgotten the Beatles for a moment and was staring at us.

At lunchtime I had a parcel to post and I told Edith I was leaving the building for a short while. I turned left out of the school gate and walked to the top of the hill. There was a shop with a sign that read:

**THE CORNER SHOP**
**K. & E. Entwhistle**
***We sell everything***

Outside on the pavement was a display of posser tubs, metal dustbins, plastic buckets, brooms and, on a wooden trestle table, a box of old bicycle parts. A Yorkshire terrier was outside too, its lead fastened to the metal railings. It barked loudly as I walked by.

The bell over the door rang as I walked in and, behind

the counter, a small man in a brown overall gave me a cautious smile and then returned to stacking tins of shoe polish next to a basket of clothes pegs. Around me the shop was a veritable cornucopia. It was crammed with sacks of potatoes, tins of beans, fresh bread, packets of cereal, washing powder and chocolate bars. The sign over the door was clearly accurate.

At the far end of the shop was a Post Office counter. A formidable-looking lady with curly blonde hair, a florid face and arms like a weightlifter was serving a customer. 'An' tell 'im Kathy sent you, Doreen, an' 'e'll fix y'pipes.' For good measure she leaned over the counter and tapped her hand in an endearing way.

'Ooh, thank you kindly,' said Doreen. 'Yurra godsend f'sortin' out m'problems. Ah've bin worryin' m'self summat rotten.'

'Well, no need. You get off 'ome an' gerrit seen to.'

The relieved lady hurried out as I approached the counter and stood behind the next customer, an elderly, stooped man with a flat cap covering his white hair.

'Now then, Mr Phizackerley, what can ah do f'you t'day?'

'Twenty Park Drive, please.'

She glanced up at me. ' 'Ello luv, ah've seen you a few times. You're one o' t'new teachers.'

'That's right, I'm Jack Sheffield.'

The old man turned to face me. 'Good Yorkshire name. Where y'from?'

'Leeds.'

'Finest tailors in t'world.'

'Yes, they are.'

'We've got it all in Yorkshire, tha knaws. Finest place on God's earth.'

'I'm sure it is.'

'Ah'm Arnold Phizackerley. Another good Yorkshire name.' He collected his cigarettes and paid. 'An' Kathy, that present y'picked were perfect.' He looked at me: 'Well, devil finds work for idle 'ands. Ah'm off t'Florence,' and he wandered out.

Puzzled, I looked across the counter. 'Florence . . . in Italy?'

Kathy laughed. 'No, 'is sister in Cleck'eaton.'

'Ah, of course.'

She grinned. 'Anyway, pleased t'meet you, Mr Sheffield, ah'm Kathy Entwhistle. That's Kathy wi' a K . . . an' laughing boy over there is my 'usband, Ernie.'

'Pleased to meet you.' We shook hands across the counter. She had a grip of iron.

Kathy was clearly weighing me up. 'Jus' so we know each other from t'start, ah tell it 'ow it is. There's no beatin' abart t'bush wi' me.'

'I'll remember that, Mrs Entwhistle,' I said. It was clear this was a woman you would want on your side. 'I've a parcel for posting, please.'

She read the address. '"Mrs M. Sheffield, 9 St Wilfrid's Avenue, Leeds 8". So . . . is this y'mother?' As the saying goes, Kathy was not backwards in coming forwards.

'Yes, it is.'

'What is it then, a gift?' She squeezed the parcel. 'It's very light.'

'Balls of wool,' I said. 'She knits pullovers for me. I always buy the wool. A sort of tradition. Though getting the right shade is tricky.'

'Problem solved, Mr Sheffield,' she said with confidence. 'Y'need t'come to me. Ah can get owt y'like. Never fear. We solve problems in 'ere. Y'should be in 'ere on pension day. Ah sort out all t'old folk.'

'That's good to know,' I said.

She glanced across at her husband. ' 'Ave y'finished that yet?' she boomed.

Ernie jumped in fright. He was taking an age to stack the tins of shoe polish.

Kathy leaned over the counter. ' 'E sez 'e's gorra nervous stomach but that won't be all that's nervous when ah get my 'ands on 'im.'

As I left Ernie gave me a shy smile.

At the end of school Connie and I left promptly and drove to the garden centre. A tall, athletic man in green overalls was expecting us.

'Hi, Connie,' he said and kissed her on the cheek. 'You're looking good.' He turned to me. 'I'm Barry. Connie says you need a tree for t'kids at school.'

'That's right,' I said. 'I appreciate your help.'

'Well, ah've gorra silver birch y'can 'ave. Come an' look. Ah've put it on one side. Ready f'plantin'. Ten feet tall.'

We walked to the delivery bay at the back of the centre.

'Perfect,' I said.

'That's just what we need,' said Connie.

'I'll deliver it tomorrow if y'like. Along wi' compost. No trouble.'

This was going too fast. 'It depends on the price.'

'Free, gratis and for nothing, Jack,' said Barry with a grin. 'Ah've gorra few that we keep for *friends.*' He gave Connie a look and she responded with a knowing smile.

Surprised at the speed of the transaction we shook hands and I followed Connie to The Cat & Kettle pub.

It was crowded but there were a few spare tables. We walked up to the bar and the barman seemed to know Connie. He nodded in acknowledgement and looked at me. 'What's it t'be?'

I glanced at the pumps. 'Well, mine's a pint of Tetley's and whatever the lady wants.'

'I'll have the same,' said Connie with a level stare at the barman.

He shrugged his shoulders and filled a pint tankard for me. Then he searched under the bar and produced two glass goblets and served Connie with two halves.

'Y'know t'policy, Connie.'

'See what I mean, Jack? Women can't drink pints.'

'Not ladylike,' muttered the barman. He picked up my two half-crowns and went to the till to get my change.

'Equality!' grumbled Connie.

We sat at a table by a bay window and supped our beer while I reflected on the transaction at the garden centre. 'Good of Barry to help us out.'

'We're old friends.'

'I guessed.'

'He's married now.'

'Oh yes?'

'Before that, a few years ago, when I first came here, we were lovers.'

I wasn't sure how to respond so said nothing. I had never met anyone quite as *direct* as Connie.

I changed the subject. 'Where are you from in the north-east?'

'Pity Me. It's near Durham.'

'Pity Me?'

'Yes, great name, isn't it? My father said it came from old English *pitte mea,* an uneven meadow. My mother was more romantic. She said it derived from Norman French *petit mere,* meaning small lake. Either way, that's where I grew up. They were happy times. We had seaside holidays at Marsden Rock in a cottage in Whitburn.'

Her voice had softened with the memory.

'I had good parents. My dad was a shop steward. Labour through and through. Then, after training to be a teacher, I moved to Yorkshire and got a job at Heather View.'

We had another drink and chatted about life and politics. Connie was an activist and had read Trotsky in the mid-sixties when her sister got eight pounds a week in a department store while men doing the same job received twelve pounds.

She asked me about my rugby and said she would like to come and see me play. I was unsure whether to be flattered or concerned and wondered where this was leading. I had enjoyed relationships at college and in my early teaching career but Connie was different. She was an intimidating presence but I was intrigued, nonetheless.

On Friday I left early for school. There was a special radiance to the morning as the low, slanting sunlight lit up the mist like a myriad of stars. I drove south with thoughts of tree-planting and Connie on my mind . . . but not in that order.

In the car park I met up with Penny.

I would have liked to spend more time with her out of school but, with boyfriend Seb on the scene, caution prevailed. We had enjoyed a meal at her cottage at the end of our first week. Her flatmate, Sue, who taught at the local comprehensive in Skipton, was engaging and a great cook. She had just started dating a science teacher on the staff. *Nerdy but nice* was the description. 'More Einstein than Elvis,' she'd said.

Since then teaching had consumed our lives and my weekends had been dominated by rugby and poorly cooked Sunday dinners. I was saving up each month with the Abbey National to buy one of the new properties on a large development in the village of Bradley near Skipton. It appeared I had a good chance of a twenty-five-year mortgage. A flat was £2,700 and it seemed a good investment.

'How did it go last night?' asked Penny.

'With Connie?'

She frowned. 'With the tree.'

'Sorry . . . yes, fine. A guy is delivering it this morning. We can get it planted today.'

'Great,' said Penny. 'I'll bring my class out to see it.'

Barry from the garden centre was bright and early and keen to impress. He had all the tools and attacked the chalked cross on the tarmac with a pickaxe.

At lunchtime everyone lent a hand and Connie, Penny and Travis took turns to shovel in the compost. Barbara made a short speech declaring our tree well and truly planted and I hammered in a wooden stake to support it.

The children stared at it as a thing of wonder.

When I drove home on that Friday evening I had no idea what lay in store.

'Sir, sir! Come look what's 'appened!'

It was Monday morning and Terry Duff and Keith Lumb were waving frantically from the playground. I looked in dismay. The tree had been ripped from the ground and tossed into the bin store next to the boiler house.

Word spread rapidly and children and staff stood silently staring at the place where our tree had been, now a circle of soil that had been trodden flat.

It was heartbreaking.

In the staff-room at morning break it was of course the main topic of conversation.

'Hooligans!' said Norman. 'That's the youth of today for you. No respect.'

Barbara was more gentle. 'Don't despair, Jack. Maybe we can plant it somewhere else.'

'Do we know who did it?' asked Penny.

'I asked my class but no luck,' said Connie. 'What about yours, Jack?'

I shook my head. 'They all went quiet. I think someone knows but they were too scared to open up.'

I went back to my class for a quiet morning of maths and writing and I noticed a few boys staring at ten-year-old Terry Speight but nothing was said.

At lunchtime I slipped out of school partly to clear my head but also to buy a loaf of bread. In the Corner Shop Kathy came to serve me.

'A loaf, please, Kathy.' I looked at the shelves behind her.

'And a packet of Kellogg's Sugar Smacks and some of that Smash Instant Potato . . . it's easier.'

'What's matter? Y'look like a wet weekend.'

I told her about the tree.

She listened stoically. 'Call in t'morrow, Mr Sheffield.' She tapped the side of her nose with a stubby finger. 'Ah might be able to 'elp.'

It was Tuesday lunchtime and I had called back in to see Kathy in the Corner Shop.

She didn't mince her words. 'Y'know what teenagers are like, Mr Sheffield, all attitude an' acne. That Kenny Speight's no different. Fourteen goin' on twenty-four. A tearaway. Not s'prisin' wi' Mad Micky for a dad.'

'I see,' I said.

' 'Is brother Terry is in your class.'

'He's a good boy, Kathy. No bother at all.'

'Anyway, ah soon got to t'bottom of it. Ah went round to t'playground when t'big lads were playin' football. By t'time ah'd finished a few of 'em were cryin' them alligator tears.'

*Crocodile,* I thought but said nothing.

'But it were 'is dad what told 'im t'pull up y'tree 'cause it were in t'way of their football. 'E's a sheep in wolf's clothin' is that one, Mr Sheffield. Jus' you mark my words.'

'Yes, I've met Mr Speight.'

'Anyway, ah've gorra s'lution.'

'Have you? To what?'

'Y'tree problem.'

'Really?'

'You 'ave t'use y'noddle,' she said, tapping her forehead. 'You 'ave t'think like them.'

'Think like them?' I shook my head. 'No thanks.'

'It's 'cause they've nowhere t'go. No youth club. No church 'all. No nothing.'

'I'm sorry about that. I agree there's no facilities but what can *I* do?'

'Well, ah walked round t'corner las' night t'watch 'em.'

'And what did you see?'

'Well, it's perfec' f'football wi' them 'igh fences an' that big wall. An' when they're playing in your yard they don't cause no bother.'

'Apart from pulling up my tree.'

'They were mekkin' a point. Y'put it in t'middle o' their football pitch.'

'I know that now.'

'Well, that's what ah mean 'bout using y'noddle.'

'I'm still not with you.'

' 'Ave a look at this.' She pulled a sheet of paper from the pocket of her pinny and placed it on the counter. It was a diagram of the school playground. At first it made no sense.

Then realization dawned and I smiled.

She looked at me as if she had just discovered penicillin. 'Reg'lation size f'goals is . . .'

'Eight feet high, twenty-four feet wide,' I said.

As a ten-year-old in the fifties I had played in goal for Coldcotes Junior Boys in Leeds and recalled that even when I jumped as high as I could I still wasn't able to reach the crossbar.

'Ah'll 'ave a word wi' 'em t'night.' Her cheerful face broke into a smile. ' 'Ave no fear, Kathy is 'ere.'

'Well, thanks, Kathy, if you think it will do any good.'

'Also . . . ah know a lad called Barry Wiggins at t'garden centre. 'E owes me a favour.'

*That man again,* I thought, although I was guessing that on this occasion they hadn't been *lovers.*

The next morning when I arrived at school there was a posse of boys waiting to greet me. Word had got round the estate and the playground had filled up quickly.

'It's great, sir. Come an' look,' shouted Keith Lumb.

At the end of the playground two trees stood proudly, each with a ring of protective stakes around them. They were in front of the centre of the far wall and exactly eight yards apart. Perfect goalposts.

A nervous Terry Speight came up to me. 'Our Kenny 'elped, sir. 'E dug the 'oles wi' that man from t'garden centre an' 'e sez 'e's sorry. 'E didn't tell m'dad but that dunt matter 'cause m'mam sez 'e'll be back in prison again soon.'

I recall this incident having a considerable effect on me. It was the beginning of the time when I learned how to teach children from some of the most challenging home backgrounds. Those who arrived at school hungry, unloved and occasionally frightened needed empathy, not anger.

I had moved on as a teacher.

In the years that followed the trees grew tall and strong and, after all this time, I still recall the smile on Terry Speight's face when he announced, 'It's great, sir, we don't use coats f'goalposts no more.'

## Chapter Four

# *The Dying of the Light*

Her name was Mary Capstick. She was five years old and, on this day, her life was destined to change.

It was Friday, 31 October, the last day before the half-term holiday. The children were excited and bonfires and fireworks beckoned. On this iron-grey morning a reluctant light spread across the rooftops of Milltown and the valley beyond.

Back in Lotherswicke village a bonfire had been built on the village green. Boys were requesting a penny for the guy outside the village store where boxes of Standard fireworks were on sale. On a bench outside The Weaver's Arms a robin had perched on a bench and trilled out a haunting song. Intricate spiders' webs laced the hedgerows while goldfinches sought seeds in the dry thatch of teasels.

Meanwhile the trees on the High Street were baring their skeletal souls. The season was moving on. Now was the time of the gathering of leaves. Nights were drawing in and darkness was a familiar companion.

It was the time of the dying of the light.

At morning break I was on playground duty and I heard a child crying. Outside the boiler-house doors a little girl was retrieving a rag doll that had fallen into a dirty puddle. The girl beside her was clearly distressed and I walked over to investigate.

'Can I help?' I said and crouched down.

Mary was a shy little girl with a pale face, spiky blonde hair and bright blue eyes. Tears were running down her cheeks as she picked up the doll and stared at her in dismay. The tiny pinafore was smeared with black stains.

Her friend, Lizzie Pickles, another five-year-old in Penny's class, was clearly used to speaking on behalf of her friend.

'Mary's dolly felled down, Mr Sheffield,' said Lizzie. 'It were an accident. It slipped. We were fast'nin' up 'er pinny.'

'I'm sure we can get her tidy again,' I said.

Mary didn't look convinced.

I changed tack. 'She's a beautiful doll. What's her name?'

'Cind'rella,' said Lizzie. 'She turns into a beautiful princess. Miss telled us t'story.'

Mary stopped crying and nodded.

'Well, I'm about to ring the bell for the end of playtime. Would Cinderella like to ring it?'

Lizzie nodded hesitantly. Mary saw her friend's reaction and smiled for the first time.

'Come on then,' I said. 'Then we can ask Miss Armitage to help get her clean again.'

After I had passed on the two girls to Penny with a brief explanation, all appeared to be well.

During morning break, Edith had collected our coffee money and was staring at the coins. 'I'm still not keen on this new fifty-pence coin,' she said.

Earlier in the month the new seven-sided fifty-pence coin had replaced the old ten-shilling note to a mixed response.

Barbara agreed. 'I'm getting it confused with half-crowns.'

Travis looked up from his Schools Council Bulletin *Mathematics in Primary Schools* and gave a gentle smile. 'Don't worry, all the old currency will be replaced and then there'll be no confusion.'

Norman looked up sharply from putting an extra spoonful of sugar in his coffee. 'Well, I think it's a funny shape.'

'Actually it's an equilateral-curve heptagon,' said Travis, 'the only coin of that shape in the world . . . so it's distinctive.'

Norman blinked. 'Well, it's still not normal.'

I had returned to the staff-room in time to hear this exchange. I had gradually come to realize that Norman was a very arrogant man: his dismissive manner proved it. Barbara had been told he had been impressive in his interview with an emphasis on discipline and that was how he had secured the headship.

The conversation moved on to *Monty Python's Flying Circus*, launched earlier in the month on BBC. There were very mixed responses. Audrey did not approve of the innuendo-laden humour while Connie thought it was brilliant. For my part I was beginning to wonder if Norman ever smiled.

After the bell at twelve noon I walked into the hall for my school dinner. It was free for teachers if you sat with the children. Everyone took advantage of this except for Audrey, who brought a packed lunch, and Norman, who flouted the rule and had a meal delivered to his office. Today it was Spam fritters, chips and peas followed by jam sponge and purple custard.

I saw Penny on the next table in animated conversation with Mary Capstick and Lizzie Pickles. Both girls were smiling and Mary had the rag doll on her lap.

I ate quickly so I would have time to prepare my room for an art lesson before afternoon school started. I put a sheet of black sugar paper on each desk along with a selection of coloured chalks that I had bought with my own money from Kathy's shop. There were only boxes of *white* chalk in the school stock cupboard. The aim was to produce firework pictures and I would have liked to arrange the children in groups but the sloping old-fashioned desks made this difficult.

Connie called in and sat down on one of the low chairs. She stretched out her long legs and gave me that familiar penetrating look. 'Jack . . . what are you doing during half-term?'

I leaned against one of the desks. 'Probably going to Leeds to see my mother. She said my father's health is getting worse.'

'Sorry to hear that,' she said. 'What's the problem?'

'He had a dreadful war,' I explained. 'He was on HMS *Prince of Wales* in the South China Sea in 1941 when it was sunk by the Japanese.'

Connie looked concerned. 'That must have been dreadful.'

'He was lucky to survive but he's suffered ever since. Anyway, what was on your mind?'

She smiled and stroked the amulet that hung around her neck with her long fingers. 'Bonfire night next Wednesday. I'm having a small party in my back garden. The usual stuff . . . jacket potatoes, toffee apples and a few rockets. Should be fun.'

'Thanks. Let me see how things go in Leeds and I'll come if I can.'

She stood up and smoothed the wrinkles in her tight skirt. 'Fine, hope you can make it. Might do you good to relax a bit.' With that she strode out, leaving behind the merest hint of perfume and a modicum of intrigue.

At afternoon break Penny was on duty and I collected a cup of tea for her and carried it out to the playground. She was wearing a bobble hat, college scarf and a duffel coat and warmed her hands on the mug.

'Thanks,' she said, 'this is welcome.'

We watched the children at play. Susan Bell and Janet Stubbs were winding a skipping rope while a group of girls jumped in and out with superb coordination. They chanted:

*'One man went to mow,*
*Went to mow a meadow.*
*One man and his dog,*

*Stop, bottle o' pop, fish an' chips,*
*Ol' Mother Riley an' 'er cow,*
*Went to mow a meadow.'*

It was bitterly cold but none of them seemed to notice. We leaned against the wall as a cloak of mist shrouded the school.

'Jack, my mum and dad always have a bonfire on the land at the back of their cottage. It's a village gathering with soup and sparklers. I'm going with my flatmate and I wondered if you were free to come along.'

I was eager to say yes but couldn't ignore the thought of boyfriend Seb blocking my pursuit of more than a friendship with Penny.

'I'm going to see *my* parents as well. So can I see how things go?'

I guessed my disappointment showed and I wondered if she knew what was on my mind.

'Just turn up if you can. My parents would love to meet you and I know you would get on with my dad. He's seen you play rugby.'

'Maybe you could come to a game with him. It's a really welcoming club.'

She smiled that familiar, confident smile that I had come to know so well. 'I'm not really into rugby, Jack, but maybe one day.'

When I walked back into school I reflected that I now had a choice of bonfires.

In Class 6 you could cut the atmosphere with a knife. The children knew what was coming. Norman arrived for his Friday afternoon handwriting lesson. He carried four skipping ropes, a cane and a stick of chalk with the tip shaped to a forty-five degree angle. It was a ritual that never wavered.

He insisted they all stand when he entered. They all sprang to their feet, thirty-six statues fearful of the wrath of their headteacher. I sat at the back of the class. Norman had insisted I observe the start of his lesson, presumably to demonstrate his absolute power over the pupils.

'You may sit,' he said.

The children sat and folded their arms, robots in absolute synchronicity.

He hung the cane on a hook on the wall, examined the blackboard to ensure it was perfectly clean and then held up the four skipping ropes. 'Woodcock,' he announced with quiet menace.

Billy Woodcock, the biggest boy in the class, hurried out to the front and took the ropes. As he did so, Norman picked up the board ruler and drew two parallel lines. Then he wrote in perfect cursive writing: 'The quick brown fox jumped over the lazy dog.' He turned to face the class: 'Today I want *perfect* ascenders and descenders.'

As I left the classroom Billy moved quickly to the four left-handed pupils and proceeded to tie their left wrist to the leg of their wooden chair.

I was furious. 'Is this necessary, Mr Little?'

Norman stared at me in astonishment. 'This is *my* lesson. Don't interrupt.'

The children looked from me to their headteacher, surprise on their faces.

'I'm sure the left-handed pupils know your rule without the need to restrain them in this way.'

'A word,' he said. He spat out the command and nodded towards the door.

I walked out to the corridor and he stared up at me. 'Never challenge me in front of the class . . . never! Try that again and I guarantee you will suffer the consequences.' He slammed the door and I was left quivering with anger.

It was well known among the staff that Norman had expressed the view that writing must be done *only* with the right hand. In his opinion left-handedness was the mark of a deviant.

We had never discussed *my* left-handedness. I looked forward to the day when I could quote the left-handed polymath Leonardo da Vinci, among other famous examples. However, I had been warned by Barbara not to interfere with this lesson. She had said the children would suffer even more if I upset him.

In Norman's world handwriting was sacrosanct in the weekly timetable.

Thirty minutes later I returned for the final lesson of the week. It was one I enjoyed and the children, released from the tedium of Norman's pedantic ritual, gathered round for story time.

It was the classic novel *The Wheel on the School* by Meindert DeJong, and we all followed the journey of Lina, one of six children in the fishing village of Shora in Holland. I loved to see their eager faces as they hung on every word and this lesson above all reminded me why I had chosen to be a teacher.

When the bell rang for the end of school the children were anxious to run out into the dusk and begin their half-term holiday.

'We're goin' to a big bonfire, sir,' said Reggie Atha.

'It's on that field, sir,' said his brother Ronnie. 'Near to t'big school.'

'It'll be great,' said Reggie.

'Wi' rockets,' added Ronnie for good measure.

I looked out of the window. Gloom had descended and smoke from the coal fires of Milltown mingled with the thick mist.

'Be careful, everybody,' I shouted after them. 'Remember what we said about fireworks.'

They grinned and waved. When you're ten years old you think you will live for ever and no one seemed daunted by my cautionary words.

Outside school, twenty yards from the main gate, was a zebra crossing. All the children from the north end of Milltown were well practised in using it. The others hurried down to the traffic lights at the bottom of the hill.

Our lollipop lady, Minnie Ackworth, was a conscientious sixty-year-old who loved her job and knew all the children. She had taken charge of the crossing on the main road two years ago. It was after the passing of the Road Traffic Regulation Act and, since then, road-safety-awareness programmes were a feature in all schools throughout the UK. We were fortunate in that our local bobby would call into school occasionally and give a talk at the end of morning assembly.

In all weathers Minnie would be there holding up her

'STOP' sign and keeping the children safe. It wasn't a particularly busy road as few parents owned a car but the road was very steep so the local delivery men had learned to drive with care.

If a child in my class had felt unwell during the day I would make sure I went out to the school gate to have a word with their parent. I soon learned that a couple of minutes communicating with parents in this way, on a regular basis, was worth countless official school open evenings. It was at those moments I would enjoy brief conversations with Minnie. She was a valuable and respected colleague.

On this particular evening I needed to speak to Mrs Bell, mother of Susan in my class. She always arrived to make sure her daughter was safe whereas most of the other ten-year-olds were confident enough to run home or were 'latchkey' children going back to an empty house. Susan had been complaining of tummy ache towards the end of the day.

Penny was also a regular at the school gate, usually in the mornings when pupils were arriving. Many of the mothers worked until five or six o'clock so had to make arrangements for a neighbour to collect their children. It was a pattern that seemed to work well. Penny always ensured a child was collected by a named parent or friend. As the infant classes finished at 3.15 p.m. and the juniors half an hour later, Penny would occasionally look after the children who had a brother or sister in one of the junior classes.

Mrs Julie Capstick was a twenty-four-year-old who worked at a local clothing factory. It was a hard life and she didn't get home until six o'clock – and she was a single parent. Her husband had departed a year ago with a leggy pub singer from Manchester. Fortunately her next-door neighbour, Mrs Elsie Pickles, came each day to collect Mary, along with her own daughter Lizzie and her eight-year-old son, Harry.

Elsie had called in to the Corner Shop before walking down the hill to school.

Kathy smiled at her regular customer. ''Ello, Elsie, what's it t'be?'

'Ah'll 'ave a Lyon's sponge sandwich, please, Kathy. Ah'm givin' it t'Julie Capstick 'cause it's 'er birthday t'morrow.'

'That's kind, luv. These single mothers need a 'elpin' 'and from time t'time.'

'Y'right there, Kathy. Poor lass spends 'er evenings wi' them catalogues lookin' for easy terms.'

Kathy shook her head in dismay. 'It's a 'ard life on t'never-never.'

Elsie scanned the shelves. 'An' ah'll 'ave a bottle o' Lucozade f'my Frank.' She smiled. ' 'E sez it puts 'airs on 'is chest.'

'An' that's not all,' added Kathy with a sly grin.

'Anyway, where's your Ernie?'

'Ah sent 'im packin' wi' a flea in 'is ear 'cause 'e 'adn't done t'day's deliveries.'

Elsie nodded. 'Men jus' don't shape up.'

The bell above the shop door rang as another customer arrived.

'Owt else?' asked Kathy.

'An' ah'll 'ave twenty Silk Cut an' some o' that new Outline margarine.'

'Low fat,' said Kathy. 'Good f'slimmin'.'

Elsie pointed to a large tray of cricket-ball-sized Energen rolls. 'An' some o' them, please, Kathy. My Frank feeds 'is face with 'em after 'is tea. Sez they give 'im get up an' go.'

Both women shared a secret smile while Elsie paid, packed her shopping bag and set off to collect Lizzie and Mary.

Kathy watched her walk down the hill and nodded in appreciation of another assertive woman. 'She knows which side 'er bread's buttered does that one,' she murmured to herself.

Except on this occasion it was *margarine.*

Meanwhile, a young man was driving a rusty 1962 Morris Mini van.

Nineteen-year-old Malachi Dodsworth never forgave his mother for christening him with the name of a Hebrew prophet. She had been told by a gypsy who told her fortune during a visit to Blackpool that it meant *my angel* and for the first few years of his young life that is exactly what he appeared to be. He soon shortened it to Mal as, during his teenage years, he became a selfish, abusive and brash young man.

Each day, as he delivered welding parts around the West Riding, he would shout obscenities at other drivers who dared to obstruct his path. One day during the summer he had enjoyed a skinful of beer in Scarborough and driven home at midnight. He was on the outskirts of Scagglethorpe when he left the road and demolished a fence. The damage was not sufficient to slow him down but his front grill was dented and the bumper bar now stuck out at an acute angle.

At exactly 3.50 p.m. Mal drove past the Corner Shop and hurtled down the hill outside the school. He had finished work early and was taking a shortcut home. His windscreen was covered in grime, his headlights were faulty and the tyres were bald. The van was an accident waiting to happen.

In the gloom ahead he saw a lollipop lady standing on a zebra crossing and he pressed on his brake pedal. The van slewed dangerously towards the kerb as the tyres failed to grip on the tarmac.

Big Jimmy Priestley was driving up the hill in his butcher's van and had pulled up well short of the zebra crossing. His headlights lit up Minnie's 'STOP' sign and her shiny coat. Minnie waved in acknowledgement as she ushered another group of children across the road.

As he peered through the gloom he saw a dirty van approaching. It was travelling too fast and Jimmy prayed it would slow down in time.

Elsie Pickles was in the group crossing the road with Harry, Lizzie and Mary. Then Mary dropped her rag doll. She stooped to pick it up and it was in that moment it happened.

The sequence of events after the bell had rung on that October evening will always stay in my mind.

I had walked to the school gate with Connie who said she wanted to call in to the Corner Shop. Mrs Veronica Bell was grateful to me for passing on my concern about her daughter's health and turned to walk to the zebra crossing. There was a screech of brakes. Everyone turned to see a van out of control.

Minnie Ackworth was standing in the centre of the crossing with her 'STOP' sign raised. She saw the danger, turned to her right and shouted, 'RUN, EVERYBODY, RUN!'

The van missed Minnie by inches but its buckled front bumper caught Mary Capstick's winter coat and knocked her off her feet. There was a terrible scream from Mrs Pickles. When the van stopped Mary had been dragged ten yards and was lying still on the pavement next to her ripped coat.

I reached the little girl at the same moment as Connie, who appeared composed as she felt for a pulse. 'She's breathing, Jack.'

The little girl was unconscious and covered in lacerations.

Connie looked up. 'You're faster than me. Run in and call for an ambulance . . . and the police.'

As I ran I shouted at Jimmy Priestley who was clambering out of his van, 'Jimmy, stop the traffic and tell Minnie to do the same.'

Connie did all the right things. She was calm in a crisis. Recalling her first aid training, she checked Mary's breathing and ensured her airways were open. It was important to move the little girl as little as possible in case of spinal injury but also to keep her warm and she took off her coat to cover her.

She was kneeling in the midst of a maelstrom. Around her, parents were screaming and children were crying. A few angry mothers were shouting at the van driver. Jimmy was standing behind his van looking out for any vehicle coming up the road while keeping an eye on Malachi, who was uninjured and too frightened to get out of his van. Minnie had recovered from her shock and continued to watch over the children who had still to cross the road.

Lizzie picked up Mary's doll.

I ran into Edith's office and telephoned for an ambulance. Barbara heard the news and ran outside with Travis and Penny. Norman was in a meeting in his office with Piers Witherspoon and both of them came out when they heard the commotion. Meanwhile, Audrey went into the staff-room to pray.

I was next to Connie once again when – thanks to Jimmy and Minnie – the ambulance arrived at the scene of the accident without any hold-up. They took great care with the little girl as they carried her away on a stretcher. A distressed Elsie wanted to go in the ambulance with Mary but Connie told her to stay with her frightened children.

Penny was now beside us and I spoke quietly to her. 'Penny, go and ring Mrs Capstick at work. Try not to alarm her and say we'll collect her and take her to the hospital.'

'OK, Jack. Makes sense.'

A police car pulled up and two policemen got out.

'It's important to speak to them, Jack,' said Connie. 'We can tell them what happened.'

I stared at the van driver, still too frightened to get out. 'And deal with him.'

Barbara was white with shock and Connie said gently to her, 'Barbara, you ought to go in the ambulance and Travis can stay by the phone.'

'Yes, of course.' She spoke with the ambulance crew

and climbed in the back. With sirens blaring it drove off down the hill.

Eventually a terrified Malachi was taken away in a police car after his van had been towed away and slowly the crowds dispersed.

It was after eight o'clock and we were sitting in the waiting room at the hospital when Julie Capstick appeared with a nurse.

'Thank you so much, all of you,' she said, her face taut with strain. 'The doctor 'as said she'll be all right an' ah can stay 'ere overnight.'

We all gave a sigh of relief. Barbara stood up, held Julie's hand and said a few quiet words.

When the young mother walked away through the swing doors it struck me in that moment we were the same age . . . but worlds apart.

One by one everyone departed. Norman and Audrey had only called in briefly but now Travis, who had stayed longer, left with Penny, and Jimmy Priestley arrived to collect Barbara. He had given his account to the police, having seen the accident played out right before him. Jimmy was a gentle giant; he put his arm around Barbara and said tenderly, 'C'mon, luv. Let me take you home.' He looked at Connie. 'Can we give anyone a lift?'

'No, but thanks anyway,' said Connie. 'I'm with Jack.'

Finally it was just the two of us walking towards the exit.

'It could have been much worse, Jack,' she said quietly. 'At least we know she will recover.'

I looked at her coat. It was stained with blood. 'Connie . . . you were brilliant today.'

'You were pretty good yourself.' Suddenly she stopped. 'Are you hungry?'

'I'm starving.'

'Let's get a fish and chips supper.'

'Where?'

'At The Cat & Kettle.'

'And a pint?'

She smiled. 'Well, maybe two halves.'

As we walked out into the cold night air we met Elsie Pickles.

'Oh, 'ello Miss Brooksbank, Mr Sheffield.' Her eyes were red-rimmed with tears. 'Word 'as it Mary's goin' t'be all right.'

'That's what we've been told,' I said.

'Ah've brought summat for 'er if they'll let me.'

'Just ask the nurse at the desk,' said Connie.

Elsie Pickles paused a moment. 'Ah'm so sorry. It should 'ave been me.'

Connie held her hand. 'It was an accident. There was nothing you could do.'

'Mebbe so. It all 'appened so fast. Poor little lass stopped to pick this up.' Elsie rummaged in her shopping bag. 'Ah tried t'clean it for 'er.'

She held it up.

It was a rag doll.

## Chapter Five

# *A Woman Scorned*

When I arrived outside Penny's home a weak sun was hidden by leaden clouds and a cold mist covered the land. The dawn frost had blackened the leaves on the climbing rose outside her cottage. In the hedgerows small creatures sought out the red hips of dog roses while leaves, gold and amber, swirled around my feet. It was Monday, 10 November and the forecast threatened sleet and heavy rain.

I had agreed to collect her on the way to school as her brother, Paul, had borrowed her Mini for a couple of days. Last night I had enjoyed a meal with Penny and her flatmate but there was still no sign of the elusive Sebastian. It was probably just as well they still hadn't chanced a visit to Ivy Cottage to sample *my* cooking. As I waited in their front room I noticed an old magazine on the table. It was the May issue of *Fashion* with a photo of Twiggy on the front cover. At four shillings it seemed expensive to me.

The radio was burbling away with news about Margaret Thatcher and her discussions with TUC leaders about a 'work experience' experiment similar to schemes in America and Sweden. It was a chance for pupils over fifteen to work in a factory. Meanwhile British Leyland was threatening to sack workers as they were finding it difficult to compete against the American car giants.

On the worktop was a book of Green Shield stamps. Penny and Sue had begun to save them. They had set their sights on a Morphy Richards pop-up toaster for eight books. Penny thought this was a realistic target . . . unlike her brother who needed 155 books for a Lambretta scooter!

The mantelpiece was filled with photos in frames. One of them featured a smiling Penny with a taller but younger version of herself, clearly her brother. He had shoulder-length hair and an Afghan coat. I knew he was reading English at Essex University but not much more and Penny filled in some of the gaps as we drove to Milltown.

'My brother is a bit wild at the moment. Going through a phase, I suppose. Spends a lot of time listening to Jefferson Airplane and the Doors and, I suspect, smoking hash. My mother is worried about him.'

'I suppose she would.'

'Somehow he survived the Summer of Love in sixty-seven, then got involved in last year's protest when Enoch Powell visited the university. So he's pretty active politically.'

'What's the university like?'

'He says it's brilliant with all the tower blocks and the smart Hexagon restaurant.' She smiled. 'I've visited a couple of times with my parents, mainly to stock him up with food. Definitely different to St John's.'

I enjoyed talking to her, particularly when our college

days cropped up in the conversation. It gave us a special connection.

'What about your father? How has he taken it?'

'Fine. He's really laid-back. Although I remember he said to him that having a degree *opens doors* but first you must choose to go through them. I think my brother is still working that one out.'

'Very true. Your dad sounds a wise man.'

She smiled again. 'Still waters run deep and all that.'

We arrived in a rain-soaked school car park. I had wanted to ask about Sebastian but couldn't find the right moment.

We rushed inside and set off for our classrooms. Connie was in the corridor outside Class 6. She looked up and smiled. 'You didn't make it then.'

'Pardon?'

She saw I looked confused. 'The bonfire party. It was great.'

'Oh, yes, sorry. I stayed over with my mum in Leeds.'

'Never mind, another time.'

It was a bleak morning but Connie always brightened up the day and looked terrific in a new purple cord maxi dress.

'Well, here we go,' she said, 'and we'll need to talk soon about what we're doing for Christmas.'

'Christmas?'

'Yes, Jack, the juniors are expected to do a Christmas entertainment while the infants sing carols and do a Nativity.'

The half-term holiday seemed to have made Connie more assertive than ever.

*

During morning break I was on playground duty and smiling at a group of children who were winding a long rope and singing a skipping rhyme to the tune of 'Frère Jacques'.

> *'Awful dinners, awful dinners,*
> *Concrete chips, concrete chips,*
> *Sloppy semolina, sloppy semolina,*
> *I feel sick, toilet quick.'*

The fact that they all devoured their midday meal each day with enthusiasm was not uppermost on their minds.

Meanwhile, in the staff-room a lively conversation had begun. As usual it was Connie making a point. She was looking at the front page of Barbara's *Daily Mirror*. The headline simply read: 'PHILIP'.

'I see the Duke of Edinburgh has put his foot in it again,' she said.

Audrey, our ardent royalist, looked up from her *Woman's Realm* in dismay. She had been engrossed in an article advertising a free thirty-two-page booklet on curtain-making. 'Why? What's happened?'

Connie scanned the newspaper. 'He's been interviewed on American television and he said the Royal Family would go into the red next year and may have to move to "smaller premises". Makes you wonder what the Queen does with her four hundred and seventy-five thousand pounds a year. Apparently, it says here, he gets forty-five thousand . . . plus perks.'

Audrey was indignant. 'But they have a lot of expensive travel and Buckingham Palace has to be kept in good repair.'

'Not to mention his polo ponies,' added Connie with feeling.

Edith was washing cups in the sink. 'It's difficult,' she said, trying to calm the troubled waters, ever the peacemaker. 'We're lucky to have such a hard-working monarch. The Queen sets a good example to us all.'

Barbara chipped in, 'You're right, Edith, but it's a shame Prince Philip doesn't *think* before he speaks. In Canada he told them he didn't go there for his health.'

Travis shook his head. 'Shame he's pleading poverty on American television.'

'Perhaps so,' conceded Audrey.

Penny thought it was a good moment to change the subject. 'By the way, everyone, Barbara and I called in to see little Mary. She's recovering well and should be back at school next week.'

'Wonderful news,' said Travis.

'We could organize a party for her,' said Connie.

Audrey brightened up. 'A lovely idea, Connie. I could bake a cake.'

'And, in all modesty, I make scones to die for,' said Travis, stroking the beginnings of a new droopy walrus moustache.

Everyone looked surprised.

'A man of hidden talents,' said Connie.

Travis smiled at Connie. 'Maybe you just need to get to know me a little better.'

Our school dinner did not resemble the skipping rhyme. It was cheese and onion pie with chips and beans and the children were enjoying every mouthful. That is until Mrs

Vera Cuthbert, the dinner lady, shouted, 'Elbows off the table, everybody! Remember your manners.' I was sure she was looking at me.

The pudding was cornflake tart and custard and afterwards the children, replete and happy, rushed back to their classrooms for indoor playtime. Mrs Cuthbert had looked up at the dark clouds and closed the door to the playground. It was a short sharp shower and the rain was coming down like stair rods. The kids delved into the box of comics, including *Shoot, Joe 90, Sally, Whizzer* and *Penelope,* and were soon engrossed.

Meanwhile, a difficult conversation was taking place in Norman's office. Eric Skinner was clutching a *Racing Mirror* and he was looking nervous.

'Sorry about Lester Piggott, boss. 'E looked a cert in that French race.'

Norman shook his head. 'You told me he couldn't lose.'

In yesterday's Grand Prix de Marseille the famous jockey Lester Piggott had finished second on New Member, one of the hot favourites.

'It were close – 'e were jus' unlucky.'

'Well, I need a change in fortune,' said Norman. 'You told me to go for Clever Scot at Sandown but Escalus beat him by four lengths.'

Eric stroked the stubble on his unshaven face. 'Yes, sorry about that but ah'm goin' to t'bettin' shop now, boss, an' ah've got all t'runners an' riders f'Wolver'ampton.' He waved his paper. It was covered in untidy markings in biro. 'Ah fancy Dumbutt in the four-thirty Sutton 'andicap.'

'Dumbutt?' Norman considered this for a moment and took a few coins from his pocket. 'Make it each way this time, not on the nose. Then I might at least get my money back.'

Eric Skinner made a hasty retreat and Norman sat back in his chair and lit up another cigarette. He had enjoyed a bet every week since he was a teenager. Now it was most days.

It added a bit of spice to life.

During the lunch break Barbara had called in to Edith's office and noticed that her friend looked troubled. 'What is it?' she asked.

'I'm getting more of these in the dinner money.' Edith held up one of the new fifty-pence pieces. 'I've got parents coming in saying they don't look as though they're worth ten shillings. They preferred the old banknote. So they get rid of a fifty-pence piece and I have to give them a half-crown change.'

'I see,' said Barbara, 'and word has it that next year the cost of a school dinner is going up by threepence to one shilling and ninepence.'

Edith considered this. 'That means a week's dinner money will cost eight shillings and ninepence. We're going to be handling a lot of threepenny bits and shillings when we're giving change.'

Barbara nodded. 'And we'll have more parents claiming free dinners.'

'Yes,' said Edith. 'Even a small increase will tip a few more over the edge.'

'Very true,' said Barbara sadly. 'For many children it's their only proper meal of the day.'

'Where will it all end?' asked Edith. She put all the

money into her metal box ready to take to the bank in town.

'I mentioned the issue to Mr Little when he was in earlier. He said he had been listening to Edward Short on the radio and that he was looking into it.'

Edith had little confidence in the Education Minister. 'He needs to spend a Monday morning in this office to see what's happening.'

Barbara nodded in agreement. 'Too true. Anyway, I called in to see if you wanted a lift to the bank. It's chucking it down out there. Saves you getting the bus.'

Edith's face lit up. 'Oh, thank you so much. Yes, please.' She checked the register, scribbled the total on a piece of paper, put it in the box and locked it with the key she kept in her handbag. It was a ritual she followed every week.

At the end of school Piers Witherspoon called in to my classroom. He was always supportive and we had struck up a positive relationship. He was a hard-working and intelligent man, dedicated to helping others. I had attended a couple of his Family Worship services at St Peter's. Travis helped out occasionally with sidesman duties and had suggested that I come along.

Piers slipped off his raincoat. It was soaking wet. 'Jack, I'm just back from the Capstick household, and things are looking up. Friends and neighbours are helping out so Mrs Capstick can go back to work. It's rewarding to see the response.'

'Good news, Piers.'

'She was fortunate that you and Connie handled the

first aid so well. I believe the Hand of God was on you that day, Jack.'

It hadn't occurred to me that divine intervention had played a part. 'We just did what we thought was needed.'

'Well, everyone is rallying round. You could say the little girl is receiving "the breath of life".' He grinned. 'Genesis, chapter two, verse seven . . . one of my favourites.'

At times he reminded me of Travis, with his quote for every occasion.

I looked at his dripping hair. 'You need to dry off before you go out again.'

He gave a wry smile. 'All part of the job, Jack.'

I studied him for a moment and wondered why he had chosen this path in his life. It was a selfless journey and he travelled it without complaint except perhaps for the incident on so-called Mischief Night on 4 November. It was the night the local children knocked on doors demanding a trick or treat. Unfortunately on occasions it was taken too far, as had been the case last week.

Piers had walked from the vicarage in Milltown towards the church on the morning of 5 November to be met with an unwelcome surprise. When he looked up he'd seen that the flag of St George had been removed from the tall flagpole on the grassy mound next to the war memorial. To their credit the vandals had not stolen the precious flag but had folded it neatly and left it draped over the noticeboard in the stone porch. In place of the flag an alternative symbol fluttered in the stiff breeze.

It was a brassiere of ample proportions.

The church cleaner had arrived at the same time. Miriam Coleclough stared up in horror. Miriam had been blessed with the largest bust in Milltown and her undergarments were a thing of wonder. It was said the washing line at the back of her cottage was almost a tourist attraction. Her neighbours would invite friends and relations to peer from their upstairs windows at the sight below them.

Miriam was a loud lady who on occasions resorted to vociferous expletives but never, of course, when she was in the church grounds. However, this day proved to be the exception.

'The cheeky little buggers,' exclaimed Miriam.

'Oh dear, Miriam,' said Piers.

'Beggin' y'pardon, Vicar, but that's my best bra.'

Miriam had recently splashed out on a Doreen Triumph International brassiere from her catalogue along with a matching panty girdle for much-needed 'tummy control' . . . or so the advertisement claimed.

Fortunately she was wearing the girdle but the bra that resembled a pair of extra-large colanders had been removed under the cover of darkness from her back garden. It must have taken a very agile teenager to climb the flagpole.

Miriam's husband, the long-suffering Archibald, who made a point of never wearing his hearing aid when his fierce wife was in the house, was called to bring his ladder. Archibald kept the church grounds neat and tidy and spent hours cleaning and oiling his lawn mower in his shed at the bottom of his garden. It was said that, in truth, he loved his mower more than his wife.

Even our caring vicar could understand why.

So it was that, as a grey morning light lit up the Norman

tower and the ancient walls, the Revd Piers Witherspoon could be seen up a ladder and grappling with a huge brassiere.

Archibald was holding the bottom of the ladder and Miriam was shouting instructions.

'Y'need to undo that big metal catch at t'back o' m'bra, Vicar.'

There was renewed laughter from the gathering crowd. They cheered each attempt until the vicar's humiliation was complete. Eventually he climbed down while gripping the garment distastefully between finger and thumb at the end of an outstretched arm. He returned it to Miriam with a look of acute embarrassment and no little distaste.

'It's all wet an' mucky now, Vicar,' complained Miriam.

'Tek it 'ome, luv,' said Archibald, 'an' dry it in front o' t'fire.'

'Ah 'ope it dunt flippin' shrink,' snapped Miriam as she walked away.

'Never mind,' muttered Archibald so only Piers could hear. 'Ah'm sure you'll soon stretch it back again.'

It took some time for the placid Piers to regain his composure.

After Piers left I made my way to the staff-room, where I found Travis concentrating on an advert in the newspaper.

He looked up. 'Hi, Jack.'

'You look intrigued.'

He held up the paper. 'Just checking this out.' It was an advertisement for Australia. 'It says here Australia is a great place to live.'

'So I've heard. Sea and beaches and a decent rugby team.'

He gave a wry smile. 'Well . . . I wouldn't get in a rugby team, Jack, but I definitely have the qualifications to go there. They certainly make it attractive. Adults can go for ten pounds and children are free.'

'Are you serious?'

'Perhaps. I've begun to consider what's keeping me here.' He closed the paper and sat back. 'No girlfriend and not much of a social life apart from the Railway Society.' He sighed and looked out of the window. The sound of the local rag-and-bone man ringing his bell could be heard from the estate across the road. 'The children here are poor as church mice but they're rewarding to teach. I have friends on the staff but working for Norman can be hell at times. He's been a complete *you-know-what* today. Absolutely no encouragement. It grinds you down after a while. Talk about using words as if they were a blunt instrument. He gave me an earful about bringing back National Service at lunchtime. Reckons that's what's needed to knock layabouts into shape. He also told me to get a haircut.'

'I'm sorry, Travis. I can see why you're feeling down.'

'You and Penny are still new but it will get you in the end.'

'Have you spoken to anyone else about this?'

He stroked his moustache. 'Not really, although I know Connie feels the same. Barbara will probably be here for ever and Audrey just trundles along hoping to find a man one day. I just feel I'll have to decide sooner rather than later what I'm going to do with my life.'

I studied him. Strong, active, bright. It seemed a shame. He was a great colleague. 'How about a pint tonight and maybe chicken in a basket?'

There was no hesitation: 'You're on.'

I shivered as I parked on the road outside The Cat & Kettle. The pub was next to the local graveyard. The rain had finally stopped and a pallid moon cast a ghostly light while lichen-covered gravestones rose like shattered teeth above the low-lying mist.

Travis had bumped into Connie as he was leaving school and invited her along as well. Inside it was warm and soon we relaxed. Travis bought a round of drinks and we were adding tomato sauce to our chicken and chips when Connie announced, 'Have you heard about Audrey?'

Travis and I shook our heads.

'She feels she's been left on the shelf.'

'That's sad,' said Travis.

'She told me and Barbara something interesting after school.'

'What about?' I asked.

'Well, she's been reading the advertisements for marriage agencies in the *Tatler*.'

This was news. Travis and I supped our beer and listened intently.

'Apparently the biggest agency is the Ivy Gibson Bureau in Oxford Street. They spend five hundred pounds each week on advertising.'

'Serious money,' said Travis.

Connie nodded. 'It's big business and Audrey has joined.'

'Really?' I said.

'Yes, and it costs eight pounds, eight shillings for a year of introductions.'

'Sounds reasonable to me,' said Travis. As usual, he was a fount of obscure knowledge. 'Particularly as women in Britain over the age of forty outnumber men by more than two million.'

'Oh well,' said Connie, 'at least there's still hope for me,' and Travis looked at her thoughtfully.

The conversation ranged from politics to rugby as we relaxed with our drinks.

'Another round?' I asked.

Travis looked at his watch. 'Sorry, must go. It's my Railway Society night and I'm working towards being a guard.' He hurried out.

'I can just see him in his uniform,' I said.

Connie picked up our glasses and smiled at me. 'Let me get these.'

I didn't mention the earlier conversation about Australia.

When she returned with the drinks I asked, 'What about you? Do you really want to get married? If you don't mind me saying, you don't come over as so conventional – more a bit of a rebel.'

'I suppose I *am* a bit of a rebel. It's just that I'm sick of inequality.' She sipped her beer. The pub was filling up and 'Honky Tonk Women' by the Rolling Stones was blasting out on the jukebox. 'Back in Durham I did A-level Economic History, the only girl in a class of twenty boys. I was better than them and the teacher wasn't pleased.'

I sensed her frustration was deeply felt. 'It's something I haven't experienced. I'm sorry it's like that for you. At least in teaching we have equal pay scales.'

'But it's the men who get promoted. Look at Norman. That's a disgrace.'

'I see what you mean. I've not come across anyone like him before.'

She sipped her drink and looked at me. 'It will be your turn one day, Jack. You'll be a headteacher and a damn sight better than him.'

'What about you? You're a good teacher.'

'That doesn't necessarily make you a good head, an effective manager.'

'But you could lead a team.'

'Maybe . . . but only with experience and some decent training.'

'You don't come over as someone who would be frightened of telling a man what to do.'

'Is that what you think?'

'Connie, when I first arrived here word had it you were something of a man-eater.'

She gave me a smile. 'That's just a front, Jack. It's easy to hide behind.'

'What do you mean?'

She stared into her glass, looking pensive. 'I'll share something with you.'

I sensed she was about to impart something of gravity.

'Back in college I was very much in love with a guy called Andy Makin; he was a PE student. It was serious and we were due to get married after we qualified. We got a flat and were living together at the time. One day, I came home and he wasn't there. All his things were gone. Just his key and a letter calling everything off. There were only six weeks to go before the wedding and I was devastated.

'Fortunately I had some good friends who had a spare room in their flat and so I moved in with them. It was only a couple of months later that Andy turned up at the flat wanting to see me. He was so sorry for his behaviour and begged me to give him a second chance, so I did. Against my friends' advice, I started seeing him again.'

I said nothing. Around us the pub was getting noisy.

Connie leaned her elbows on the table and clasped her hands together. 'Eventually he proposed again and we planned to get married in the summer. Three weeks before the wedding I went to my parents' home to do some final preparation for the big day. Andy drove me to the station and said he had to call in to the Post Office on the way. He had a letter to post. As he dropped me off he gave me a big hug.'

Connie paused; the thoughts were obviously flooding back to her as if it had all happened yesterday. 'A few days later I received a letter. I remember my mum bringing it up to me. I was finishing off the bridesmaids' dresses in my bedroom. The letter was the one Andy posted on the way to the station. He was calling off the wedding . . . again.'

She looked at me with a penetrating stare. 'He was a tall man, Jack . . . like you. But for all his stature and imposing looks, he was a coward and always will be. It was hard but I realized there was no place in my life for a man like him and there never will be.'

'I'm so sorry, Connie.'

She put her hands flat on the table and studied me again with those familiar steel-grey eyes. 'So a man-eater? No, not really . . . more a woman scorned.'

## Chapter Six

# *A Mouse Called Brian*

There was just a flicker of movement that caught my eye as I was writing the date, Friday, 5 December, on the blackboard.

It was from the direction of Terry Speight's desk.

I paused and stared at Terry, who was a picture of blissful innocence.

His right hand was covering the circular hole where the inkwell should have been. Before school our caretaker had collected all the inkwells for cleaning prior to Norman's handwriting lesson later in the day. Norman was fastidious about his inkwells.

Then I saw it.

A tiny grey head suddenly appeared from out of the hole.

It popped up between his fingers.

I looked in astonishment.

There could be no doubt.

It was a mouse!

*

Back in Ivy Cottage that morning my day had begun like many others. I had eaten my bowl of Kellogg's Sugar Smacks while listening to the Tony Blackburn show on BBC Radio 1. Elvis Presley was singing 'Suspicious Minds', which seemed appropriate when I considered some of the stories concerning Norman that had begun to circulate in the staff-room. By the time I had put on my duffel coat and old college scarf, the Beatles were blasting out 'Come Together', which put me in a more cheerful mood to meet the new day.

When I walked outside the world was different. The first snow of winter had fallen on the high ground of the Pennines and the frozen earth was gripped in an iron fist. As I drove out of the village the fields beyond the hedgerows were covered in a cloak of silence. All sounds appeared muted as the creatures of the countryside had sought refuge in the night. The distant hills were a washboard of smooth white folds while above me the rags of cirrus clouds raced across a gunmetal sky that promised more snow.

By the time I was driving up the hill towards Heather View a brisk north wind was sweeping through the Milltown estate and frost had dusted the cobbles of the back streets.

It had been a tough journey on the slippery roads but, as I reached the top of the hill, I saw a strange sight. The teenager Kenny Speight was crossing the road and it was clear he had a problem. He was wearing an old overcoat meant for a much taller person and limping noticeably. He appeared to be walking with a stiff straight leg.

As I slowed up he grinned at me and I wondered why.

However, there was no time to dwell on it – I just had enough time to call at the Corner Shop before driving into school.

Mrs Pickles was being served as I walked in and her daughter, Lizzie, was clinging to her mother's hand.

'Ah've run out o' washing-up liquid, Kathy.'

Kathy slapped a bottle on the counter. 'Large Fairy Liquid, Elsie. That's two bob.'

'An' ah want summat special f'my Frank's tea. It's 'is birthday.'

'What d'you fancy?'

'Ah were thinkin' about one o' your Ernie's pork pies wi' some chips and mebbe a tin o' them *mandolin* oranges.'

'Perfec',' said Kathy.

'So ah won't be at bingo tonight.'

'That's a shame,' said Kathy, 'it's jackpot night.'

'Ah know,' said Elsie mournfully. 'Ah love m'bingo. Out o' m'kitchen. No one tellin' me what t'do, a gin an' tonic . . . an' all for four bob a week.'

'An' no men!' exclaimed Kathy, sending a disparaging look towards the downtrodden Ernie, who was stacking boxes of Kellogg's Puffa Puffa Rice on the cereals shelf. She glanced up at me. 'Present company *discluded*, o' course.'

*Excluded,* I thought but said nothing.

Mrs Pickles packed her shopping bag, collected her change and smiled at me. 'Morning, Mr Sheffield.'

'Good morning, Mrs Pickles. Winter seems to have arrived.'

Both women glanced out of the window. 'Nowt but a sprinklin',' said Kathy. It would need a lot more snow to impress these two tough Yorkshire ladies.

'So . . . what can ah do for you, Mr Sheffield?' asked Kathy.

'A packet of Scott's Porage Oats, a loaf of bread and a jar of strawberry jam, please.'

I paid with a fifty-pence piece. Kathy stared at it. 'Ah'll miss m'ten-shilling notes when they go,' she said sadly.

'I know what you mean,' I said. 'A nostalgic thought,' I added with a supportive smile.

'Nostalgia,' said Kathy bluntly. 'That's all in the past!'

*I suppose it would be,* I thought as I left the shop.

I met Penny in the school car park. Her Mini had managed to get up the steep hill on this frosty morning. I smiled. Last week she had been into C&A and splashed out on a black midi 'wet look' coat in crushed PVC for eight pounds nineteen shillings. With her red bobble hat, long scarf and high leather boots she looked terrific.

'Love the coat,' I said appreciatively.

'It's an early Christmas present to myself,' she said with a grin.

'Looks great.'

I wondered if Seb would be buying her a Christmas gift.

Suddenly there was a sharp *ping* from the direction of the 'SCHOOL' warning sign on the other side of the fence. It was as if someone had thrown a small piece of glass against the metal pole that supported it. I noticed Minnie Ackworth, twenty yards away on the zebra crossing, look curiously towards the sudden sound. Then the cries of lively children, undeterred by the bitter weather, filled the air as they swarmed through the school gate.

Connie and Travis were in the entrance hall.

'Norman looked out of sorts this morning,' said Connie. 'It was as though he had all the worries of the world on his shoulders when he walked in from the car park.'

Travis gave a wry smile. '"Creeping like a snail unwillingly to school."'

Connie narrowed her eyes. 'Sounds a bit like your friend Shakespeare again.'

'I know that one,' I said. 'It's from the "All the world's a stage" speech in *As You Like It*.'

'Well done, Jack,' said Travis. 'Hard luck, Connie.'

She dug him in the ribs and we set off for our classrooms.

At nine o'clock the children in my class had filed into Class 6 and waited patiently while I completed the register. Their behaviour was, as usual now, excellent and I was pleased with their response. They appeared to enjoy their work as I gradually encouraged a love of learning in them and, for me, their enthusiasm confirmed that teaching was the best job in the world, even in the tough environment of Milltown.

I intended to start the day with a writing lesson concerning the activities they enjoyed during their spare time. We began with a discussion. The range of interests was wide. The quietest girl in the class, Margery Duckworth, had one of the new talking Barbie dolls while Susan Bell never missed an episode of *Coronation Street*. The Atha twins, Ronnie and Reggie, apparently spent a lot of time sitting outside local pubs eating crisps while waiting for their parents to emerge. Billy Woodcock was the proud owner of a James Bond 100-shot cap pistol, complete with a silencer, and would take imaginary pot shots at the milkman each morning from the safety of the outside toilet in the back yard.

Thankfully, Matthew Hesketh was into gentler pursuits. He was the proud owner of a Subbuteo set. His father would cover their kitchen table with the green cloth marked out like a football pitch and together they would flick the little footballers around the surface and try to score a goal. His father had begun a league championship and now many of the dads were turning up to play.

It was when I turned to write the date on the blackboard that I saw the mouse!

Terry Speight closed protective fingers over the unexpected visitor.

I walked slowly over to his desk and crouched down to appear less intimidating. 'What have you got there, Terry?'

It was incongruous that, with a psychopath for a father and a tearaway teenager for a brother, Terry was always open and honest.

'It's Brian, sir.'

'Brian?'

There were giggles from the children close by, who were clearly aware of Terry's rodent companion.

'Yes, sir . . . 'e's m'friend.'

'I'm sure he is but why is he in your desk?'

'That's where ah 'ave t'keep 'im 'cause m'mam dunt want no mice in our 'ouse.'

'I can understand that,' I said, ignoring the double negative.

'She sez she'll 'it 'im wi' m'dad's 'ammer if she sees 'im again.'

I paused for thought. This was an unwelcome dilemma. To remove Brian into the wild could be unkind, keeping him in a school desk was unthinkable and sending him home meant a violent death.

The little boy looked anxious.

It was clear the bond between Terry and Brian could not be ignored.

I reflected that my teacher training had not prepared me for moments like this. There was a metal pencil case on my desk and I picked it up and slid it carefully under Terry's hand and over the hole in the desk. Brian was secure . . . at least for now.

Our discussion took a different turn as others made their views known.

'Sir, let's keep 'im,' said the sympathetic Sandra Asquith.

'In a box,' suggested Janet Stubbs.

'A cage would be better,' said Charlie Dewhirst. 'Then 'e won't eat 'is way to freedom.'

I was impressed. 'Good sentence, Charlie. Well done.'

Suddenly everyone was speaking at once. I held up my hands for silence.

'Right, boys and girls, I'll have a chat with Terry at morning break. In the meantime I want you to write a story. Make it an exciting adventure.'

I turned to the blackboard and wrote the title 'A Mouse Called Brian'.

Everyone set to with enthusiasm.

Terry's face was wreathed in smiles. His furry friend was not only famous . . . he had a future.

When the bell rang for morning break the children were excited to see it had begun to snow again and they ran outside. Only Terry remained behind and he looked up at me expectantly.

'Terry, I need to talk with Mr Little first. Then we can decide what to do with Brian. Just keep him safe for the time being.'

'OK, sir . . . and thanks.'

We walked out to the cloakroom area and he pulled his coat off his peg.

A thought occurred to me. 'Terry, what's the matter with your brother?'

Terry looked puzzled. 'Nowt, sir.'

'Well, he was limping across the road this morning. I thought he must have hurt himself.'

Terry grinned. 'No, sir. It allus looks as though 'e's limpin' when 'e's got 'is rifle down 'is trouser leg.'

I thought I had misheard. 'Rifle?'

'Yes, sir, 'is air rifle. 'E teks it out t'practise.'

'Your brother has an air rifle?'

'Yes, sir,' said Terry as if it was perfectly natural. ' 'E's a good shot is our Kenny.'

'I imagine he is,' I muttered.

The cheerful little boy was eager to get out to play with the others. 'Can ah go now, sir?'

'Just something else, Terry. Where does Kenny keep his rifle?'

'In our bedroom. 'E 'as the top bunk an' 'e shoots out of t'window.'

This was getting serious. 'What at?'

'That "SCHOOL" sign across t'road, sir. 'E sez it's good target practice.'

I had heard enough and hurried to the head's office.

Norman was reading a golfing magazine and smoking a cigarette when I tapped on his door and walked in.

He looked up angrily. 'You haven't got it yet, have you?'

'Pardon?'

'Show some manners and wait until I say *come in*.'

'Sorry, but this is urgent.' I related my conversation with Terry Speight.

'Bad family,' said Norman.

'We need to contact the police as a matter of urgency.'

Norman was still irritated. 'I don't need you to tell me my job.'

'Will you ring or shall I?'

He stubbed out his cigarette. 'Leave it with me.'

It was as the dinner bell rang at twelve o'clock that Billy Woodcock announced, 'Copper coming in, sir.' Billy was tall enough to see out of the window and he had become a useful early-warning system.

A policeman on a motorbike was riding carefully through the school gate towards the car park. I followed the children out of the classroom and walked to the entrance porch and out into the bitter cold. The policeman parked his bike. It was impressive: a BSA C15 250cc with a black Avon fairing.

He walked up the steps to the shelter of the entrance

porch and removed his helmet: a tall, athletic man with short-cropped ginger hair; I recognized him as the pacy winger for Skipton rugby club. We shook hands.

'I'm Jack Sheffield, Terry Speight's teacher.'

He smiled in recognition. 'Hello, Jack. I remember you from the last Wharfedale–Skipton game.' He glanced around. 'I'm PC Moxon but call me Phil in private conversation.' He shivered. 'Bloody cold on that bike, Jack. Shall we talk inside?'

We walked into the relative warmth of the entrance hall.

'I had better tell the head you're here.'

He glanced at the door to Norman's office. 'Before that, Jack, just tell me what you know.' He took out his notebook. 'All I've got here is a report of a teenager with an air rifle.'

It occurred to me that Barbara had been right. We were fortunate to have a good local bobby.

After a warming school dinner of beef stew and carrots Sandra Asquith and Janet Stubbs seemed anxious to speak to me. I had seen PC Moxon depart, riding his bike purposefully up the drive.

'What is it, girls?'

'Can we stay in, sir, 'stead o' goin' out?' asked Sandra.

I looked out of the window. Snow had begun to sweep across the playground. I couldn't blame her for asking. 'What will you be doing?'

Sandra gave me an engaging smile. 'Me an' Janet were goin' t'read m'*Jackie* in our classroom.'

'*Jackie*? Yes, I suppose so.' I knew this was a popular magazine among the older junior girls. Both Sandra and

Janet had just passed their eleventh birthdays. 'Do you get it every week?'

'Yes, sir,' said Sandra. 'M'gran gives me sixpence from 'er pension.'

'It's brilliant,' said Janet. 'There's a poster of t'Rollin' Stones in this one.'

'Las' month it said it were t'paper f'young lovers,' said Sandra.

'Oh, did it?'

'Yes, sir . . . but me an' Janet jus' like it f'pop stars. Mick Jagger is my fav'rite an' Janet likes 'im what plays a guitar in the 'Ollies.'

'The Hollies? I like them. They were on the radio this morning.'

The girls looked surprised. It hadn't occurred to them that their teacher might also like pop music. They hurried off to dream of sixties pin-ups along with the problems that awaited them in the future as teenage girls while I walked to the staff-room. There I met a hubbub of conversation as Barbara and Audrey had claimed their usual chairs nearest to the two-bar electric fire.

'Did you see the news last night, Barbara?' asked Audrey.

'Yes,' said Barbara, 'and in colour.'

Regular broadcasts in colour had been a feature on BBC and ITV since last month.

'I was thinking of all those poor young men in America.'

'Oh yes,' said Barbara, 'I see what you mean.'

The first Draft Lottery in the USA had taken place to choose conscripts for Vietnam.

'What a dreadful waste of life,' said Audrey. 'Let's hope it's over quickly and they're all home again soon.'

'There will be a lot of worried families this Christmas,' said Barbara.

Connie leaned over to Penny and spoke quietly: 'I went on the anti-Vietnam War demonstration last year in London.'

'I remember it,' said Penny, 'and I can understand why John Lennon returned his MBE.'

Ten days ago his chauffeur had delivered handwritten letters to the Queen and Prime Minister Harold Wilson in protest at the government's support of the US in Vietnam.

'So, what was it like?' asked Penny.

'Quite an experience,' said Connie. 'A bit scary, to be honest. We gathered in Grosvenor Square until the police horses barged us away. It felt like a cavalry charge.'

'Oh dear,' said Penny.

Connie sighed. 'Yes, a pity . . . I like horses.'

Afternoon school began with the three infant classes sitting cross-legged in the hall and waiting expectantly. It was the first rehearsal for the Nativity play and the experienced Barbara was taking it all in her stride. Penny's children were the stars with the youngest children taking the main parts. Audrey's class were the angelic choir and Barbara's children were taking turns to read the timeless story. So every child was involved.

Two of the seven-year-olds in Barbara's class, Karen Swales and Susan Holbeck, were looking at the large poster on the wall featuring the Virgin Mary and baby Jesus.

'She doesn't look too 'appy,' said Karen thoughtfully.

'Ah s'ppose she's a bit fed up 'avin' a baby in a stable,' said Susan.

'Ah were born in a 'ospital,' said Karen.

'Best place,' said Susan, 'wi' nurses an' suchlike.'

There was a pause while they both studied the picture.

'Where's 'is dad?' asked Karen.

Susan pursed her lips. ' 'E must 'ave been taking the picture.'

Barbara called the two of them over just as the Revd Witherspoon arrived to lend support.

'Wonderful,' said Piers. 'You do this so well every year.'

'Thank you,' said Barbara, who was delighted to see him. 'At least they should know the story by now.'

There was a break while Penny arranged the children to create a tableau of the scene in the stable with the shepherds and Wise Men.

Piers smiled at the children. 'Now, girls and boys, can you tell me what presents the Wise Men brought for Jesus?'

Six-year-old Claire Lofthouse raised her hand, bursting with enthusiasm. Audrey smiled. Claire was one of the most hard-working children in Class 2. 'I know, sir, I know!'

'Very well, Claire, what do you think?'

'Was it one o' Mr Priestley's pies?'

Audrey flushed as Piers gave her an inquisitive look.

Back in my class the children were busy with their project work. Billy Woodcock was staring at the poster of the moon on the noticeboard.

'Where's the Ocean of Storms, sir?'

It was where astronauts Charles 'Pete' Conrad and Alan Bean had landed on the moon last month on Apollo 12. I had asked Billy to produce a project folder dedicated to space travel and he had responded well.

I took Billy over to the large poster of the moon. 'It's here, Billy.'

'Thanks, sir.'

I gave him one of the newspaper cuttings I had brought in. 'And I want you to read this and tell me about the moon's gravity.'

Billy grinned. 'Well, ah know it's a lot less than Earth.'

'Well done, Billy. See if you can find out the difference between the moon's gravity and Earth's gravity.'

He hurried off, intent on solving the task.

I had encouraged each child to do their own research on a topic of their choice. This was in addition to our staple daily diet of maths and English. Teaching at Heather View was proving to be an interesting journey, and I felt that my teaching skills were developing.

At afternoon break I called in to Connie's class to discuss the air-rifle incident. It had dominated my thoughts and Norman hadn't spoken to me since his interview with PC Moxon. When I walked in she was busy talking to two nine-year-olds, Natalie Winthrop and Mandy Hardisty.

The two girls were enjoying a copy of *Sally*. Natalie had called in to the Corner Shop that morning and spent sixpence on her favourite weekly comic.

She was sharing it with her friend. It was advertised as 'The comic for the adventurous girl' and the two girls loved their favourite super-heroines. Natalie was a fan of 'Cat Girl' whereas Mandy favoured the incongruously named 'Legion of Super Slaves'. Either way, they loved their weekly journey of make-believe.

Connie suddenly said, 'I heard about the mouse, Jack.'

'Oh yes,' I said. It hadn't been uppermost on my mind since reflecting on a certain teenager taking potshots with his air rifle.

'I've got a cage at home if you want it.'

'Thanks. Yes, please.'

'I could take the mouse home with me over the weekend, feed him, then bring him back in his new home next week.'

'That would be perfect.'

She smiled. 'I used to have a gerbil called Robby.'

'Good name,' I said and then wondered if Robby had been another of Connie's boyfriends.

When we returned to our classrooms Billy Woodcock made his familiar announcement. 'That copper's back, sir.' Billy didn't miss much.

'It's Police Constable Moxon, Billy,' I said, hoping the correct title for our local law enforcer would sink in.

As Norman had cancelled his weekly handwriting lesson I finished off the day with an extra-long story time. Then, at the end of school, the children dispersed into the darkness and I told Terry that Miss Brooksbank had offered to look after Brian for the weekend and bring him back in a cage.

'Cor, thanks, sir.' He made sure my pencil tin was secure over Brian's escape hole before he left.

It was later when I was in the staff-room that Piers called in.

'Hello, Jack, I heard about the rifle incident. Just had an informative conversation with PC Moxon. He's confiscated the weapon and no doubt Kenny will receive a stern warning.'

'Good news. It needed dealing with.'

'We're lucky to have such a good local policeman,' he said. 'PC Moxon is a force for good in a dark world and a friend in time of need.'

'Very true.' It struck me that Piers often spoke as if he were addressing his congregation.

'But Kenny's not a bad lad,' he went on.

I agreed. 'Maybe it's just that he's never been brought up knowing right from wrong and, of course, he's totally fearless.'

He patted me on the shoulder. 'If you think about it, Jack, nobody's afraid of what they don't know.'

'Really?'

Piers nodded knowingly. 'Everything passes through, Jack. We are but fleeting shadows on this earth.'

I was still considering this as he hurried out and I went to collect my dinner register from Edith. I was in the entrance hall when PC Moxon stepped out of Norman's office.

'Hi, Phil, any news?'

He looked left and right and nodded towards the entrance door. I followed him out and we sheltered under the porch. His motorbike was parked at the foot of the steps.

'One minute, Jack.' He walked to his bike, picked up the telephone handset cradled on top of the petrol tank and reported a brief message. Then he walked back up the steps and we stood under the porch light.

'I've spoken to the head, Jack, and I can bring you up to date if you like . . . off the record, so to speak.'

'Thanks, Phil. So, what's happened?'

'Well, first of all, there are laws about air guns and you might be surprised to hear they can be used by fourteen-year-olds but you have to be over eighteen to buy one. Even so, a fourteen-year-old like Kenny can receive one as a gift.'

'That's worrying.'

He sighed. 'Too true.'

'That means Kenny can use one.'

He leaned back against the wall. 'Sadly, yes, but not within fifty feet of a public highway. On private land he could fire pellets but there's no way he should be firing shots from his bedroom window.'

'So have you confiscated it?'

He grinned. 'Yes. In my report it will say I saw it through a crack in the door.'

'And did you?'

'No, it was in the bedroom so I quoted the Ways and Means Act.'

'Never heard of it.'

He gave me a wry smile. 'It doesn't exist, Jack. Just a ruse to get into a property. My sergeant uses it all the time.'

'I see. So what happens next?'

'I have to go back to see Kenny when an adult is present so I'll be going there later tonight. Then it will go into the log for the day down at the station.' We both looked out into the darkness as fresh snow began to fall. 'So long as I can ride in this stuff.'

'What will happen to Kenny?'

'Depends.' He stroked his chin. 'He'll be reported and fined or maybe just given a warning.'

'Either way, let's hope he won't be taking potshots at our school sign again.'

We shook hands and he mounted his bike with extreme care. The radio was fixed to the mudguard over the back wheel but the aerial was sticking up near the seat. He saw me staring and laughed. 'You could do yourself an injury with this bloody thing.'

'Might slow you down a bit when we next meet on the rugby field,' I said.

'No chance, Jack,' he retorted and roared off.

I walked back into the entrance hall as Norman appeared from his office. He paused to button up his coat.

'Good night, Mr Little, have a good weekend,' I said politely but without conviction.

He muttered something under his breath that I couldn't quite hear.

It was at that moment that Eric Skinner suddenly burst through the swing doors leading to the hall as if the hounds of hell were chasing him. His face was ashen.

'What is it, Eric?' asked Norman.

'Ah couldn't believe m'eyes,' he said, shaking his head.

'What's happened?' asked Norman, clearly irritated by the interruption.

Our caretaker gave me a steely look. 'Ah were jus' puttin' yer inkwells back in Class Six.'

'Oh yes?' I said with a sinking feeling. I recalled what it was I had intended to discuss with Norman.

'Then, large as life, there it was starin' at me.'

'What was staring at you?' asked Norman, trying to remain composed.

'You'll never guess in a month o' Sundays . . . It were a mouse . . . a bleedin' mouse!'

## Chapter Seven

# *Three Wise Women*

A world of silence awaited me as I looked out of the bedroom window. Snow drifted weightlessly in the still cold air like countryside confetti and the pantile roofs of the cottages on Lotherswicke High Street were covered in wavy white patterns. The hedgerows sparkled and, in the far distance, the trees were like frozen sentinels. High in the elms, a parliament of rooks surveyed the bitter landscape with beady eyes. Undeterred, I dressed quickly. It was Friday, 19 December, the last day of the autumn term, and the Christmas holiday beckoned.

A difficult journey was in store. The road out of the village was a causeway of blue crystal and the grassy mounds were rimed with frost. The world was changed and even Milltown looked fresh and clean under its blanket of snow. When I drove through the school gates children were building snowmen, skimming over icy slides and enjoying snowball fights. They didn't seem to feel the cold and their tireless winter games were a sight to behold.

As I crunched over the snow into the school car park Barbara's husband, Big Jimmy, was carrying a Dansette record player into the school entrance. Barbara was scurrying behind with a large shopping bag. The children's Christmas party with music and games was in store and Barbara, as always, was well prepared.

Edith had arrived very early and was in her office writing out her Christmas cards for the staff. It was a ritual that she followed with great care. Last night she had posted all the cards to her friends and relations. However, each year a name was crossed out, a deceased family member or a friend who was no longer there.

It was always a sad moment. With a stroke of the pen she was erasing a life.

Deep down, however, there was another concern in her life. Her usual peaceful equilibrium had been disturbed. Edith had always taken a pride in her work and knew her accountancy was impeccable. During the past term, however, it had happened three times . . . the unthinkable. The amount in the total column in her dinner register did not match the sum she handed in to the bank. On each occasion she had been fifty pence short. Ten shillings in old money. Each time she had made up the difference from her own purse. It couldn't go on. There had to be a resolution.

There was a tap on the door and Barbara walked in. 'Good morning, Edith, how are you?'

Edith took a moment to compose herself. 'Fine, thank you, Barbara. Just engrossed in my registers.'

Barbara recognized when her dear friend had a problem and determined she would support her if she could. 'Can I help?'

'Perhaps,' said Edith cautiously. She was starting to believe that a lifetime of adding up columns of figures was beginning to take its toll. Everything fades in time.

She looked up at Barbara and knew there was no one else she could speak to about this.

Suddenly a parent appeared in the open doorway. It was Mrs Peggy Stubbs, dragging a reluctant Gary behind her.

'Mrs Priestley, sorry t'bother you. Ah know y'busy but can ah 'ave a quick word. It's about t'Nativity.'

Barbara smiled at Edith. 'I'll catch you later.' She closed the door and addressed the red-faced Mrs Stubbs. 'Is there a problem?'

'Well, my Gary said 'e were a big white fairy in this play o' yours.'

Barbara took a deep breath. 'He's the *Angel Gabriel*, Mrs Stubbs,' she said with feeling.

'Is 'e?'

'It's a very important part.'

'Is it?'

'Mrs Clegg told me he's tried really hard.'

''As 'e?'

'He has.'

'Well, 'e's mekkin' a big fuss about nowt then. 'E's like 'is dad, a big soft ha'porth. So ah'm sorry to 'ave bothered you, Mrs Priestley. Thanks for y'time.'

She dragged Gary out to the playground. 'Off y'go and play,' she said and pushed him in the direction of his friends. Then she went to the school gate, lit a cigarette and smiled.

Betty Sweet ushered little Willy through the school gate, leaned on the fence and took out a cigarette. 'Give us a light, Peggy.'

They puffed away contentedly. 'So what are you lookin' so 'appy about?'

'My Gary.'

'What about 'im?'

'You'll never guess,' she announced proudly. ' 'E's only t'chief bloody angel in t'Christmas play.'

At morning break we gathered in the staff-room. Out of the window I could see Travis on playground duty stamping his feet to keep warm. Barbara had brought in a huge Victoria sponge cake and was serving generous slices while Edith passed around mugs of coffee.

We sat in a circle like contented kittens enjoying the welcome treat.

'Thanks, Barbara,' said Penny, 'absolutely delicious.'

'So . . . any special plans for Christmas?' asked Barbara.

'The usual,' said Penny. 'Christmas Day with my parents. Lots to eat and drink and, oh yes . . . Seb said he would take me to the new Bond film.'

The sixth James Bond film, *On Her Majesty's Secret Service* starring George Lazenby and Diana Rigg, had just premiered in London.

'Not sure about the new Bond,' mumbled Connie through a mouthful of crumbs.

'He's certainly no Sean Connery,' said Barbara.

'True . . . very true,' agreed Audrey with a faraway look in her eyes. The tough Scot was another of Audrey's heart-throbs.

'Anyway, I'm going back to Pity Me for Christmas,' said Connie. 'What about you, Jack?'

'Similar to you and Penny. I'll be in Leeds with my

parents on Christmas Day. Then I'm playing rugby in Grassington for the annual Boxing Day fixture.'

'My dad will be there,' said Penny.

'I'd like to meet him. Perhaps he could stick around after the game for a drink.'

Penny smiled. 'I might come along as well.'

'That's great.'

'Unless Seb has other plans. He's not really into rugby. I think he played squash and croquet at university.'

Connie looked up with a mischievous grin. 'I thought you said he was *good at simply everything*.'

Penny sighed. 'Did I?' She crumpled up her paper napkin and tossed it in the bin.

'Anyway, don't forget, everybody,' said Connie, 'you're all welcome to see in the New Year at my house.'

'I'll be there,' said Travis.

'What about you, Jack?'

I paused before replying. 'There's a party at the rugby club.'

She gave me that familiar *direct* look. 'Then . . . come on later.'

In Connie's class, the children were writing their letters to Santa.

Connie looked down at Mandy Hardisty's writing. The little girl had filled the page. 'That's a long list, Mandy.'

Mandy sighed deeply and looked up. 'Yes, Miss, 'cause it's well, y'know . . . just in case.'

'Just in case?'

'Yes, Miss . . . just in case ah don't believe in 'im nex' year.'

'I see,' said Connie cautiously.

'An' ah were thinkin' 'e mus' spend a fortune on Sellotape.'

'I suppose he does,' agreed Connie but without conviction.

'Ah'm jus' wond'rin', Miss . . .' said nine-year-old Barry Piggott.

'What about, Barry?'

Barry was a quiet boy and it was unusual for him to speak up. 'Well, m'mum told me she's gettin' our Rocky a whistle f'Christmas.'

'Rocky?'

'Our dog, Miss.'

'That sounds a good idea.'

'Yes, Miss, but that's why ah'm wond'rin'.'

'And what are you wondering about?'

'Well, Miss, 'ow's Rocky gonna blow it?'

'Ah,' said Connie. 'Let me explain . . .'

Penny was in her classroom sitting in front of a giant Christmas frieze. Santa was in his sleigh being pulled by a long line of reindeer. The names were pinned underneath each one and the children were reciting their names: Dasher, Dancer, Prancer, Vixen, Comet, Cupid, Donner and Blitzen . . . plus Rudolph.

For a finale they sang 'Rudolph the Red-Nosed Reindeer' with the exception of Willy Sweet who sang 'Rhubarb the Red-Nosed Reindeer.' Willy loved rhubarb.

At the start of afternoon school all the children gathered in the hall. Barbara had plugged in her Dansette record player and Travis was acting as disc jockey. His first record was 'Twist and Shout' by the Beatles accompanied by frantic dancing by all the boys and girls. This was followed by Musical Chairs and a more sedate Statues competition.

Meanwhile the ladies in the kitchen had worked hard to provide a simple party tea including crab-paste sandwiches, iced buns and orange juice. It had been a happy and hectic end of term and the day ended with children running out into the darkness with thoughts of presents and Christmas stockings.

Now it was time to clear up and prepare for our own Christmas break and we gathered in the school hall again. There was one exception. Norman had a golf dinner in Leeds and had almost beaten the children to the gate when the bell went.

Barbara and I were dismantling the Christmas tree.

'Seems odd taking down the decorations before Christmas.'

She smiled. 'Thanks for your help, Jack. You're the only one tall enough to take down the fairy from the top . . . apart from my Jimmy that is,' she added with a grin. 'This will be decorated again tonight in my front room.' She wrapped a couple of baubles in tissue paper and placed them carefully in a shoe box. 'I've done this for years. Some of these children won't see a Christmas tree otherwise.'

'It's a special time,' I said as I handed over a model fairy with a damaged wing.

Barbara gently straightened the angel's wing. 'The beauty of it is that I get *two* Christmases, one with the children and one with my family.'

'Yes, I suppose we do.' It hadn't really occurred to me before.

When the hall was clear of balloons and paper hats we set about stacking the dining tables. Eric Skinner ambled in carrying a black bag.

'Any chance of some help, Eric?' asked Barbara pointedly.

'Bad back,' he muttered and walked on to collect the waste paper from the bins.

'And a merry Christmas to you too,' said Connie as she pushed a dining trolley back into the kitchen.

'Tea and cake, everyone,' shouted Edith from the double doors that led to the entrance hall. We didn't need asking twice.

Ten minutes later we were enjoying one of Edith's specialities, a Dundee cake packed with currants and sultanas and covered in almonds. With a cup of hot tea it was a feast at the end of a busy day.

After half an hour of relaxed conversation we put on our coats and scarves and walked out to the car park. It was left to Barbara to lock the school as Eric Skinner had long since departed.

Connie was giving Travis a lift home, Audrey climbed into Edith's car and Jimmy Priestley arrived in his van to collect Barbara.

Penny and I stood side by side, two souls in the darkness looking out on a desolate world.

'Well, we've survived our first term,' I said.

She looked up at me and smiled. Her cheeks were flushed in the bitter cold. 'Yes, I suppose we have and it was good to see the children so happy today.'

A whisper of breeze ruffled her hair and I longed to put

my arms around her beneath this eternal sky; I wanted to tell her how I felt but the thought of Seb waiting for her in the shadows flickered through my mind.

'Are you happy?' I asked quietly.

She looked at me and her eyes were soft with sadness. 'Most of the time, Jack . . . not always.'

'If you need a friend, I'm here.'

'I know that. It's just that life is confusing at times.'

'We could meet up for a drink sometime if you like. Maybe even tonight if you're free.'

There was a pause. 'I'm seeing Seb later. The young doctors are having a party.'

'Another time then.'

I guess she sensed my disappointment. 'Yes, Jack. Another time.' And she stretched up and kissed me on my cheek before hurrying away. I scraped the ice from my windscreen, breathed on my car key to warm up the lock and climbed in my car. Finally I watched her drive away; the red lights disappeared as she turned on to the road and out of my life.

It was Tuesday morning, the day before Christmas Eve, when I drove into Skipton to buy some presents. Christmas Day with my parents in Leeds was always a special time, particularly now as my father's health was failing. My mother, Margaret, always prepared a spectacular Christmas dinner and her sister, my aunt May, was joining us this year.

I had saved up over the past months and had fifteen pounds to spend on presents for them. Skipton High Street was at its festive best as I scanned the brightly lit shop windows. As usual, I didn't take long. The main gift was a Morphy Richards Easimix Food Mixer at ten pounds nineteen shillings. I knew my mother would be delighted and it was worth standing in the queue and having to listen yet again to the Christmas number one, 'Two Little Boys'. I also purchased a bottle of RSVP sherry for twelve shillings and a Timothy White's Home Diary for my Aunt May. A market trader sold me some cheap wrapping paper and coloured ribbon and, with a sense of a job well done, I walked into one of the local pubs and ordered a pie and mash lunch and a pint of John Smith's.

I glanced at my wristwatch and shook my head. My Christmas shopping had taken forty-five minutes, much longer than usual.

On Christmas Eve I drove to the far side of Milltown. St Peter and All Angels Church was in the market square and close to the comprehensive school. Since then sprawling rows of Victorian terraced dwellings had been added along with the back-to-back houses of the early twentieth century.

Piers had told me that the parish church of St Peter's was the oldest building in Milltown and could be traced back to the Saxon period. He was proud of its history with the first known reference in the Domesday Book of 1086. From the Norman Conquest onwards the church had gradually been enlarged with its huge square bell tower dominating the skyline. Today a fresh fall of snow curved gently against its ancient walls. The church bells were ringing as I followed patterns of scumbled footsteps to the haven of the church.

The annual Crib Service was one of the best supported in the church calendar with parents of the youngest children in school coming along for their annual pilgrimage.

The children from the infant classes were gathering in the choir stalls, getting ready to perform the Nativity. While Barbara, Penny and Audrey adjusted tea-towel headdresses and cardboard crowns, I watched Penny and the tender way she helped each child. It was clear to me that the kiss on the cheek confirmed I was a friend, nothing more.

Barbara spotted me and beckoned to me to help. 'Jack, will you wrap the gifts for the Three Kings, please?' She passed over a shopping bag. 'There's some tissue and a roll of Sellotape in there.'

I smiled when I looked in the bag and duly wrapped a tin of Crosse & Blackwell Spaghetti Rings, a packet of Kellogg's Frosties and a tin of Marvel instant non-fat milk. Soon all was ready and we settled in our pews as the organist, Maisie Butterby, launched into the first bars of 'Little Donkey'.

Piers welcomed the congregation and smiled at all the children. He was standing next to a thatched model crib filled with hand-painted clay figures.

All seemed to go well with the exception of Mary dropping baby Jesus into the cardboard manger with all the grace of a coalman delivering a bag of nutty slack. Audrey was perched on the bottom step of the pulpit acting as prompter. She had spent an age with six-year-old Gary Stubbs, who appeared to be a dubious choice for the part of Angel Gabriel.

Gary had been told to say, 'A baby is born and his name is Jesus.' The spiky-haired little boy got it almost right.

He stood on a chair wearing a white sheet, a pair of droopy cardboard wings and a piece of tinsel tied round his head, spread his arms as if he were about to address a Trade Union Conference, and announced, 'Yer 'avin' a baby an' you 'ave t'call 'im . . .'

There was a pause.

'Jesus,' whispered Audrey.

'CHEESES!' shouted Gary.

On the back row Mrs Hardisty leaned over to her friend, Mrs Winthrop, and muttered, 'Y'can't beat a bit o' Wensleydale wi' a slice o' Christmas cake.'

'Y'reight there, Maureen.'

Mrs Swales had arrived early with her daughter, seven-year-old Karen, and had secured a front pew.

When the tableau in the stable was assembled Karen looked puzzled. 'Ah don't reckon much t'them gifts f'baby Jesus, Mam. Joseph dunt look too pleased.'

'It's 'ow it was f'baby Jesus.'

'Well, ah bet 'is mam would've wanted a blanket.'

'Mebbe so,' said Mrs Swales while wishing her daughter wouldn't be so persistent.

'Where's their telly, Mam?'

'They didn't 'ave no tellies in the Bible.'

'Why not, Mam?'

The angelic choir burst into a chorus of 'Away in a Manger'.

' 'Cause they were too busy singing.'

The narrator stood up and stared at his script. 'And Joseph arrived in Bethlehem with the Virgin Mary.'

'What's *virgin,* Mam?' asked the curious six-year-old Claire Lofthouse.

Mrs Lofthouse was speechless.

Her husband tried his best to rescue the situation. 'It's what y'mam was afore ah met 'er.'

'That's right, luv,' said a relieved Mrs Lofthouse.

Her husband was unaware of her pre-marriage relationship with a certain carpet-fitter from Rotherham . . . not to mention at least half the brass section of the Barnsley Swingtime Big Band.

At the end Piers reminded us of Midnight Mass and wished us all a merry Christmas. As we filed out into the bitter cold, Barbara suggested that all the staff should gather that evening for a drink in The Cat & Kettle. I was delighted. It would be another opportunity to spend time with Penny . . . even as a friend.

Bernard Stubbs was one of the fathers who had vacated The Crooked Billet in Milltown market square. He met his wife and children outside the church.

' 'Ow did it go, luv?'

His wife was not impressed with the smell of Tetley's Bitter on his breath. 'You would 'ave been proud of 'em. They both spoke up well. Pity y'weren't there.'

'Christmas drink wi' the lads . . . it's tradition,' said Bernard.

'So is t'Crib Service,' she retorted.

Bernard looked down at his daughter. 'What part did y'little brother play?'

' 'E were a big white fairy, Dad.'

'Flippin' 'eck.'

Mrs Stubbs held little Gary's hand. 'But it were a big part.'

As they turned to trudge home Mrs Stubbs reflected that it was probably just as well he hadn't seen the performance.

In the cobbled market square outside the church the Christmas Eve market was in full swing. Stalls had been set up and a choir was singing 'Hark! The Herald Angels Sing' accompanied by the Milltown Brass Band. A tall Christmas tree had been erected next to the war memorial and swirling flakes of snow had begun to fall. A malevolent wind was blowing and a few shoppers had gathered for warmth beside the roast chestnut stall while supping hot tea from tin mugs.

Outside Santa's little wooden grotto Lizzie Pickles, now just past her sixth birthday, was shouting a cheerful farewell to Lennie Chisel in his red suit and long white beard. Lennie, a retired drains inspector, was a member of the Social Committee of Milltown Working Men's Club and was always first choice to act the part of Father Christmas.

'Don't fret, Santa,' said Lizzie, 'ah'll come back later wi' m'mam's cat'logue.'

Lennie had never heard of a Tressy doll with hair that could actually 'grow'. He was more of a Meccano man. Times were changing and it was hard to keep up.

We met in The Cat & Kettle for our Christmas drink and all the staff were there with the exception of Norman who was visiting friends and, in any case, hadn't been invited.

A television stood on a high shelf in the far corner of the lounge bar. It was tuned to BBC 1 and the choir from King's College, Cambridge, was singing carols. It added to the festive occasion. The drinks flowed and everyone relaxed.

Connie, Audrey and Penny were sitting together on a bench seat. Travis and I sat on carver chairs on either side of Edith while Barbara was at the head of the table and determined to ensure everyone had a good night. It was noticeable that Audrey was coming out of her shell and becoming more voluble with every glass of Babycham. Travis arrived with another tray of drinks and seven bags of Golden Wonder crisps. By half past eight the television was still burbling away and Cilla Black was introducing Cliff Richard and Dusty Springfield.

Connie was deep in conversation with Penny. 'So, how's your love life?'

Penny sighed. 'To be honest, these days I seem to spend most of my evenings sitting at home preparing lessons and listening to Joan Baez on my record player.'

'Maybe we both need a night out,' said Connie.

Penny stared into her glass of gin and tonic. 'I remember being in London with another girl from college. I was walking down the King's Road in a pelmet skirt and my posh Courrèges boots and we were invited to a bottle party.'

'What was it like?'

'Great.' She smiled and sipped her drink.

'And?'

'I smoked pot for the first time with a guy called Quentin.'

Connie nodded knowingly.

A slightly inebriated Audrey was chatting happily. 'I'm going to buy two chairs from Habitat in the Boxing Day sales.'

'That's wonderful,' said Barbara. 'I'm so pleased for you.'

Audrey was moving into a previously unseen whimsical

mode. 'Come to think of it, Barbara, I think Mary and Joseph would have appreciated a couple of decent chairs after such a long journey.'

'You're quite right.' Barbara smiled. She looked around at everyone and knew this gathering had been a good idea. It seemed a shame that Norman was not sharing this special time. Miss Tipple would certainly have been here. She missed her old headteacher.

Edith leaned over the table and squeezed Barbara's hand. 'You're in a reflective mood.'

'Just thinking how it used to be.'

'Different times, Barbara.'

It was then that Barbara recalled their earlier conversation. 'By the way, Edith, what has been troubling you?'

Edith shook her head. 'Perhaps another time, Barbara – let's enjoy this evening. It's going well, isn't it?'

Barbara nodded and glanced at Penny, Audrey and Connie. She tapped her wine glass and stood to make an announcement.

Everyone stopped talking and looked up at our rosy-cheeked deputy headteacher.

'Well done, everybody,' she said. 'Thanks for all your support today and especially to Audrey, Connie and Penny who worked so hard to produce another successful Nativity.'

'A formidable trio,' said Edith.

'Pity they weren't around in Bethlehem,' said Travis. 'Things would have been different.'

'In what way?' I asked.

'Well . . . we would certainly have tidied up the stable,' said a determined Audrey.

'And brought some *useful* gifts,' added Penny.

'And we could have helped Mary deliver the baby,' said Connie with a grin.

'There's no doubt,' said Barbara, effervescent now, 'that the Nativity didn't really need those three Wise Men. What was required was *three wise women*.'

There was laughter and cheers and it occurred to me I would always remember these happy times as the sixties drew towards their close.

## Chapter Eight

# *Goodbye to the Sixties*

'Jack, this is Seb.'

It was Penny and she was smiling.

'Pleased to meet you,' he said with the confidence of the innately gifted.

So this was Sebastian Courtney, the man I had heard so much about. He was an inch or two shorter than me and I could see what Penny saw in him. With his handsome chiselled face, high cheekbones and long wavy blond hair he looked like a Greek god.

We shook hands. 'Hello, Seb. Welcome to Wharfedale.'

It was Boxing Day and we were in the clubhouse before the rugby game.

He looked me up and down as if assessing me. 'Penny mentioned you help her out a bit at school.'

*A bit*. For me it was always more than that.

'Yes, we support each other whenever we can. It's a tough place to teach.'

He laughed. 'Really? You want to try my job for a day.'

The room was filling up with the players, girlfriends and supporters. In this North Yorkshire farming community Seb's extravagant style of dress was causing interest. He was wearing a patterned voile shirt with a large collar, heavily pleated corduroy trousers and suede boots. However, it was the embroidered Afghan coat that stood out like a sore thumb. It made him look like a Russian prince in *Doctor Zhivago.* A long university scarf was draped like a badge of office around his neck and a 'Ban the Bomb' badge completed the ensemble.

I felt a little inadequate in my Aran sweater, jeans and duffel coat. Kick-off was an hour away. 'So are you here to watch the game?' I asked.

'Maybe,' he said casually. 'We're going into Grassington for a bite of lunch.'

Penny looked concerned. 'We ought to get back for the game, Seb.'

He shrugged his shoulders. 'I'm not really into rugby.'

'Connie and Travis are coming, Jack.' She gave Seb a stern look. 'I said we would see them here . . . and my dad should be along later.'

Seb glanced at his wristwatch. 'Let's see how the time goes.'

I watched them walk out to the car park and climb into Sebastian's rusty yellow Citroën 2CV with its distinctive bug-eyes. They bounced up the rutted drive out towards the village of Grassington and I was left with an empty feeling. I looked out across the fields while a nimbus of frozen droplets covered the land with a cloak of sadness. With a heavy heart I stood there in silence reflecting on misty memories.

Suddenly a familiar voice shattered my reverie. 'Jack, Jack!' It was the 1st XV captain. 'Stop daydreamin'. Team talk. C'mon. Move y'self!'

I picked up my sports bag and set off for the changing rooms.

'I've brought a flask,' said Travis, opening his duffel bag.

'Wow! A man of many talents,' said Connie with a smile.

They were sitting on one of the tiered wooden seats in the grandstand. It provided a perfect view of the pitch while in the distance the endless limestone walls of Yorkshire criss-crossed the hill farms of God's own country. A stiff breeze flushed their faces.

'Coffee,' said Travis. 'White with sugar.'

'Perfect.'

'Well, I know that's how you like it. We've worked together long enough.'

He poured the steaming drink into two plastic mugs and produced two Mars bars from his anorak pocket.

'Thanks, Travis.' Connie grinned. 'You know how to treat a lady.'

Travis looked down at his coffee. 'I try.'

'Good crowd,' said Connie, looking around at the packed grandstand and the hardy supporters who had gathered behind the barriers close to the touchlines. On the far side of the field a few farmers had arrived with tractors and trailers. The trailers were stacked with straw bales to provide extra elevated seating for spectators.

Travis opened the programme and looked at the team-sheet. 'J. Sheffield' was listed as the number 6 for Upper Wharfedale.

As usual Travis was a fount of knowledge. 'So this means Jack is a wing forward, Connie. His job is to nullify their scrum half and tackle everything above the grass.'

'Actually, Travis, to be more precise, Jack is the *blind-side* wing forward in contrast to the *open-side* wing forward.' Back in Durham an earlier boyfriend had played rugby.

Travis smiled. 'Behave. I've got two sausage rolls for half-time.'

It was five minutes before kick-off and the kit man was walking round the changing room with a large tin of Vaseline. I took a dollop and began to spread it over my ears. It eased the wear and tear when in the scrum.

'OK, boys,' shouted our team coach. 'Warm up.'

We stood up and began to jog on the spot. The metal studs in our boots made a fearsome cacophony of noise on the concrete floor. This was the usual ritual before a game and was also intended to put the fear of God into the opposition in the next-door changing room.

The team talk was brief and to the point.

'Big crowd today, lads, so let's give 'em hell and smash the buggers.'

'Hey, it's Audrey,' said Travis. He stood up and waved. A breathless Audrey squeezed on to the seat beside them. She was a vision in yellow with a matching bobble hat, scarf and coat.

'Made it,' she gasped. 'Sorry, busy morning, but I was keen to come along. My neighbour gave me a lift. She has a daughter in Skipton.' She looked around in wonderment. 'I've never been to a rugby game before.'

Travis grinned. 'Coffee?' he asked.

'Thanks. You're an angel.'

Audrey fell silent as she sipped her hot drink; meanwhile, Connie and Travis were both wondering about her introductions agency and if, at long last, there was a man on the scene.

The two teams emerged from the tunnel and, after tossing a coin, the captains shook hands and shouts of 'C'mon Wharfedale' echoed around the ground.

'There's Jack,' said Audrey, full of anticipation. She surveyed the wearing pitch. 'Oh dear, he's going to get awfully muddy.'

Connie gave Travis a wide-eyed stare; he smiled back in acknowledgement.

The referee blew his whistle to start the game while Audrey sat back and sipped her coffee. 'Now, can someone explain the rules?'

On the row in front the diehard supporters with their green Upper Wharfedale scarves turned towards her in astonishment.

'Teks all sorts,' one of them muttered.

It was a fiercely fought game on a frozen pitch and the final score was Upper Wharfedale 15, Hull Ionians 9. After spending eighty minutes knocking seven bells out of each other the players shook hands and trooped off the field to the changing rooms. Muddied and battered, we stripped off and headed for the warmth of the huge communal bath with a single bar of soap shared between fifteen men.

*

Travis and Connie led the way down the steps to the clubhouse with Audrey close behind. As they reached the doorway Audrey stumbled at the same moment that the touch judge, Arnie Crabtree, with his green flag and muddy knees, appeared alongside.

'Oh, dear!' cried Audrey as she fell into his arms.

Arnie held her firmly. 'Now then. Don't fret, Miss. You're safe.'

Audrey looked up into the ruddy face of this unexpected Good Samaritan. 'Oh, thank you.'

'Y'nearly came a cropper there, luv,' said Arnie. Her yellow bobble hat had fallen and he picked it up. 'Here you are, my little buttercup,' he said with a smile.

Arnie was a tall, genial greengrocer from Skipton. His ears stuck out like taxi doors and wisps of black hair covered his balding head. A forty-five-year-old bachelor, his life revolved around selling fruit and veg, woodwork evening classes in the Skipton Institute and supporting local rugby.

Audrey looked up into the blue eyes of this gentle stranger. 'You're very kind.'

'A pleasure,' he said and he watched her walk away.

Joe Butterworth, a sixty-year-old local farmer and long-standing member of the rugby committee, was propping up the bar when I arrived to buy a round of drinks.

'This one's on me, young Jack,' he said, slapping a pound note on the bar. 'Y'played a stormer t'day.'

'Thanks, Mr Butterworth. It was touch and go until Michael scored that winning try.'

Joe drained his pint, wiped his lips with the back of his hand and nodded. 'Should play f'Yorkshire, that lad.'

'I agree, Mr Butterworth.' I picked up the tray of drinks and nodded towards our table. 'I'm with my teacher friends.'

He didn't take the hint. 'So 'ave y'got y'self a young lady yet?' This bluff Yorkshireman didn't beat about the bush.

'Nothing to speak of,' I replied cautiously.

He removed his flat cap and scratched his head. 'That's t'problem wi' women. Y'don't know where you are wi' 'em.'

Joe had been married three times.

'I'm sure you're right.'

'Y'see, young Jack.' He put his hand on my shoulder in a fatherly way. 'We 'ave *experience* but we don't allus 'ave *wisdom*.' He shook his head. 'An' you 'ave t'be careful what y'say. Problem wi' words is once they've passed y'lips y'can't tek 'em back.'

'Very true.'

'So tek care. My eldest 'as been a proper barmpot since 'e started courtin'.'

I gave an apologetic smile. 'Well, I had better deliver these drinks, Mr Butterworth. Many thanks for the advice.'

As I turned to weave my way through the crowd he called after me, 'An' remember, when you 'ave a lass a threepenny bun costs sixpence.'

It was half an hour later that Travis and Connie decided to take their leave.

'A shame that Penny couldn't make it, Jack,' said Travis. 'She would have enjoyed the game.'

Connie frowned. 'Yes, but when you've got God's gift to

women by your side you tend to get distracted.' The sarcasm was clear.

Travis smiled. 'I've never been called that before.'

Connie shook her head. 'I was referring to Prince Charming. He had no intention of coming back.'

'Maybe so,' I said and Connie gave me a searching look.

'Anyway,' said Travis, 'shall we ask Audrey if she wants a lift?'

'Let's go and see,' said Connie, 'but from the look of things she may have another offer.'

At the far end of the clubhouse Audrey was deep in conversation with Arnie Crabtree . . . and she was smiling.

The crowd around the bar was thinning out now and I returned our glasses when a tall, slim man with greying hair and keen eyes stood before me.

'Hello, Jack, I'm Penny's dad.'

'Pleased to meet you, Mr Armitage.'

'Call me Peter.' We shook hands. His grip was firm. 'You played well today.'

'Thanks, I enjoyed the game.'

He scanned the room. 'I thought Penny might be here.'

'She was here earlier but went off with Sebastian into Grassington.'

There was a flicker of understanding and he sighed. 'Fine, so can I get you a drink?'

'Thanks, just a half of bitter, please.'

Peter Armitage was good company. We discussed rugby and the future of the club, which was the heartbeat of this farming community.

'You must come and visit us soon, Jack. My wife and I

live in Askrigg. It's a great place and Viv does a terrific Sunday dinner with all the trimmings. Her Yorkshire puddings are to die for.'

'Really?' My mouth was watering.

'Yes, Jack, and swimming in onion gravy.'

'You're on,' I said with a smile. 'Another pint?'

'I'll have a Chestnut Mild,' he said. Then he stared out of the window as a familiar yellow Citroën pulled up into the car park.

Penny and Seb had enjoyed a leisurely lunch in The Devonshire pub in Grassington's cobbled market square. Penny had been in a hurry to get back to the rugby but Seb had preferred to finish the bottle of white wine at a leisurely pace.

They walked towards the bar.

Penny looked a little flustered. 'Have the others gone?'

I pointed to where Connie and Travis had found a table and were sitting with Audrey and Arnie. 'Not yet.'

'You missed a good game, Seb,' said Peter.

'Did I?'

'Jack played well,' he added.

'Well done, Jack,' said Penny. 'I'm sorry we didn't make it.'

'No problem, Penny. Perhaps another time.'

Seb glanced at his watch. 'Well, things to do, everybody.' He rested his hand on Penny's shoulder. 'Shall we make tracks?'

Penny's cheeks flushed. 'I was hoping to have a drink with my dad and Jack.'

Seb took his car keys from his pocket. 'Let's leave them to talk about the finer points of rugby.'

Penny sighed. 'I had better go, Dad.'

Peter remained impassive. He kept his thoughts to himself and kissed his daughter on the cheek. 'Drive safely,' he said to Seb.

'Always do,' said Seb.

Penny had a brief word with the others before Seb ushered her towards the door. She turned and called over her shoulder, 'Maybe see you at Connie's party, Jack.'

Then they had gone as darkness fell over the distant hills.

'Daughters,' murmured Peter with a sad smile. 'You love them more when they leave you.' He shook his head and gave me a knowing look.

Suddenly Joe Butterworth was alongside breathing beer fumes over us. 'Now then, Peter. What did y'think of this young lad?' He slapped me on the shoulder.

Peter grinned. 'Bit like me thirty years ago.'

Joe Butterworth put his arm around Peter's shoulders. 'We were good back in the day.'

Peter winked at me. 'Well . . . one of us was.'

Finally, when I left and walked towards my Morris Minor, frost-frozen leaves crunched under my feet. Above me was a vast sky that promised more snow and, as I drove home on that lonely road, my thoughts were of Penny.

It was New Year's Eve and there were lots of cars outside Connie's house. I rang the bell and Connie opened the door.

'Come in, Jack. Glad you could make it.'

When I stepped inside the heat and noise rushed over

me. She spied my can of Watney's Party Seven. 'Let's take that into the kitchen. It needs to settle first. The last one showered everybody when we opened it.'

'We never did get the chance to talk about Christmas when we met at the rugby. So, how was it up in Pity Me?'

'Yes, usual stuff. *Top of the Pops* on the telly. My mother asking how someone can be daft enough to call themselves Creedence Clearwater Revival and Dad complaining that Fleetwood Mac aren't a patch on Glenn Miller. But they love every minute. A huge meal and more telly with a couple of eggnogs. We finished up with cold turkey sandwiches, watching *The Morecambe & Wise Christmas Show.* What about you?'

'Similar, except my dad's really poorly now so festivities were quite gentle. A lovely Christmas dinner, crackers and party hats, the Queen's speech, Billy Smart's Circus and a game of whist with a few bottles of stout. I drove back again to Leeds to stay for a couple more days.'

She picked up a cocktail from a worktop full of bottles and glasses.

'What's that?'

'One of my specialities.' She held up the glass. 'A sidecar . . . cognac, orange liqueur and lemon juice. Audrey loves them and guess what? She's brought her new man with her, Arnold, the guy from the rugby. She calls him Arnie. He's lovely. Keeps calling her *my little buttercup*.'

'That's great news.'

'What an irony. She goes to London to pay an agency for introductions and then finds a man who lives five minutes from her front door. I've never seen her looking so happy. Anyway, help yourself to a drink. You know most people. Travis is regaling a couple of potential railway enthusiasts and Barbara and Jimmy have brought enough pies to sink a battleship.'

I looked around at the clutter of bottles. A huge bowl of festive punch stood on the worktop and the scent of cinnamon hung in the air. I picked up a ladle, poured the pungent liquid into a tumbler and joined the party. When I looked around there was a notable absentee . . . Penny.

A television was on in the corner and snippets of news filtered through.

At 10.35 p.m. Connie switched over to BBC for *Pop Go the 60s!* with Cilla Black, the Kinks, Lulu, Cliff Richard, the Rolling Stones and the Who. Soon the room was full of memories of a decade of great music that defined our generation and everyone began to dance.

Connie had left Travis breathless with her energy and soon they both collapsed on the sofa next to me.

'Is Penny coming?' I asked.

'Hope so,' said Connie. 'Last I heard she was meeting Seb in The Cat & Kettle then coming on here.'

'What did you think of him?' I asked.

Connie thought for a moment. 'I liked his Afghan coat. Very trendy. Penny said he bought it at the Chelsea Antiques Market.'

'Evasive answer, Connie,' said a slightly inebriated Travis. 'Bit too sure of himself for me.'

'Well, she's old enough to make her own decisions.'

'I heard he had moved in with her,' said Travis.

Connie gave Travis a determined look. 'Well, thankfully, times and attitudes are changing. Do you remember that last year on *Coronation Street* Dennis Tanner and Jenny Sutton slept together before marriage and it caused an uproar in the press? You may have noticed that women are more emancipated now and that's how it should be. In fact, if you're on the pill you can do as you please.'

Travis and I were simply staring at her – Connie was never anything but frank – when the doorbell rang. Penny had arrived and she was alone. Connie took her coat and led her into the relative peace of the kitchen.

The door remained closed for five minutes while Travis and one of Connie's neighbours had a headstand competition. Connie reappeared looking concerned. She shut the door behind her and sat beside me. On the television the Who were blasting out 'Pinball Wizard'.

'How's Penny?' I asked.

Connie just shook her head and sighed. 'Not good.'

'Shall I have a word?'

'It might help, Jack.'

I stood up and opened the kitchen door. Penny was standing facing the window, hands gripping the worktop. I closed the door and stood next to her. Her shoulders were shaking.

'Penny,' I said softly.

She turned. Tears were streaming down her face.

'What's wrong?'

She covered her face with her hands and continued to sob.

I put my hands on her shoulders. 'Tell me. I want to help.'

She looked up at me. In the sharp fluorescent light her skin appeared almost translucent. 'It's Seb. It's over.'

'I'm so sorry,' I whispered.

'He ended it. Said we were going nowhere. I don't know what he wants.' She rested her head on my chest. 'Oh Jack, why do these things happen?'

It seemed natural to put my arms around her. She responded and held on to me.

We stood there for what seemed like an age. Penny was in my arms and it felt right.

Suddenly the door opened and Connie walked in. She stood there transfixed, taking in the moment. I looked at her over Penny's shoulder and slowly shook my head. I mouthed, 'She's upset.'

Connie nodded, held up a hand in understanding and slowly walked out. She closed the door and the party sounds were muted once more.

Then it was just the two of us again, holding each other, a tableau in time.

Her face was close to mine. She stared at me for a long moment; then I leaned towards her and kissed her gently. We kissed again and she responded. Then suddenly she leaned back. 'I'm sorry, Jack. I didn't mean . . .'

A sense of guilt filled my heart. 'Penny, I didn't mean to take advantage of the situation . . . but you must know how I feel about you.'

She stepped away. 'Yes, I guessed. You're a lovely man, Jack.' She walked to the door and paused. 'I'm confused at the moment. Let's see how things go.'

She dabbed her eyes with her handkerchief one final time, opened the door and walked back into the party.

I stared at my reflection in the kitchen window.

*What just happened?* My thoughts were in a whirl.

Moments later Connie was beside me. 'Are you OK?'

I had no words. Just a sense that something exciting and unexpected had occurred.

'I guessed,' said Connie quietly. 'Seb's moved on to pastures new.'

'Yes . . . and she's taken it badly.'

Connie squeezed my arm. 'Jack, please be careful. Penny has been hurt but it might be *you* that gets hurt next.'

In that moment I didn't fully understand and silence fell between us.

Finally she took my hand and led me to the door. 'Now, come on and let's say goodbye to the sixties.'

As midnight approached we were sitting around swapping our memories of the past decade. Travis was telling me that he had once thought it was cool to roll liquorice paper Old Holborn cigarettes and then he grew out of it.

Audrey and Arnie were deep in conversation with Barbara and Jimmy about the Boxing Day film they had all watched. It had been the classic *Breakfast at Tiffany's* with Audrey Hepburn. Barbara was listening carefully but was more interested in this kindly new greengrocer who had appeared in Audrey's life.

Meanwhile, a few of Connie's neighbours were sitting on the stairs discussing the morbid subject of the death penalty, the abolition of which had recently been confirmed, while supping the last of my can of Watney's.

By the time we all gathered together for the chimes of Big Ben it was a happy group that linked hands to sing 'Auld Lang Syne'.

Connie released a bag of brightly coloured balloons and suddenly everyone was milling around wishing each other a happy 1970. Barbara kissed me on the cheek; Travis shook my hand and suddenly I was standing in front of Penny. She looked at me and hesitated as if she would kiss me . . . But it was not to be. She smiled . . . and then she left. Yet the closeness between us that night had been special and I wondered what it meant.

Surrounded by a crescendo of colour and sound I felt I had found a moment of peace in a mad world.

# Chapter Nine

## *Days of My Life*

It was 6 a.m. on a dark winter morning when I got out of bed and stood shivering by the bedroom window. There had been a heavy snowfall during the night and by the light of the street lamp I saw that my Morris Minor was buried under a snowdrift. The first day of the new term beckoned and a hostile world was spread out before me. It was the dawn of a new year, a new decade, and I wondered what it would bring.

There are days of my life that I remember well and Monday, 5 January 1970 was one of them.

A decision had to be made. I considered clearing the snow from around my car but I wouldn't have got out of the village. The High Street was silent and there was no sign of a snow plough. I resigned myself to the fact that a difficult journey to school was in store, beginning with a one-mile walk to the bus stop on the main road from Skipton.

I made a hasty breakfast of steaming hot porridge laced

with golden syrup and then dug out my hiking boots and thick socks. My only hope of getting to school on time was to leave an hour earlier than usual and hope the buses were running.

I pulled on my duffel coat, college scarf and knitted bobble hat, slung my leather satchel over my shoulder and set off. It was seven o'clock and the snow was ankle deep. Soon I was panting as I trudged along the High Street. There was no traffic moving out of Lotherswicke village and, after ten minutes, I was in a world of darkness. A bitter, malevolent wind blew gusts of snow that stung my face until I covered it with my scarf. I felt like Scott of the Antarctic as I battled my way through the snowdrifts.

Above me the leafless branches of oak and beech creaked in the wind and formed a jigsaw sky of snow and stars. Beyond the frozen hedgerows the land was silent and still, for the creatures of the countryside had sought a safe haven. A sudden Siberian winter had scoured the land of life. The villages of Yorkshire were held in its grip and the temperature had dropped to minus eight degrees. The frost was cruel and my breath steamed before me.

When I reached the bus stop there was no one else there. The main road from Skipton had been cleared but traffic was moving very slowly. By 7.30 a.m. there was no sign of the bus and I felt my fingers and toes slowly freezing. Finally, fifteen minutes later, the lights of a bus emerging from the darkness were a welcome sight. Once on board there was a blessed warmth and the handful of passengers huddled gratefully in their seats.

The minutes ticked by as we crunched through the frozen snow towards the southern outskirts of Milltown.

Finally, at 8.30 a.m., we pulled up outside the bus station in the valley bottom. The driver leaned out. 'Sorry, folks. That's as far as I can go. It's not safe. We've done well to get here.'

I had a quiet word with him as I passed his cab. 'I'm guessing nothing will be going up to Heather View?'

He smiled. 'It's Shanks's pony from 'ere, mate. Good luck.'

There was still a mile to go up the steep hill to the Milltown estate and I set off. Eventually, fingertip softly, a grudging light spread across the distant hills and lit up the bleak world. It was almost nine o'clock when I reached the school gate and with great relief staggered into the entrance hall. I stamped the snow from my boots and unwrapped the scarf from my face.

Norman was there to greet me and he didn't look pleased. A thick pullover under his suit covered his ale-house belly and his cheeks were flushed with the cold. I should have known that it was unlikely he would wish me a happy new year or congratulate me on arriving at school in such difficult conditions. However, his response was crass in the extreme. He looked at me with an aloof superior grin, held up his wristwatch in my face and tapped it. Then he shook his head in a dismissive manner.

'What time d'you call this?'

I was furious.

He looked up at me with a supercilious smile and prodded my chest. 'I've not been late since I started here.' He turned and strode back into his office and slammed the door.

Barbara had appeared out of Edith's office and saw the look on my face. I dropped my satchel on the table, took a deep breath and grabbed the door handle.

'Jack, don't!' she exclaimed and held my arm.

'Barbara, I've gone through hell to get here this morning. I'm not going to be spoken to like that.'

'If you act hastily you may regret it later.' She let go of my arm and stepped back. 'He's in a bad mood for some reason and I don't think it's anything to do with the weather.'

'Whatever it is, I don't deserve that.'

'Jack, we need to act professionally.'

I felt the anger building up inside me. 'You mean like *him*?' I turned the handle and walked in.

Norman had lit a cigarette and was standing by the window. He was staring out at the bleak world beyond.

'I'd like a word,' I said.

He didn't move. 'Not now.' He spoke with threatening restraint.

I stayed where I was. 'We need to talk.'

He turned slowly and pointed to the office clock. It was nine o'clock. Then he rested his cigarette in the ashtray on his desk, sat down, linked his fingers and cracked his knuckles. 'I said . . . *not now*.'

Fury suddenly built up inside me, a primitive urge for retribution. I'd almost forgotten I could feel like this. On occasions it was a reflex response during the ferocity of a rugby match – in the heat of battle, as it were. These were emotions that had never emerged in my professional life . . . until now. It took everything I had to keep control.

I breathed deeply and said stiffly, 'The children will be in my classroom so I'll leave . . . but I'll be back.'

He fixed me with a cold stare.

I felt like grabbing him by the scruff of his collar. Instead I gritted my teeth and walked out.

Barbara and Audrey had begun to put out tables and chairs in the hall. Barbara hurried over to me. 'Are you all right?' She looked concerned.

I had a face like thunder. 'I'm fine, thanks,' I said through gritted teeth.

Audrey waved from the other side of the hall. 'Well done for getting here, Jack.'

I called back, 'Yes, just a bit difficult this morning. I had to come on the bus and walk the last mile.'

Parents and children were wandering in and a few of the mothers had realized what was happening.

'Do you want a 'and, Mrs Priestley?' asked Mrs Pickles. 'Me an' Peggy can put some tables out if y'like.' Peggy Stubbs grinned and joined in. They were pleased the school was open.

'Yes thank you,' said Barbara. She turned back to me and gave a reassuring smile. 'By the way, Jack . . . happy new year.'

I spotted Connie and Travis in the junior corridor supervising the children hanging up their coats. 'Are we all here?'

'Penny rang in,' said Barbara. 'She couldn't get out of her village. The rest of us arrived one way or another. Audrey and I are looking after the three infant classes here in the hall . . . so we'll manage.' Barbara's dedication always shone through.

I walked through to the junior corridor as the bell rang. Connie and Travis were pleased to see me. 'Hey, Jack, you made it,' said Travis with a grin. 'The abominable snowman returns.'

I was still fuming from my altercation with Norman. 'Thanks, Travis, a difficult morning.'

Connie could see that something was wrong. 'What's happened?'

I shrugged. 'Just Norman. You know what he's like.'

The children were filing into their classrooms.

'We had best get on,' said Travis and set off for his classroom. He gave me a thumbs up. 'Cheer up, Jack.'

Connie hung back and gave me an inquisitive look. 'We can talk later.'

I nodded but without enthusiasm.

She smiled and hit me playfully in the ribs: 'Come on, Jack. Happy new year, let's hope it's a good one,' and strode off in that purposeful style of hers.

It was only then I noticed she was wearing trousers.

The children in my class were already at their desks when I entered my classroom. They were excited and full of stories about their experiences in the snow.

'Mr Sheffield . . . my mam pulled us 'ere on a sledge,' said Sandra Asquith.

Charlie Dewhirst was wreathed in smiles. 'Isn't snow great, sir?'

Keith Lumb was holding up a multi-coloured creation from whatever balls of wool his mother had left over. 'Ah've gorra new balaclava, sir. M'mam knitted it. She said it'll keep m'brains warm.'

As his mother had recently told me she thought her bristle-haired son was a sandwich short of a picnic I guessed it was more in hope than expectation.

Reggie Atha called out, 'Can we build . . .'

'. . . an igloo, sir?' Ronnie completed the sentence.

'We saw one on telly,' said Reggie.

'It were a funny shape, sir,' said Ronnie.

'Like a ball cut in 'alf,' added Reggie for good measure.

I picked up a stick of chalk and drew on the blackboard. 'What could we call that shape?' I asked.

Matthew Hesketh's hand shot up. 'A hemisphere, sir. Like that dome in St Paul's in London. It's in my *Look and Learn* annual I got for Christmas.'

Along with Sandra Asquith, Matthew was probably one of the brightest pupils in my class. Significantly, both had supportive mothers who took them to the Milltown Library on Saturday mornings.

Soon we were discussing shapes and making a list on the blackboard. It was the fact that every hexagonal snowflake had a unique pattern that created most interest. I sent Sandra to borrow Connie's magnifying glass to test it outside. It took my mind off the dispute with Norman . . . at least until the bell went for morning break and the children donned coats and scarves. It was noticeable few of these tough children owned gloves. They seemed impervious to the cold and rushed out to play in the snow.

I walked to the entrance hall, tapped on Norman's door and stepped inside his office. 'Can we talk now?'

He put down his pen. 'Make it quick. I'm busy.'

'I didn't like what you did this morning.' I held up my wrist and tapped my wristwatch. 'There was no need to accuse me of lateness.'

'You should have got up earlier.'

'I left home at seven.'

'Then make it six thirty tomorrow.'

'I'm relying on buses. I've no control over their timetable, particularly in this weather.'

He picked up his pen again. 'Is that it?'

'So long as we understand each other.'

'What does that mean?'

'That you need to act professionally towards me in future, particularly in front of others.'

'*You* need to remember that I'm the head and you do the job you've been given to do.'

'A bit of civility wouldn't go amiss.'

He leaned back in his chair and shook his head. 'Keep up that attitude and you'll be looking for another job.'

I could see he meant it. 'I might not be the only one.'

'You're pushing your luck now, Sheffield.' He stared at me defiantly. 'And while I'm thinking about it, Eric has complained about your classroom. He says the rows aren't in straight lines and sweeping up is difficult.'

'I move them for different lessons.'

'Well, don't. There's no need.'

'And a bit more effort from him wouldn't go amiss. He doesn't even go into the infant classes apart from emptying the waste bins.'

'We're lucky to have him and you're in no position to complain.'

We were getting away from the reason I had confronted him. 'All I'm asking is for you to treat me with respect.'

'Then earn it.'

'That goes both ways,' I said and marched out.

Connie appeared from the stock cupboard as I closed the door of Norman's office behind me. She put down the ream of sugar paper and beckoned me towards the double doors that led to the hall. 'What's happened? I heard raised voices.'

'Yes, we had *words*.'

'Best to ignore him and just do your best for the children.'

I realized she was trying to help. 'Why is he like this? I felt like punching him this morning.'

She smiled. 'He's got issues, Jack.'

'*Issues?*'

'Yes, he wasn't pleased with me when I arrived.'

'Why?'

'Can't you guess?'

'You've lost me.'

'You're missing the obvious, Jack. Look at what's in front of you. I'm wearing *trousers*.'

The penny dropped. There appeared to be an unwritten rule that female teachers only wore dresses and skirts. Connie was wearing a cord trouser suit.

'Of course,' I said with a smile.

'I knew I would have to walk the last mile so I thought: *Stuff the rules and keep warm.*' She grinned. 'Equal rights, Jack. Why should women be treated differently?'

'I agree.'

'So when I arrived we had a flaming row in his office. He wanted to send me home. Even said women should know their place. I told him he was *old school*. It's the seventies, not the fifties, and attitudes to women have changed. He wasn't pleased.'

I was beginning to understand why Norman had been in a bad mood when I arrived.

She glanced up at the hall clock. 'Anyway, come on. Let's enjoy what's left of morning break.'

Edith served us with steaming mugs of coffee. 'By the way, everybody,' she said, 'Penny has been in touch. Her father is bringing her in. He's got a decent Land Rover that can get through this weather.'

'Good news,' said Barbara. It had been a demanding morning with two of them looking after ninety children.

Edith looked at Connie with approval. 'I like the trouser suit.'

'You're brave,' said Barbara. 'It's a first for this school.'

'Yes, Norman wasn't keen.'

Barbara gave her a knowing look. 'So that accounts for his mood this morning. I wished him a happy new year and he ignored me.'

Edith looked out of the window as Travis rang the bell for the end of playtime. A Land Rover had pulled up outside school. 'Oh, good, Penny's here,' she said.

I thought back to our last meeting as Connie and I walked back to our classrooms. She touched my arm and spoke to me in a hushed whisper: 'Jack, I saw what happened between you two on New Year's Eve.' She gave me that familiar inquisitive stare. It felt as though she could read my soul. 'Do take care. I don't want to see either of you hurt.'

Then she turned and walked into her classroom.

My mind was elsewhere until Sandra Asquith and her friends brought me back to the present; they were eager to discuss the hexagonal shape of snowflakes.

After a warming school dinner of liver and onions and mashed potatoes I was hoping to catch up with Penny but she always seemed to be in conversation with groups of children. I sat in the staff-room by the electric fire, drinking a cup of black tea while staring out of the window at the wolf-grey clouds that promised more snow.

It was a sombre scene on that first school day of the seventies.

I decided to prepare for an afternoon art lesson based on hexagonal patterns. I went back to my classroom – and Penny walked in.

'Happy new year,' I said with a smile.

'You too, Jack.' She studied me cautiously.

'So your dad helped out.'

'Yes. After the snow plough turned up in Cold Beck he arrived in his Land Rover and brought me in. He'll be back at the end of school. How about you?'

'I had a rotten journey on the bus.'

'Well, come back with us. My dad will get you home.'

'Thanks. That's a great help.'

We were engaging in one of those polite conversations where you discuss everything but what is on your mind.

Silence fell as she looked around the room. 'So I had better let you get on.'

'Penny . . . about New Year's Eve.'

She sighed. 'Yes, it was . . . complicated.'

'I'm sorry if I made things difficult for you.'

She walked towards the door and paused, holding the handle. 'I understand.'

'But I don't regret the kiss,' I said quietly.

She opened the door and turned back. 'Neither do I.'

Suddenly the argument with Norman was forgotten and life was filled with a new expectation.

At afternoon break Audrey was full of news about the new man in her life. The relationship had clearly moved on at a rapid pace.

'So how's Arnold?' asked Connie.

The other conversations ceased.

'He's been talking about a holiday.'

'That's wonderful,' said Barbara. 'Where are you thinking of going?'

'Well, he saw an advert in the *TVTimes* for the Paris Travel Service.'

'Paris?' said Barbara in surprise. 'That sounds romantic.'

'He said it was a bargain at only eleven pounds.'

Barbara gave a wry smile. 'Well, he is a Yorkshireman after all.'

'What about you, Barbara?' asked Connie. 'Have you any plans?'

She sighed. 'Yes, it's the Norfolk Broads again. My Jimmy always gets the Hoseasons catalogue in January and we spend the dark nights planning a summer holiday. Then he hires another houseboat and we do the same thing again. So it's not exactly Paris but it is a break away from the shop so I'm thankful for small mercies.'

'A houseboat sounds wonderful, Barbara,' said Audrey.

Barbara grinned. 'And like your Arnold he's always looking for a bargain.'

'So how much is *your* holiday?'

'Top of the range, Audrey. *Twelve* pounds for a week!'

They both sipped their afternoon tea and dreamed of warmer days in the far-off sun.

At the end of school the children were torn between playing in the snow and their regular television programmes. 'It's *Blue Peter,* sir,' said Janet Stubbs. 'Me an' Susan never miss it.'

*Blue Peter* with Valerie Singleton, John Noakes and Peter Purves along with the mongrel, Petra, was popular viewing for many of the children in my class except, of course, for the Atha twins. They were looking forward to an episode of *Superman* on ITV.

As the last of the children filed out of the cloakroom area Travis appeared. 'How are you, Jack? I heard our leader was behaving like a pig when you arrived this morning.'

'Yes, he's not spoken to me since.'

'Best to ignore him.'

'Apparently Connie caused him some concern when she arrived wearing trousers.'

'Yes, but doesn't she look great?'

He smiled and it struck me that it would be sad if he decided to go to Australia. He had become a true friend. Then he walked on and I called in to the office to collect my dinner register. I found Edith looking concerned. She was adding up her dinner money before putting it in her metal tin.

'Hello, Edith, will you have trouble getting home?'

'No problem, Jack. Travis is giving me a lift. Living at the north end of Milltown means we avoid the steep hill.'

I looked at the piles of coins on her desk. 'You're working late.'

'Just double-checking, Jack. The amounts haven't added up.' She refrained from saying *again*. 'And Mr Little had a lot of letters for me to type up this afternoon. It's been hectic.'

'I see,' I said. But Edith wasn't her usual calm self, so I asked, 'Is everything all right?'

There was a long pause. 'You'll hear anyway. He discussed it with Barbara and Connie before he left.'

'Sounds ominous.'

She pursed her lips in disapproval. 'Yes, he's written to all the governors and County Hall complaining about Connie wearing trousers. The way it's going it will finish up in the local papers.'

The day seemed to lurch from one crisis to another.

I left her counting her money once again and returned to my classroom to tidy up before Penny appeared to say her father had arrived.

There was an awkward silence so I took the plunge as I packed my satchel. 'Penny, I'm sorry if I caused you any confusion on New Year's Eve.'

She gave me a gentle smile. 'Not a problem, Jack.'

'If you want to talk sometime I'm happy to listen.'

'Thanks. Maybe later. Life is a bit confused at present.'

We walked out into the bitter cold towards the welcome warmth of her father's Land Rover.

It was a journey of polite conversation as we drove north towards Skipton. I sat in the front with Peter, who talked about the effect of the weather on the local farmers. Meanwhile, I was aware of Penny in the back seat, deep in her own thoughts and wrapped in a mantle of silence.

Peter dropped me outside the fish and chip shop in Lotherswicke village. 'Enjoy your supper, Jack, and I'll call by in the morning if this weather keeps up.'

'Thanks,' I said, and added a hesitant farewell.

Penny waved briefly as they drove away.

I enjoyed my supper along with a tin of pears and a huge mug of black tea with a slice of lemon. On the radio Peter Sarstedt was singing 'Where Do You Go To (My Lovely)' and I thought of Penny. Then I settled down to watch David Vine on BBC 1 introducing *A Question of Sport*.

After marking the children's books it was almost eleven o'clock when I finally got into bed. I turned on my bedside light and opened Joseph Heller's classic satirical novel, *Catch-22*.

It seemed appropriate, considering the dilemma surrounding my feelings for Penny.

At that moment, ten miles away in Cold Beck, Penny was curled up on the sofa in her dressing gown drinking hot Ovaltine. Her flatmate, Sue, had switched to ITV to watch her heart-throb, the American actor Ryan O'Neal, in *Peyton Place*.

Suddenly, there was a knock on the door.

'Who can it be at this time?' said Sue.

'Could be the lady next door,' murmured Penny. 'She may have a problem.'

Sue made sure the security chain was attached before she opened the door a few inches.

On the doorstep was a figure she knew well.

It was Seb.

## Chapter Ten

# *The Girl with Pink Hair*

It was a frozen dawn and a monochrome snowscape stretched out to the far horizon. In Lotherswicke village trails of wood smoke settled on the pantile roofs of the cottages on the High Street before drifting off into a pewter-grey sky. There had been a fresh fall of snow during the night while a cold wind blew in from the north-west and bent the skeletal trees. As I looked out of my window the bitter rhythms of winter rattled the roof tiles and, across the road, snow had gathered in gentle curves outside the walls of The Weaver's Arms.

On the radio Engelbert Humperdinck was singing 'Winter World of Love'. I switched it off, not least because Penny had barely spoken to me for the past two weeks. It was Monday, 19 January and an eventful day lay ahead.

When I pulled into the school car park parents and children were hurrying in through the gate. Their breath steamed as they trudged up the driveway towards the entrance porch. As I walked across the playground a woman I didn't recognize approached me.

'Excuse me, are you one of the teachers?'

She was tall and slim with long blonde hair under a knitted bobble hat.

'Yes, I'm Jack Sheffield. I teach Class Six.'

'Sorry for troubling you but I'm Donna Clayton and this is my daughter, Sherri. We've come to live in Milltown and I wanted Sherri to come to school here.'

She looked like a Scandinavian skier and moved with an athletic grace. Holding her hand was a mini version of herself, a leggy six-year-old.

'That's fine. Come with me and we'll see Miss Verity in the school office.'

She gave me an engaging smile and, as we walked in, I looked down at the girl and was surprised. Underneath her bobble hat strands of hair were sticking out . . . and they were pink.

Edith was standing by her filing cabinet with a handful of County Hall circulars.

'Excuse me, Miss Verity,' I said. 'I have a new admission for you.'

Donna removed her bobble hat and studied me with a level gaze. 'Thank you for your help, Mr Sheffield.'

We shook hands. She had a firm handshake.

I smiled. 'A pleasure. I'll leave you to it.'

'Welcome to Milltown,' said Edith. 'I'm Miss Verity, the school secretary. Please take a seat.'

'Good morning,' said Donna. 'I'm Donna Clayton . . . *Miss* Donna Clayton and this is my daughter.'

Edith was used to single parents and unmarried mothers.

She sat down, opened her new-admissions register and unscrewed the top of her Platignum pen.

Donna looked down at her daughter. 'Sherri, take your hat off, please,' she said quietly.

When Edith looked up her eyes widened. In her long career it was the first time a new starter had sported pink hair.

Donna had noticed the reaction. 'I'm a hairdresser,' she said as if by way of explanation. 'Sherri likes pink.'

'Yes, of course,' said Edith.

'My mummy is the best hairdresser in the world,' said Sherri with the absolute confidence of youth.

'I'm sure she is,' said Edith.

'Actually, Sherri was going to a party yesterday as a candy-floss girl. It was my mother who dyed her hair. She thought it was a good idea. Sadly she didn't understand the products I use. I'll make sure it's soon back to normal.'

Edith smiled at the little girl. 'Well, I think you have beautiful hair.'

'You're very kind,' said Donna.

Edith opened the register, pen poised. 'So . . . could I begin with your name and address?'

Donna visibly relaxed and smiled. 'Would you tell the kind lady, Sherri?'

'Yes, Mummy.' She looked across the desk at Edith.

'What a polite daughter you have, Miss Clayton,' said Edith, clearly impressed.

'Thank you,' said Donna. 'I try to encourage her to have good manners.' She looked down with pride at her daughter. 'Go ahead, Sherri.'

'My name is Sherri Clayton and I live at 15 Jubilee Grove, Milltown.' She saw Edith hesitate. 'I can spell it if you like.'

'Yes, please,' said Edith, who was wondering how Norman would respond to a child with such unconventional hair colouring. 'That would be very helpful.'

'It begins with a capital S,' said Sherri.

Connie was in the school hall setting up for morning assembly. Her recorder group and choir were to perform a version of 'Kumbaya'.

'Morning, Jack, who was that with you?'

'An interesting new admission.'

Connie paused in erecting a music stand. 'How so?'

'She has pink hair.'

'Brilliant!'

'I was just wondering what the reaction would be.'

'Just as it always is, Jack. The non-conformists will love it and others will think it strange. My hair has been all the colours of the rainbow over the years.'

'Norman will have an opinion.'

'Yes, trouble ahead no doubt,' said Connie with a grin.

'Do you want a hand?'

'Yes, please – just sort out a few more music stands. It's the *full* orchestra this morning.'

It sounded very grand but was really just four children playing recorders, Sandra Asquith on a xylophone, Lizzie Pickles on a triangle and Terry Speight beating a drum as if his life depended on it.

I put down my satchel and started to open up the folded metal struts. 'They're all bent,' I complained.

'Sorry, they are a bit of a mess. Penny put them away last. I guess her mind wasn't on the job.'

I looked at Connie wondering if there was a subliminal message in her words. As always, she guessed my thoughts. 'Have you spoken to her recently?'

I shook my head.

'Perhaps you should, Jack.'

I proceeded to do battle with the strips of twisted metal in silence.

Morning assembly went well. Audrey played the piano to accompany 'When a Knight Won His Spurs' and Penny's class held up their snow pictures from the previous week and received a round of applause. Connie's orchestra gave an ear-shattering performance and Barbara led everyone in the Lord's Prayer followed by a few notices about keeping safe in the slippy conditions.

Our experienced deputy head knew full well that as soon as the children went out for playtime they would create a slide that resembled frozen glass and throw snowballs at each other with little care for personal safety.

At morning break Penny was on duty and it appeared another day would go by without us having a conversation. Meanwhile Audrey was keen to tell everyone that she had been to London with Arnie and he had spent twenty-four pounds on a present for her, a top-of-the-range fur coat.

Audrey was clearly thrilled and we were all pleased she had found romance at last. I reflected it was something that didn't appear to be part of my life.

Meanwhile Norman had spotted Sherri's pink hair when

the children went out to play and had shared stern words with Barbara in his office.

'I told him that her mother is going to put it right,' said Barbara. 'She seems a very sensible lady. Norman wasn't pleased . . . said he was going to have a word with her.'

'I said there would be trouble ahead,' said Connie.

After lunch, when we met up in the staff-room again, Audrey's love life and Sherri Clayton's hair were once more the centre of conversation.

'Pity she can't leave it as it is,' said Connie. 'The girls in my class definitely approved.'

'It would suit you,' said Travis with a smile. 'Might show you had confidence in your self-image.'

Connie wagged her finger at him. 'I might just surprise you.'

'Can't wait,' said Travis.

Barbara looked mischievously at Connie and Penny. 'Ladies, perhaps we should all have a purple rinse and see what Norman has to say.'

'Well said. I might join you,' said Travis.

'I'm game,' said Penny, 'and I've just got a new hair-dryer with multiple attachments. It's great. Seb took me shopping.'

After years of ironing her hair under a brown paper bag to get it really straight, a myriad of styles was suddenly possible.

I saw Connie glance at me but I said nothing.

'So Sebastian knows his way to a woman's heart,' said Barbara with a wide-eyed smile.

Penny looked thoughtful. 'He's lovely but sometimes he's twenty-five going on fifteen.'

'That's *men* for you,' said Barbara. 'Present company excluded, of course.'

At 3.15 p.m. Connie and I were in the hall with our two classes. It had been Connie's idea to introduce the children in the upper juniors to a foreign language. Norman had said it was a waste of time and they could do with learning English first. However, Connie had gone ahead anyway and we were watching the ITV programme *Ici la France.* Connie was holding up flash cards and the children were repeating basic greetings.

This was the time that the infant classes headed home. Through the double doors that led to the entrance hall I saw Norman talking to Donna Clayton. Norman was pointing his stubby finger at Sherri's hair and Donna was standing impassively and towering above him. Her nostrils had flared in annoyance.

I sensed trouble. 'Connie, just need to pop out for a moment.'

Norman was in a foul mood. 'We have standards of dress here . . . so we can't have this.'

Somehow Donna kept her tone neutral. 'I've tried to deal with it, Mr Little.'

'What sort of a school do you think we have here?' Norman was becoming aggressive.

Donna's cheeks were flushed and she took a step back. 'Sherri can wear a hat.'

'What? In school?'

I felt I had arrived in the nick of time. 'Excuse me, Mr Little, just a quick message.'

Norman was surprised at my appearance. 'Yes?'

'The staff were discussing Miss Clayton's positive response to the request regarding Sherri's hair and said what a delight it was to have such a polite and hard-working little girl at Heather View. I wanted to reassure Miss Clayton before she left that we'll do all we can to ensure her daughter settles in well.'

At that moment the telephone rang and Edith popped her head around the door to her office. 'County Hall, Mr Little.'

Norman was not pleased, nor did he want to leave without the last word, but the rug appeared to have been pulled from under his feet and he hurried off to take the call.

Donna smiled. 'Good timing, Mr Sheffield. It was getting awkward.'

Suddenly Connie appeared. 'We're going back to class now.' She stared thoughtfully at our new parent.

'I must go,' I said.

Donna Clayton gave me that level stare again. She stretched out her hand. 'Thank you.' We shook hands. Her grip was a little firmer than last time.

At the end of school I walked into Connie's classroom. She was busy tidying the books in her book corner. She had brought in an off-cut of carpet and created an attractive space for children to sit and read.

She smiled and held up a copy of *The Lion, the Witch and the Wardrobe*. 'Most of these books are mine, Jack . . . collected over the years from jumble sales.'

'It looks great. Perhaps I could do it as well in my classroom but it would mean rearranging the rows of desks.'

'I see what you mean. Our idle caretaker wouldn't be pleased.'

'It's getting to the stage where I would prefer to do the tidying up myself. He does so little anyway it's barely worth him coming in apart from emptying the bin.'

'You're still faced with Norman wanting the desks in four straight rows for his handwriting lesson.'

I sighed. 'It's such a pity. I teach handwriting anyway. His lesson is a waste of time. He caned Charlie Dewhirst last week for smudging his work. It's a lesson from the Dark Ages . . . well, the fifties at least. The children are frightened of him.'

Connie stood up from the book corner, walked to the door and closed it. 'Did you know Eric Skinner goes to the betting shop most days?'

'No I didn't. He's not often around in school when we need him. So is he a gambler?'

Connie shook her head. 'Not him, Jack. It's Norman.'

'Norman?'

'Yes, the barman in The Cat & Kettle told me. He has the odd flutter but he says Eric is in nearly every day putting on bets for Norman and loses money hand over fist.'

'Bad news.'

'That's Norman for you.'

'I had words with him again when I slipped out during our last lesson. He was giving the new parent a hard time.'

'Barbara says Sherri enjoyed her first day and the other children thought her hair looked amazing.'

'That's good to hear. I felt a bit sorry for her mother when Norman was giving her a dressing-down. To her credit she handled it well.'

'She looks a confident woman,' said Connie. 'It's a breath of fresh air having a parent who doesn't worry that her daughter has got pink hair.'

'Yes, I was impressed. Anyway, I'll let you get on,' I said, and walked to the door.

Connie looked at me thoughtfully but said nothing.

It was 7 p.m. and I was exhausted. Our coach, a retired PE teacher, had put the team through a tough session. We were training in a local sports hall and it was a relief to use the new showers and wind down.

When I left to drive home I was tired and hungry and, as I drove into Lotherswicke High Street, the bright lights of The Weaver's Arms were a welcome sight. I made a quick decision and pulled up outside my cottage and walked across the road.

The pub was having a quiet evening. Only a few of the regulars were in, playing dominoes along with a lively group of farmers enjoying a well-earned pint by the huge log fire. I looked up at the specials board as I approached the bar.

'Good evening, Mr Sheffield, what can I get you?'

I looked across the bar. It was Sherri Clayton's mother. 'Oh, hello. This is a surprise.' She was wearing a white blouse and tight blue jeans. 'A pint of Chestnut, please, and chicken and chips.'

'Coming up.' She leaned through the doorway to the kitchen. 'Chicken and chips, please, Gary.' Then her lips pursed in concentration as she pulled the perfect pint.

I passed over a fifty-pence piece. 'So when did you start here?'

She smiled after ringing up my order and passing my change over the bar. 'Yesterday. My mother spotted the advert in the local paper for extra bar staff.'

'Your mother?'

'Yes, Sherri and I moved in with her last week.'

'So, you're doing this as well as your hairdressing.'

'I need to save up. I want to train to be a teacher, which means losing the money I earn from hairdressing.' She sighed. 'It's just that I'm not eighteen any more. I would have liked to have gone on to university after school but I took a different path.' She gave me a knowing look. 'As you have probably guessed.'

I supped my beer and looked at her with new interest. 'Mrs Priestley trained at Bretton Hall near Wakefield. They encourage so-called "mature" students.'

'*Mature?*' Her face lit up with amusement. 'I'm not twenty-five until Easter.'

It hadn't occurred to me that we were almost the same age. 'I'm told it means those students who have had other life experiences before settling on a course of higher education.'

'Life experiences?' she said with a wry smile. 'Well, I've certainly had plenty of those.'

'Four more pints of Tetley's, please, luv,' shouted one of the domino players.

'Excuse me, duty calls.' She hurried to the other end of the bar while I found a quiet table in the corner and picked up a discarded copy of today's *Daily Mirror*.

Under the front-page headline 'INHUMAN' Ted Heath had blasted Enoch Powell's recent speech on immigration and, on the sports page, Don Revie, manager of Leeds

United, said he wanted his team to be 'loved' on the day they returned to the top of the First Division. Meanwhile it was reported more than 250,000 people would miss work today because of a weekend hangover. It was then that the entry for my star sign – Leo – caught my eye. It said it was a time to enjoy good company but to beware of making important decisions.

'Another pint, Mr Sheffield?' asked Donna. She was rearranging bottles of stout on the shelf behind the bar.

I glanced at my wristwatch. 'Yes, please.' I was warm and well fed and it was good to relax. As Donna served me my second pint I wondered how and why her life had brought her here. But it was only later that I was to learn of her story.

Donna had met Barty Withinshaw in a coffee bar when she was seventeen. He was a trendy mod with a Lambretta and a window-cleaning round in Easterly Road in north-east Leeds. At that time she lived with her mother, Betty, a single parent, in Chapeltown.

Donna was one of the more able students at her comprehensive school and destined to do well in her A-levels, as well as being a promising athlete. Her mother recognized Barty for what he was but her warnings fell on deaf ears. Donna was simply repeating her mother's mistakes.

On their first date Barty took Donna to the Bee Gee Club in White Horse Yard in Leeds. They danced all night to the Steam Packet and the other acts, then spent the following day buying matching jeans in one of the shopping arcades.

A few weeks later, when they were drinking frothy

coffee in the 'New' Mecca, Barty told Donna that he loved her. The disc jockey was playing the Beatles' 'I Want to Hold Your Hand' and Donna thought she was in heaven. It was a happy time until she realized she was pregnant. Then her life changed; joss sticks and coffee bars were replaced by nappies and night-time feeds.

At about that time Barty lost interest and took up with a girl from the perfume counter in Lewis's. They left on his Lambretta for Halifax where he had no responsibilities and there were more windows to clean.

So it was that Donna, as a teenage mother, began a career as a part-time hairdresser and life became a struggle.

It was late when I left The Weaver's Arms. I had enjoyed the warmth and the peace, the hot food and a second pint of Chestnut Mild. I waved farewell to Donna. She looked up expectantly for a moment before returning to cleaning glasses behind the bar.

The sharp cold took my breath away as I stepped outside into a land of white silence. Stretching out before me the snow lay deep and smooth. The prints of a midnight badger and a prowling fox were the only disturbances to the smooth wasteland.

As I set off towards my cottage across the road there was a shout from the pub entrance. 'Mr Sheffield.' I turned. It was Donna. 'Just wanted to thank you for your support today.'

'I was glad to help.'

She stepped forward and pushed a strand of blonde hair from her face. 'But I'm grateful . . . It meant a lot.'

'Thank you for saying so.'

I sensed she wanted to talk and I would have enjoyed the company but this was neither the time nor the place.

'Goodnight and a safe journey home,' I said.

When I reached the door of my cottage I paused and fumbled for my key. The High Street was still and sepulchral, reflecting the light of the full moon. I looked up. In the ink-black firmament white light bleached the pale orb and marked the craters on its lonely surface. It was hard to believe that man had walked on its surface.

When I opened the door I looked back to the lights of The Weaver's Arms. Donna Clayton was still standing there, statuesque, looking up at the moon. I wondered what was on her mind.

Soon she would be driving back to Milltown to the life she had chosen and a daughter with pink hair.

## Chapter Eleven

# *A Liberated Woman*

'Shut up an' be'ave!'

The shout rang across the playground as Travis and I walked from the car park. It was Friday morning, 13 February, and another bleak and bitter day had dawned.

A small girl was crying. She had spiky blonde hair and was wearing an old anorak that was too big for her. It was a child I didn't recognize. A young but haggard woman in an ancient overcoat and headscarf was gripping her hand.

'Stop cryin'. Y'mekkin' a fuss,' she said as she took a final puff of her cigarette, pinched the glowing tip and put it back in her pocket.

'I'll check this out, Jack.' Travis walked over to them. 'Good morning. I'm Mr Farthing, one of the teachers.'

'Ah'm Dorothy Nuttall,' the woman said.

He glanced down at the little girl. Her eyes were red with tears. 'What's the matter?'

The woman looked up, caution in her eyes. 'Nowt. Phoebe's jus' upset 'cause she fell this morning.'

There was a bruise on the little girl's cheekbone.

'Are you Phoebe's mother?' he asked.

'Yes, ah'm Mrs Nuttall. We've jus' moved 'ere from Castleford.'

'It's 'urtin',' said the little girl, rubbing her ear.

Travis paused, trying to weigh up the situation. 'Let's go into the school office and we can see about getting Phoebe registered.' He crouched down and spoke quietly. 'It's nice and warm in school. Follow me. It won't take long.'

I followed them into school.

So began a day – and a weekend – I would never forget.

Barbara was in the staff-room when Travis and I walked in to hang up our coats.

'Morning, Barbara,' said Travis. 'There's a new girl with Edith that you might want to meet. Phoebe Nuttall. About five years old. Mother was apprehensive when I spoke to her and the little girl has a bruise on her face.'

'I saw it as well, Barbara.' I looked across at Travis. 'We think it's important for you to take a look for yourself.' He nodded in agreement.

Barbara took this in her stride, as she did everything. 'Thanks. Better to be safe than sorry. I'll call in and check it out.' She paused in the doorway, assessing our level of concern. 'And, if necessary, I'll contact Di Matlock.'

The formidable Mrs Matlock was our Education Welfare Officer. She had links with Social Services and was always quick to assess a problem and solve it.

*

Meanwhile, in the school office, Edith closed her new-admissions register and looked up at Barbara when she walked in.

'We have a new starter, Mrs Priestley. This is Mrs Nuttall. Phoebe is five and will be going into Miss Armitage's class.'

'Welcome to Milltown, Mrs Nuttall,' said Barbara. 'I'm the deputy head.' She looked down. 'Oh dear, have you had an accident, Phoebe?' she asked gently.

'She's allus 'avin' accidents,' said Mrs Nuttall quickly. 'A reight tearaway, aren't yer, luv?'

Phoebe said nothing, just stared up at her mother.

'If you come with me,' said Barbara, 'I'll take you to Class One. Then Phoebe can meet her teacher and start to make friends.'

It was ten thirty when I sent Charlie Dewhirst to ring the bell for morning break and I hurried across the hall to Penny's classroom.

The children were finishing their morning milk. Before school, blue tits had perched on the crates outside the entrance door. As usual Eric Skinner had been slow to bring them into the classrooms and the eager birds had pecked through the foil tops of the one-third-of-a-pint milk bottles to get at the layer of cream. The girls and boys didn't care and sucked their straws eagerly. When they had finished they blew milky bubbles until Penny smiled and told them to behave.

We stood by the classroom door as the children rushed out, unconcerned by the frozen wasteland that greeted them.

'How's it going with the new girl?' I asked.

Penny frowned. 'A lot has happened, Jack. Barbara was quick off the mark. She called in the Welfare Officer and Social Services. Apparently, Mrs Nuttall was really defensive, almost scared. There's clearly a problem with her husband. His name's Gary and he sounds a bit of a thug. When I talked to Phoebe she said he puts her in the cupboard under the stairs when she's naughty.'

'Oh dear. Is there any evidence of physical abuse?'

'Possibly. She has bruises on her arm as well and it looks like a patch of hair is missing from the crown of her head.'

I considered this for a moment. 'This could be important, Penny. Be careful how you handle it and start a log of the events. It may be crucial later.'

She looked thoughtful. 'Have you come across this before?'

'A couple of times at my previous school. I recall that Social Services and the police soon sorted it.'

'Well, Barbara is on the case.' She glanced at her watch. 'Anyway, must go. Talk later. I'm on duty.'

When I walked into the staff-room I thought of taking a hot drink to Penny but Edith had beaten me to it and was already back and serving up steaming mugs of coffee.

Out of the staff-room window the morning was bright and cold and, in the distance, a thin light bathed the frozen hills. The stillness of winter lay heavy on the land and snowflakes drifted on the north wind. Penny was out there speaking with a group of girls, including Phoebe Nuttall, and for a moment, once again, I felt the ache of distance.

Suddenly, a triumphant Connie made an announcement. 'It's happening, everybody. Women are finally fighting back.'

She had brought her copy of yesterday's *Evening Post* into the staff-room. Under the headline 'Strikers march on 5 clothing firms in Leeds' was a photograph of women demanding a better deal. 'It says here "Shilling-an-hour rejection sparks off mass revolt". At long last women workers are united against a man's world.'

'I've got cousins who work in the clothing industry,' I said. 'They make terrific suits. I get them cheap.'

'Are they men or women?' asked Audrey.

'Men,' I said. 'Three brothers who sit cross-legged on the floor all day in a sweatshop. They deserve a pay rise.'

'Jack, you're not up to date,' said Barbara. 'Men are paid more than women for doing the same job.'

'Well, clearly that's wrong,' I said. 'So what's caused this strike?'

Connie scanned the article. 'The unions agreed a pay deal without consulting the workers. Men were to receive six shillings and seven pence per hour while women were offered four shillings and ninepence.'

'I didn't realize,' I said. 'That's a scandal.'

'What are the women demanding?' asked Audrey.

'A shilling an hour increase,' said Connie. 'It's the least they deserve.'

Travis had been listening carefully and contributed his usual nugget of information. 'I read that half the working women in Leeds are employed in the clothing industry and sixty per cent of suits sold in Britain are made there. So we're talking about an industrial powerhouse.'

'And one that runs on the backs of cheap labour,' added Barbara fiercely.

'"O most *pernicious woman*",' said Travis with a grin.

I was learning a lot about Travis; he possessed an acerbic wit.

Barbara gave a wry smile. 'I know that one, my learned friend. We did *Hamlet* at college.'

'Sorry, Barbara,' said Travis. 'It just flicked through my mind but you're right. We need to speak up. After all it's the *seventies* now. We've moved on from the oppression of the forties and fifties.'

There was a rattle of crockery and Edith turned away from the sink. 'Tell that to some of the parents who come in to see me,' she said. 'Their husbands don't give them enough of their wages to pay for dinner money. The pittance they earn themselves might cover the rent and a few meals but for many of them, life is a struggle.'

'It's time for women to be liberated, fight back and assert themselves,' said Connie.

I noticed Travis staring at Connie in admiration. The sound of Penny ringing the bell brought the discussion to an end and we trooped back to our classrooms, each with our own thoughts.

It was lunchtime when I saw PC Phil Moxon in the entrance hall speaking with Barbara. Norman was away on a headteacher course at Woolley Hall and I wondered about the cost of these courses with their extravagant lunches when there were schools in our area without indoor toilets. Meanwhile Barbara was in charge.

Phil smiled when he saw me. 'Hello, Jack. Are you playing tomorrow?'

'Yes, local derby up at Wharfedale against Otley.'

'We're away at Doncaster.'

'Hope it goes well. Have a good game.'

He grinned. 'You too.'

'I guess you're here about the Nuttall girl.'

'Yes. Just getting the details before reporting back to the station. I'll probably follow up with Social Services and call at the house later.'

I could see anxiety mixed with anger etched on his face. It was all part of his job but it must affect him when children were at risk. He nodded and I knew there was an understanding between us.

It was afternoon break and I was on duty. Around me the children, oblivious to the biting cold, were playing happily and sliding on the ice-covered tarmac.

A sudden movement by the school gate caught my eye. A man I didn't recognize appeared and began striding across the playground. He was tall and heavily built and dressed in a lumberjack shirt, jeans, boots and a biker's leather jacket. Phoebe Nuttall looked up in fright when he grabbed her by the shoulder and began yelling. Then he turned quickly and ran up the steps to the entrance door with me in pursuit.

'Ah want t'know who sent t'Welfare t'my 'ouse,' I heard him shout as I burst through the entrance door. He was banging his fist on Norman's door but the room was empty. Edith ran out of her office, alarmed by the commotion.

The stranger swayed as if drunk and leaned over our diminutive secretary in a threatening manner. 'Ah want an answer an' ah want it now!'

The rest of the teachers poured out of the staff-room as I pushed myself between the angry stranger and a frightened Edith.

'Calm down and tell me who you are,' I said.

'Piss off!' He almost spat in my face.

'I'm ringing the police,' said Barbara and ran into Edith's office.

He placed a fist under my chin. 'Move away or you'll get some o' this.'

Travis stepped forward. 'Hey! Stop that.'

The man turned, placed a large hand in his face and pushed him savagely. Travis fell backwards on the floor and cracked his head on the leg of the table.

Penny screamed, 'No! No!' while Connie knelt beside Travis and held his head.

'Stop him, Jack!' Connie shouted.

It was time to act. I grabbed the intruder's wrist, twisted it round his back and pushed him to the floor.

'Gerroff me, y'bastard!' he yelled.

I pressed my knee in the middle of his back and held him there. 'Stay still,' I said, 'and I won't break your arm.'

He understood my intent and lay still.

Connie looked up at Audrey. 'Ring the bell and bring all the children into the hall. We can look after them there until this is sorted.'

Barbara appeared from the office. 'The police are on their way,' she said. Then to me: 'Can you handle this, Jack?'

The man had stopped struggling and was breathing heavily.

I nodded. 'Don't worry. I'll keep him here until they arrive.'

Travis was sitting up holding his head but appeared to be fine. 'I'll stay here with Jack,' he said shakily.

The bell was ringing.

Barbara looked at Penny, who was shaking. 'Penny, get a drink of water, take a few deep breaths and then come into the hall when you feel ready.' She turned to Connie: 'Make sure Travis is recovered, Connie. If there's any doubt we'll need to ring for an ambulance. In the meantime I'll go into the hall with Audrey.' She strode off purposefully.

Minutes later a police van drove down the school drive. PC Moxon walked in with a huge constable by his side.

'We'll take over,' he said quietly.

His colleague handcuffed the man, lifted him up effortlessly and pinned him against the wall. 'Name?'

'Nuttall,' he spluttered. 'Gary Nuttall.'

They read him his rights and marched him outside.

In the hall Audrey was playing the only three chords she knew on her battered guitar while Barbara led the children in an extended version of 'You'll Never Go to Heaven'.

For Gary Nuttall it seemed appropriate as I watched the police van drive him away.

At the end of school Barbara gathered us together for a meeting. Edith served tea and we settled in the staff-room.

Barbara looked at us all and smiled. 'I wanted to thank

you all for coping with a difficult situation. I telephoned Norman and he's up to date with everything that's happened. Mr Nuttall is now in custody. I've spoken to Mrs Nuttall and Phoebe and they're fine. In fact Mrs Nuttall looked distinctly relieved.'

'I'm not surprised,' said Connie. 'She was living with a violent and abusive man.'

'He needed locking up,' added Travis, who appeared completely recovered.

'You were brave to challenge him, Travis,' said Penny.

'Or perhaps foolhardy,' said Connie with a grin.

'Lucky we had Jack's rugby skills,' said Travis.

'It could have been dangerous, Jack,' said Barbara. There was caution in her voice. 'Remember Mad Micky . . . he was carrying a weapon.'

'I understand, Barbara. I just reacted when he pushed Travis.'

The conversation ebbed and flowed, centring on the incident, until gradually everyone relaxed and we began to think ahead to the weekend.

It was Connie who changed the subject. 'So any plans for Valentine's Day, everybody?'

'Well, not so much Valentine's Day,' I said, 'but I'm playing rugby up at Wharfedale tomorrow if anyone fancies an afternoon out.'

'I'll be there,' said Audrey. 'Arnie will be running up and down the touchline again and we're going for a drink in Skipton afterwards.'

'Sorry, Jack,' said Barbara, 'I'll be helping my Jimmy in the shop.'

'How about you, Connie?' said Travis. 'I'd like to go.'

'Sounds good so long as you don't pick an argument with any rough rugby types.'

Travis stroked the bump on his head. 'No chance.'

Connie looked across at Penny. 'What are your plans? Is Seb taking you out?'

'He's coming round,' she said quietly. 'After that I'm not sure. I know my dad is going to watch the game. He offered us a lift up to Wharfedale so maybe we'll see you there.'

Connie looked to see my reaction but I kept my thoughts to myself.

On Saturday afternoon I set off for Wharfedale. I always loved the drive from Skipton to Grassington. Today the hills were topped with snow and the limestone walls rimed with frost. The air was clear and sharp and, as I drove through Cracoe village, two farmers appeared amused as my Morris Minor struggled up the High Street. It was a day for tractors not family cars.

When I arrived at the rugby ground I saw volunteers clearing the last of the snow from the pitch and the groundsman was marking out the lines with blue paint. It was an uplifting sight as a pale sun gave a bright ethereal quality to the light across the fields and the distant Dales.

The visiting team's bus was parked and the Otley team were welcomed by the club president. There was always a lot of hand-shaking and cheerful camaraderie prior to thirty young men knocking the stuffing out of each other. A few spectators had already arrived wrapped in warm coats and scarves while seeking out the best vantage points. I wondered if Penny and Seb would be joining them.

Back in Cold Beck Penny was not happy.

Seb had settled with his feet up on her sofa. The television was blaring away and he was engrossed in an interview featuring the Manchester United footballer George Best. Last week the Irish wizard had returned from a suspension after kicking the ball out of the referee's hands and he had celebrated by scoring six goals in an 8–2 thrashing of Northampton Town.

Penny stared at the mantelpiece. There was a single Valentine card.

Seb saw her looking at it. 'Thanks for the card, darling. Sorry I didn't get you one. I've been rushed off my feet.'

Penny hid her disappointment. 'We ought to be getting ready to go,' she said evenly.

'Go?'

'Yes, to the rugby. My dad is calling by to give us a lift. I told you last night. Travis and Connie will be there.'

Seb glanced out of the window. 'It's bloody freezing out there.'

'A bit of fresh air will do us good. We don't want to stay cooped up in here all day.'

Seb picked up the copy of *TVTimes* from the coffee table. Tom Jones was on the front cover. He considered the image of the handsome Welsh singer for a moment and decided it was time to grow his sideburns a little longer.

'There's something I want to watch on TV.' He flicked through the pages, only pausing to study the photograph of Sandie Shaw. The pop star and trendsetter had decided to give up on miniskirts. 'Have you ever thought she looks a bit like you?'

Penny shook her head. 'I don't want to stay in and watch television.'

Seb was unconcerned. 'Here it is. Golf at its best. Tony Jacklin and a host of other top golfers.' He glanced at his watch. 'Starts a little after three.'

There was the sound of a car horn outside.

Penny grabbed her coat, scarf and bobble hat. 'So . . . are you coming?'

Seb patted the cushion beside him. 'Darling. It's Valentine's Day. We should spend time together, not with a group of boring teachers and a rough bunch of rugger types.'

'You can see yourself out,' she shouted and stormed out of the door.

A raucous crowd greeted the two teams as we walked out on to the field. I glanced up in the stand and saw Travis sitting next to Connie and Audrey. He gave me a thumbs up and Connie and Audrey waved. Two rows in front Penny was sitting with her father. He was intent on the forthcoming game while Penny had her head bowed. There was no sign of Seb and I wondered why.

The match was another fierce encounter against our local rivals but the Wharfedale pack proved too strong and eventually we ran out easy winners. Afterwards the hot bath was welcome on this bitterly cold day.

In the clubhouse Audrey was in an animated mood when Arnie Crabtree joined her for a post-match meal of shepherd's pie and garden peas swimming in onion gravy.

'How are the apprentices?' asked Audrey as Arnie wolfed down the last of his hot food.

Arnie's fruit and veg business was booming and he had taken on two sixteen-year-olds. He shook his head. 'Ah'm working wi' people who are younger than m'coat. Ah think ah'm gettin' old.'

'Nonsense, Arnie,' said Audrey. 'You're in your prime.'

He looked at her, his eyes full of admiration. 'D'you really think so?'

'I do,' said Audrey.

Travis and Connie were at the bar and smiling at the pair of them. Audrey and Arnie were now definitely an 'item'.

'It's been a whirlwind romance for Audrey,' said Connie. 'Good to see her looking so happy.'

'I wonder if he'll propose to her?' said Travis with a smile.

'Or perhaps *she* will propose to him,' retorted Connie defiantly.

Travis considered this for a moment. 'Officially, she would have to wait until the next leap year.'

Connie frowned. 'Why on earth wait that long?'

'It's one of those old traditions,' said Travis with gravitas. 'Women can propose to men on the twenty-ninth of February and the next leap year is 1972. It's always the same year as the Olympic Games. The next one is in Munich. In fact, I'm hoping to go there.'

'Really? That would be special.'

'Yes. I've come to the conclusion that life's for living. I'm happy being a teacher but working for Norman drains me of enthusiasm. I want a new challenge.'

'Really?'

'Yes, I've even been looking at Australia.'

Connie looked at his eager face and realized there was more to Travis than met the eye. 'Sounds as if you're chasing rainbows.'

'Maybe I am,' he said quietly.

'And maybe your pot of gold is already here.'

Travis's eyes were full of curiosity but he said nothing because at that moment Penny walked over to the bar. She appeared subdued. 'My dad is going now so I'll see you on Monday.'

'Aren't you waiting for Jack?' asked Travis. 'He should be here any time.'

Penny sighed. 'Dad is taking my mum out for a meal. He promised not to stay too long.' She turned towards the exit.

Connie hurried after her and took her arm. 'Penny, tell your dad you want to stay a while. We'll give you a lift home.'

'I'm not sure. Seb might still be back at my place watching TV.'

Connie looked determined. 'He should have been here with you.'

Suddenly Penny's expression was fierce. 'You're right. I'll tell my dad.'

I'm not sure how it happened but after I joined my colleagues in the bar Connie suggested we buy a couple of bottles of wine and all go back to my cottage.

Now Penny was curled up in an armchair in her stockinged feet and sipping a glass of wine. Connie and Travis were sharing my battered sofa and watching my Radio Rentals black-and-white television. They were laughing at Tommy Cooper and his special brand of comedy and magic whereas Penny seemed preoccupied.

When *Match of the Day* began Connie and Penny disappeared into the kitchen and they began to talk quietly.

'He's just selfish, Penny. I can see why you're so angry.'

Penny had shared her latest confrontation with Seb.

'You can do better than him.'

There was a cheer from Travis in the lounge. Peter Lorimer had just scored for Leeds United in the one-all draw with Tottenham Hotspur.

Penny looked at the clock. 'I should be getting home.' She sounded dispirited. It was late but I was sad to hear her words. They meant a relaxed evening was over.

Finally they collected their coats and we gathered in the hallway.

'Thanks, Connie, this was a lovely night – great idea of yours. I've enjoyed the company.' I had a thought and grabbed my duffel coat. 'Let me take Penny home. It's in the wrong direction for you.'

To my surprise Connie simply smiled. 'Good idea, Jack. Come on, Travis. See you on Monday, you two.'

We stood in the doorway and waved them off. Penny was standing close to me and then she shivered.

'We ought to go,' I said. 'Seb might wonder where you are.'

There was a long silence. 'He won't be there, Jack.'

'I'm sorry.'

Penny shook her head. 'I'm not.'

We stayed there, hesitating.

'We'll freeze here, Penny.'

She stared up at the sickle moon watching over us like a silent sentinel. 'Jack . . . I think I'd like a nightcap.'

We closed the door on a desolate world and a sky that promised more snow.

It was Monday morning and Connie had arrived in the car park at the same time as me. We walked across the playground together when we saw Mrs Nuttall waiting for us on the entrance steps. Phoebe was playing nearby with her new friends.

Mrs Nuttall looked strangely relaxed. 'Ah've come t'say thank you,' she said with a grateful smile.

'We're pleased you're safe, Mrs Nuttall,' said Connie.

'And Phoebe looks happy,' I said. The little girl was playing a game of tag with her new friends and ran around as if she didn't have a care in the world.

' 'E were a bully, Miss Brooksbank. Me an' Phoebe were frightened t'death of 'im.' She paused as if seeking the right words. 'So now . . . we're free.'

We watched her give Phoebe a hug before she set off for the school gate.

'There goes a *liberated woman*,' said Connie.

Penny had just parked her Mini and waved to us.

Connie looked at me steadily. 'And maybe here comes another one.'

## Chapter Twelve

# *Rumours*

It was Friday, 27 February and the half-term holiday beckoned. As I drove out of Lotherswicke the land was no longer held so fiercely in the grip of winter. The season was moving on and, although the morning was bleak and grey, new life was stirring beneath the frozen fields and hedgerows. Rooks squawked in the high branches of the elm trees while an early dawn had caressed the land with pale sunlight. The first signs of spring touched the distant hills and the dark days were receding.

All seemed well as I arrived at school and walked across the car park . . . that is until I spoke to Connie.

'Jack, there's a few rumours going around about you and Penny.'

'*Rumours?*'

'Well, idle gossip really.'

'What sort of gossip?'

'The usual,' said Connie nonchalantly, '. . . *relationships*.'

'I see.'

'Thought you ought to know.'

'Well . . . thanks.'

We reached the school entrance. 'Do you mean gossip in the staff-room?'

'No, Jack. It's the parents. Elsie Pickles saw the two of you in the Berni Inn last weekend and she was talking to Julie Capstick in the Corner Shop. Kathy Entwhistle overheard them and had a quiet word with me.'

'Thanks, Connie. For the record . . . there's nothing going on. We're just friends. Penny has gone through a difficult time. I was just giving support.'

Connie smiled. 'I know that, Jack. No problem. Just watching your back.' She walked into school with her usual confidence and left me wondering about my relationship with Penny.

Mostly it was fine.

Other times it was like treading on broken glass.

Last weekend Penny had been keen to talk. We had visited a Berni Inn and she had poured out her troubles over chicken in a basket, a glass of red wine and an Irish coffee.

'Sometimes I feel as though my world has been turned upside down,' she had said. 'It's hard to bear.'

On the jukebox the current number-one record, Edison Lighthouse singing 'Love Grows', accompanied our meal and for me it seemed appropriate.

It was good she felt she could confide in me, but it did make me wish I had a partner by my side.

Meanwhile, in the school office, Edith was concerned. There was a problem with the dinner money once again. The total in the right-hand column of her register didn't match the amount in the money tin. She was fifty pence short. Her computational skills had always been excellent . . . or so she thought. Now she wasn't so sure. When she walked into the staff-room to prepare the morning hot drinks she felt confused.

Barbara was the first to arrive. 'Hello, Edith,' she said cheerily, 'I need a fortified coffee, please.'

'*Fortified?*'

'Yes, I've got infant hymn practice coming up.'

'A strong coffee coming up,' said Edith, 'with three sugars.' However, she said this without her usual enthusiasm, and Barbara noticed her friend appeared troubled.

'What's the matter, Edith?'

Edith continued to stir the milk in a pan over the single electric ring. 'I'm afraid it's happened again. I'm fifty pence short in the dinner money.'

'Let me do the coffee,' said Barbara. 'You sit down.'

Edith passed over the wooden spoon, lined up the mugs on the worktop and sat down dejectedly. 'I just don't know how it's happening. It can't be any of the children. They just hand in their teacher's tin of money and walk straight out again.'

'Has anyone else been in?'

'Only Mr Sheffield asking for change for a pound note. That Mrs Stubbs never gives him the right money. In fact she's in school so often she's becoming a nuisance.'

Barbara kept her thoughts to herself as she prepared the coffee.

*

At the end of morning break, as I was leaving the staff-room, Barbara rattled the coffee-money tin. 'Sorry, Jack. You're overdue with your coffee money.'

'Oh, sorry, I forgot.' I rummaged in the pocket of my old sports coat and pulled out a handful of change. 'Things are a bit tight this week.'

I had some shopping to do and checked I had enough.

'Ah, yes, here's fifty pence.'

'Thank you,' said Barbara and she gave me change from the tin. 'Sorry if you're feeling the pinch.'

'No, it's fine, really.'

I didn't mention that I had just paid another instalment into the bank as I sought to secure sufficient savings to apply for a mortgage. I was being cautious with my money.

Barbara nodded but said nothing.

At lunchtime it was beef stew and mashed potatoes and evil-smelling cabbage. It was followed by roly-poly pudding and custard that burned the inside of your mouth: a feast on a cold day. I was sitting with a group of children from Penny's class.

Lizzie Pickles and Mary Capstick had both passed their sixth birthdays but it was another birthday that was on their minds.

'It's my mummy's birthday tonight, Mr Sheffield,' said Lizzie.

'That's lovely. Are you doing anything special?'

'We've got a surprise,' said Lizzie, her eyes shining with excitement.

'We made 'er a cake at our 'ouse,' said Mary. 'My mummy 'elped us make it.'

'It's covered in Smarties,' said Lizzie. 'It looks really pretty.'

'Well, I'm sure she will enjoy it.'

It was when we were clearing away our plates that Mary looked up at me and said proudly, 'My mummy loves me more than anyone.'

'That's good to hear, Mary,' I said quietly.

I could see her thinking about this. Finally she said, 'Well she's the only one who kisses me t'sleep at night.'

It struck me that it was as good a reason as any to believe someone loves you.

After lunch a canopy of ragged cirrus clouds drifted on a bitterly cold wind as I walked towards the school gate. More snow was forecast. I needed to call in to the Corner Shop and the bracing air cleared my thoughts.

Kathy was serving Mavis Piggott, mother of nine-year-old Barry in Connie's class. Mavis worked in the local bookmaker's and was regularly referred to by the other mothers as 'mutton dressed as lamb'. She was wearing skin-tight blue jeans, heavy make-up, huge hooped ear-rings and a hat that resembled a dead raccoon.

' 'Ello, Mavis,' said Kathy. 'Ah see y'got a new 'at then.'

'It's m'*Doctor Zhivago* look,' said Mavis, glancing at me and stroking it lovingly. 'It's that *stimulated* fur what looks like t'real thing.'

'Definitely looks real,' said Kathy without a hint of sar-casm. 'So, what's it t'be?'

'Jus' a packet o' twenty Kensitas.'

' 'Ow's it goin' wi' y'gift coupons?'

Mavis unwrapped the packet. 'Nearly there, Kathy.' She took out a cigarette and lit up. The coupons were inside and she smiled through a haze of cigarette smoke. 'Another couple o' weeks an' ah'll 'ave enough for a Morphy Richards 'airdryer.' She gave Kathy a disparaging look. 'It's important to allus look y'best.'

*An' some 'ave t'work 'arder than others,* thought Kathy.

Mavis scanned the shelves behind the counter. They were stacked with cigarettes: Consulate, Embassy, Benson & Hedges, Rothman's and many more. 'An' ah'll tek a packet o' Rizla. My Claude 'as started rolling 'is own.'

'Owt else while yer 'ere, Mavis?' said Kathy, aware she had a customer waiting.

'Well, ah'm thinkin' about m'figure.'

*Ah wouldn't think about it too long,* thought Kathy. 'Well, we've got this Outline low-fat margarine, Mavis.' She put a tub on the counter. 'It's f'customers who want t'keep slim.' Kathy was always quick to spot a vulnerable shopper.

'Ah'll 'ave it, Kathy. Need t'keep m'self in trim f'my Claude.' She gave me a lascivious look and fluttered her false eyelashes. ' 'E's very *demanding*, if y'know what ah mean.' She paid and sashayed to the door.

Kathy shook her head. 'Fancies 'erself summat rotten does that one.'

'Who's Claude?' I asked.

' 'Er 'usband,' said Kathy with a grin. 'An' 'e's camp as Christmas.'

'Oh, I see.' I wasn't sure how to respond.

'Nowt so queer as folk, Mr Sheffield.'

'So it's just a loaf and some milk and a tin of corned beef, please, Kathy.'

I paid and as I was leaving she gave me a knowing look. 'And do be careful, Mr Sheffield.'

I walked out slightly puzzled.

That morning Travis had called in at the Corner Shop and spent four shillings and sixpence on his weekly magazine, *The New English Encyclopedia*. He was scanning the pages when I walked back into the staff-room.

'It's wonderful,' he said. 'Eventually it will grow into twelve volumes and I'll have a huge source of knowledge at my fingertips.'

'Impressive,' said Connie quietly.

Travis was clearly thrilled. 'For example, you never know when someone might ask you what a quasar is.'

No one spoke.

'Go on then, ask me,' pleaded Travis.

'Don't need to,' said Connie.

'Why?' asked a puzzled Travis.

'Because a quasar is a "luminous active galactic nucleus",' said Connie with deliberate emphasis and without looking up from her *Daily Mirror*.

Travis shook his head and walked out.

Barbara stared at Connie in amazement. 'So, come on. How did you know that?'

Connie looked up and grinned. 'He left his magazine open at that page and it was the only sentence I read before giving up on it.'

'So,' said Barbara, 'have you got any more gems of knowledge to share?'

'Yes,' said Connie looking back at her newspaper. 'It says here there's sixpence off Choosy cat food.'

Audrey, our resident cat-lover, nodded in appreciation. 'Now that *is* interesting. I'm looking after my niece's cat while she's on honeymoon.'

Penny put down her *Art & Craft* magazine. 'Who's that, Audrey?'

'Our Becky,' said Audrey, 'from the wild side of the family in Hunslet. She got married last Saturday. Certainly an eventful service.'

'How come?' asked Penny.

'I know the registrar, Benedict; he's a sidesman at our church. He said some are *weddings* and some are *marriages* and he wasn't sure if this was a new category.'

'Oh dear,' said Barbara.

'So what was eventful about it?' asked Penny.

By now Audrey had everyone's attention.

'Well, Benedict said the groom was distinctly nervous and the last time he wore a suit was when he was in court for being drunk and disorderly in Leeds city centre.'

'Not ideal husband material then,' said Barbara.

'And his best man handed over a loop of insulation wire instead of a ring.'

Travis grinned. 'So romance is not dead.'

'Wonder why they got married,' said Penny.

Audrey smiled. 'Benedict thought it might have something to do with the bride being six months pregnant.'

'Yes, I guess that would have been important,' said Connie.

'It got worse,' said Audrey.

'How?' said Barbara.

'When Benedict declared them as man and wife Becky

looked up at the groom and said with a triumphant smile, "You're a prisoner now."'

'Scary,' said Travis. 'That will never happen to me.'

'Don't be too sure,' said Connie. 'There may be someone out there who wants a quirky train buff to control.'

Travis stood up. 'On that note I'll return to Class Four's model of Oakworth Station.' He strode towards the door, giving Connie a wink on his way out.

'That tall blonde lady's 'ere again, sir,' announced Billy Woodcock.

It was just before afternoon break and I was pinning on the noticeboard a spectacular collection of charcoal drawings that the children had completed on large sheets of sugar paper.

I looked out of the window. It was Donna Clayton striding purposefully up the drive. This was her third visit this week. 'Thanks, Billy. You can ring the bell now.'

Billy hurried out, wiping his charcoal-smeared fingers down the seat of his grey shorts.

Donna was waiting for me in the entrance hall. She was wearing a cord trouser suit, duffel coat and long scarf. Her boots were flecked with snow and her cheeks were flushed with the cold. She was holding a large brown envelope and looked anxious.

'Hope you don't mind, Mr Sheffield, but I wondered if you would look at my letter of application for teacher training. There's an open day coming up at Bretton Hall.'

'Of course. I would be pleased to help.'

I could see the relief on her face. 'I was concerned about coming in again to see you. You must be getting sick of me.'

'Not at all.'

She handed over the envelope. 'I should be really grateful.'

'Let me check it out over the weekend.'

There was a pause while she gave me that familiar direct stare. 'Well, I'm working in the pub again tonight and tomorrow so maybe see you then.'

Suddenly Norman appeared out of the secretary's office and frowned when he saw us. He walked into his office and closed the door.

'Sorry,' she said. 'Bad timing. I'm clearly not his favourite parent.'

'Well, must get on,' I said hurriedly.

'Thanks again,' she said, 'and hope to hear from you.'

She shook my hand. It appeared unnecessary but I noticed once again the firmness of her grip.

When the bell rang for the end of school the children were excited about the forthcoming half-term holiday. I stood in the cloakroom area as they collected coats, scarves and balaclavas.

'It's *Banana Splits* on telly t'night, sir,' said Billy Woodcock. 'Me an' Keith are goin' t'watch it round 'is 'ouse.'

Keith Lumb held up the door key that hung from a loop of string round his neck. He was one of our many latchkey children.

'Does your mother know you're going there?' I asked.

'Yes, sir.' Billy was always honest.

'Well, enjoy it, boys, and have a good holiday.'

'We will, sir,' said Keith. 'We'll be 'elpin' Billy's dad on 'is milk round.'

' 'E wants us t'deliver them books 'e's fed up wi',' said Billy.

Normally this would have made no sense but lately local milkmen had been delivering *The Dairy Book of Home Cookery* and its companion *The Dairy Book of Home Improvement* for twenty-one shillings the pair. It was advertised for the 'adventurous housewife'.

Mavis Piggott had been first in the queue and had proved to be particularly *adventurous*. First you had to buy six extra pints to receive the special offer but it was said Mavis had found an alternative way of offering payment.

Meanwhile, Reggie and Ronnie Atha were taking their time putting on their coats. Matthew Hesketh was standing next to them, waiting patiently.

'Have a good half-term holiday, boys,' I said cheerily. 'You don't seem to be in much of a hurry.'

It was strange. The Atha twins were usually first out of the door at the end of school.

'We're goin' round t'Matthew's 'ouse, sir,' said Reggie.

' 'E lives nex' door,' explained Ronnie.

'And why is that?' I asked.

'We've got visitors, sir,' said Reggie.

Ronnie shook his head. 'Well, we *think* we've got visitors. An' they mus' be comin' t'stay.'

'Why do you think someone is coming to stay?'

'M'mam was *'ooverin'* when we left,' said Reggie.

'She only 'oovers when we 'ave visitors,' said Ronnie.

However, vacuum cleaners were far from their minds as they trudged off into the darkness to watch television at Matthew's house.

When they finally returned home they spent the rest of the evening in stockinged feet collecting the various parts of their Scalextric set from under the kitchen table. Mrs Atha also made sure the boys went to bed earlier than usual to avoid meeting her flighty sister and her new boyfriend, a carpet-fitter from Bradford who was likely to cast judgement on her tufted pile.

I called in to Class 4 to see if Travis wanted to go for a drink. He wasn't in so I paused to admire his classroom. Travis had a gift for display and the walls were full of children's paintings and poems.

I stood by his desk and noticed an envelope next to his diary. The address read 'Chief Migration Officer, Canberra House, LONDON' and I wondered whether he had come to a decision about his future.

It was then that Connie popped her head round the door. 'Jack, I noticed Miss Clayton was in again.'

'Yes, she was.'

'You need to watch out for her.' Connie was always forthright.

'Why?'

She smiled. 'Jack, it's obvious she's got a crush on you, so take care.'

I simply shrugged. 'Thanks, Connie. I know you mean well but it's fine.'

Back in my own classroom, there was no sign of Eric Skinner so I spent the next half-hour tidying before setting off to collect a broom from the caretaker's store. Norman was in the entrance hall looking agitated. He beckoned me with a stubby finger towards his office. 'Sheffield, inside.'

I walked in and he closed the door and gestured towards the visitor's chair.

I declined the seat and said, 'Yes?'

'I need a word.'

'I'm busy cleaning my classroom and there's no sign of Mr Skinner.'

'Eric's doing a job for me.'

'I'd like to get on so will this take long?'

There were no pleasantries between us any more.

'It'll take as long as I need it to take.' He sat down and lit up a cigarette while he composed himself.

*And keeps me waiting,* I thought.

He viewed me with cold appraisal. 'There're *rumours* going round that do the school no good.'

I presumed he was talking about Penny and recalled the conversation with Connie, but I said nothing as I knew this irritated him.

'Anything to say?'

'No.'

'It has to stop.'

'What has to stop?'

He sat back in his chair and puffed furiously on his cigarette. 'This blonde woman who keeps calling in. People are talking. Eric said she's been in your classroom talking all lovey-dovey.'

'Mr Skinner is incorrect.'

'Well, it has to stop.'

It was just after six o'clock and the lights of The Weaver's Arms glowed brightly in the darkness as I drove into Lotherswicke village. I was tired and hungry and although

I didn't have much change in my pocket I knew there was enough for a pint and the daily special, whatever it might be.

I parked outside my cottage and hurried across the frozen High Street.

The television in the corner above the bar was burbling away to a disinterested audience. Graham Kerr was presenting *Entertaining with Kerr,* the latest in his Galloping Gourmet programmes. A few local farmers were supping the first of many Friday-night pints. Donna Clayton was behind the bar and staring up at the screen. The celebrity chef was preparing Iced Rum Husks and she was cleaning glasses with metronomic boredom.

'Good evening, Miss Clayton.'

She turned and swept a lock of blonde hair from her face. Her eyes were red with recent tears. 'Oh, hello, Mr Sheffield. Good to see you. What will it be?'

'A pint of Chestnut, please, and whatever the special is.'

She gave a sad smile. 'It's Friday, Mr Sheffield, so you've got fish, chips and either garden peas or mushy peas.'

'Fine, mushy peas, please.'

She turned and called through the door behind her, 'A special, please, Gary, with mushy peas.' She pulled the pint with expert care and set it on a John Smith's coaster on the bar. 'How are you, Mr Sheffield? Any plans for your half-term?'

'Nothing special, probably visit my parents in Leeds along with rugby up at Wharfedale. How about you?'

She clenched her hands together tightly and I could see she was seeking the right words. 'I've just said goodbye to Sherri. My mum is taking her to her sister's in

Bridlington for a couple of days. Sherri wanted me to go as well but I've got my hairdressing and this job. I can't afford to be away.'

I sipped my pint and felt compassion for this intelligent and caring young woman. 'I can see why you're upset but you have so much to look forward to and you've begun the journey towards becoming a teacher. I'll have a look through your letter tonight.'

She took a small lace handkerchief from the cuff of her cardigan and wiped her eyes. 'Thank you so much. You give me hope.' She stretched across the bar and squeezed my hand. 'I'll bring your meal to your table.'

Half an hour later I was feeling relaxed and comfortable. The meal was excellent, the pub was warm and filling up with young couples seeking a cheap meal and the company of friends. *Crossroads* was on the television with the sound turned down while Neil Diamond's 'Sweet Caroline' was on the jukebox with some of the inebriated locals singing along.

I picked up one of the morning papers. The twenty-five-year-old actress Mia Farrow, former wife of singer Frank Sinatra, had given birth to twins. The father, forty-year-old André Previn, was filing for divorce from his wife. I glanced across at Donna, working furiously behind the bar, and considered that relationships can always throw up the unexpected.

I was about to leave when Phil Moxon walked in with his girlfriend, Thelma, daughter of the Skipton Rugby Club chairman. They walked over to join me and persuaded me to have another drink. Our conversation ranged far and wide from the safety of North Sea Gas to the plans for a first test tube baby but mainly it was about rugby and tomorrow's games.

It was almost nine o'clock when I left.

Back in Ivy Cottage I threw a few logs on the fire and soon there was a cosy glow. Then I settled in my armchair to watch the *Forsyte Saga*. The character Philip had been killed in a fog and I wanted to see what happened next.

At ten o'clock Peter West introduced *Come Dancing* and the competition between Wales and the West Midlands. I decided to forgo the synchronized whirl of sequined frocks, crisp dress shirts and bow ties and switched off. I opened my leather satchel and took out Donna's envelope.

She had obviously completed a huge amount of research and the letter of application was convincing. The minimum qualifications required were listed and there was no doubt about her commitment. She was fortunate to have a mother who was prepared to help with childcare but it was clear her current life was not what she wanted. I was determined to help as much as I could.

It was almost eleven o'clock when there was a knocking at my front door.

Outside stood a shivering Donna Clayton. Snow had begun to fall again.

'What's wrong?'

She pointed across the road at her car. 'So sorry to trouble you. I saw the light on. Flat battery. I need a push and there's no one left in the pub that's capable. Can you help?'

'Of course. Come in out of the cold while I get my coat.'

She stepped inside and I closed the door. My duffel coat and scarf were hanging on a peg in the hallway. It was then I heard her sobbing. When I turned she had her head in her hands.

'Look, just sit down for a moment by the fire.'

'I'm so sorry. It's just been a rotten day and the car was the last straw.'

'Let me get you a hot drink. Warm yourself up while I put the kettle on. You'll feel better soon. Then we can see about your car.'

Five minutes later we were both drinking hot chocolate. She had dragged off her bobble hat and her blonde hair hung free.

'You're a kind man, Mr Sheffield.' She sipped her hot drink. 'It seems strange sitting here by your fire and calling you Mr Sheffield.' She smiled. 'So, well . . . *formal*.'

I stared at her. She looked so vulnerable. 'Donna,' I said gently, 'your letter of application is excellent. You should be proud of what you've achieved. You must pursue your dream of being a teacher.'

'Perhaps.' She looked at me earnestly. 'There are times when life seems so complex.'

The log fire was crackling and we were bathed in its warmth as I considered a response. 'It can be for all of us but you have so much to look forward to: a talented daughter, a good career and a professional life.'

She finished the hot chocolate and stood up. 'I've taken up too much of your time. I ought to go.'

We walked into the hallway and I put on my duffel coat.

When I turned she was standing close. Her blue eyes gazed steadily at me. She reached up and pulled down my old college scarf from the hook and slung it lazily over my head. She held it and stared at the gold and green stripes. 'I might have a scarf like this one day,' she said softly.

'I'm sure you will.'

Then she gripped the scarf a little tighter, moved closer and kissed me lightly on the cheek. There was the musky hint of Chanel No. 5. 'Thank you. You're a good man.'

I opened the door. The snow was falling more heavily and we both looked out at her car and the drift of snow forming against the back wheels. A difficult job was in store.

She looked at me again, this time with an intensity in her eyes.

Then she was in my arms and I held her closer.

We kissed and she responded.

'Jack . . .'

'Yes?'

'If you like . . . I could stay.'

## Chapter Thirteen

# *Silence Is Golden*

An eventful half-term holiday was over and the spring of optimism was in my step as I left Ivy Cottage. It was Monday, 9 March and the pale light of a new dawn had touched the land with gentle fingertips.

Across the road outside The Weaver's Arms the bright yellow petals of forsythia sparkled as the earth warmed again after a long winter. When I drove out of Lotherswicke village a warm breeze caressed the trees and the blue-grey arrowheads of daffodils were bursting through the new grass by the village pond. There was new life in the hedgerows and the fields beyond where tiny lambs were taking their first tentative steps.

All seemed well until the bell went for morning break. I was on duty and I walked into the entrance hall to collect my cup of coffee.

A visitor was standing there. He was a skeletally thin, taciturn man with a permanent frown. His sunken cheeks were flushed in the bitter cold.

'Good morning, I'm one of the teachers. Can I help?'

'Ah've come t'make a complaint.' He held up a sheet of paper. 'It's about y'jumble sale.'

'Yes, it's next . . .'

'Saturday! Ah know when it is.' He pointed at the poster.

'So how can I . . .?'

'Help? That's easy. You'll 'ave t'cancel it.'

'Well, Mr . . .'

'Wormley, Maurice Wormley.'

'Pleased to meet you, Mr Wormley, I'm Jack—'

'Sheffield. Ah know who you are.'

'So do you want to . . .?'

'Discuss? Yes ah do. Let's gerron wi' it.'

I was getting irritated with this annoying little man who completed my sentences, particularly as he seemed to be correct almost every time.

Suddenly Barbara arrived. 'Good morning,' she said. 'Can I help? I'm Mrs—'

'Priestley,' he said. 'Ah know 'cause that 'usband o' yours s'pplies pies for our functions.'

'That's good to hear,' said Barbara evenly.

'This is Mr Wormley,' I said. 'He has a complaint.'

'So it's like this,' he ranted on. 'Ah'm on t'c'mmittee of t'Milltown Working Men's Club. It's our bring-an'-buy sale on Sat'day so we've gorra clash wi' your jumble sale.'

Barbara remained calm. 'I see. Let me look into this, Mr Wormley, and I'll do my best to get back to you with a solution.'

'Well, ah shall look forward t'your s'lution, my dear.'

Barbara took a deep breath. The calm exterior vanished.

'Come back tomorrow, Mr Wormley, and, for the record . . . I'm not your *dear*.'

For a moment Maurice thought he might have met his match but he recovered quickly. 'Very well,' he declared loftily. 'Ah shall return tomorrer an' ah'll give what you 'ave t'say my *judicious consid'ration*.' As he strode out Maurice smiled. He liked using the occasional *big word*. It impressed people.

'Oh dear, just what we didn't want,' said Barbara.

Edith appeared from the staff-room. The door had been ajar and she had heard the conversation. 'Coffee time, everybody,' she said cheerfully.

It was lunchtime and we were in the staff-room. Connie was reading her *Daily Mirror* while Travis was flicking through the pages of his *Guardian* newspaper.

'Did you see that Neil Armstrong has been given an Oscar?' he said.

Penny was surprised. 'An Oscar?'

Audrey looked up. 'I thought they just went to film stars.'

'Well, he had the biggest television audience in history so presumably that qualifies. Most of the world watched that special moment when he landed in the Sea of Tranquillity.'

'Anyone else get one?' asked Audrey.

Travis scanned the page once again. 'Yes, Morecambe and Wise were voted TV's funniest comedians in spite of Eric's heart attack.'

'Well deserved,' said Audrey. 'They've known the hard times and survived to enjoy a better future.'

'Bit like us,' quipped Travis. 'Although we're not quite there yet.'

He looked across to Connie, who had moved on to an article by Marjorie Proops. The forthright journalist wanted birth control to go on the National Health and Connie looked up and stared out of the window at the children playing on the playground. Her thoughts would remain private for now and, amidst the lively chatter that whirled around the room, Connie was silent in her private reverie.

Suddenly Audrey made an announcement: 'I've finally got a telephone.'

This was news. Thirty-five per cent of the population now owned a telephone although often on a party line which they shared with their neighbour.

'That's wonderful,' said Barbara, 'I can ring you now from our shop.'

Audrey smiled. She was clearly thrilled with the prospect. 'I'm on the same line as Mrs Longbottom across the road so we've agreed to be considerate. Mrs Longbottom says we'll both be paying one pound forty-five pence each month.'

'I'm so pleased for you,' said Penny. 'We still use the public box at the end of our road.'

'One day everyone will have a telephone,' said Travis. 'It's the future.'

Edith looked up from the sink. 'Talking of the future, what are we doing about the jumble sale?'

'Or more to the point,' said Connie, 'what are we doing about that dreadful Mr Wormley?'

'Yes,' said Barbara. 'He'll be back tomorrow and I promised him a solution.'

'Leave it with me,' said Edith. We all turned to her in surprise. 'I know his long-suffering wife, Isabella. A lovely lady and not a bit like her husband.'

At the end of school the children were in good spirits.

'Ah'm lookin' forward to t'jumble sale,' said Susan Bell.

'That's right, sir,' added Terry Duff. 'There's allus lots o' toys an' games.'

'Me an' Terry are watching telly tonight at our house,' said Keith Lumb.

'Is it *Blue Peter*?' I asked.

'No, that's jus' f'little kids, sir. We'll be watching *David Nixon's Magic Box*.'

They ran off and I reflected that they were growing up fast. It appeared the *Blue Peter* trio of Valerie Singleton, John Noakes and Peter Purves were now a poor second to vanishing playing cards.

Meanwhile, a tall well-dressed lady tapped on the secretary's door and walked in. Her warm smile disguised the crow's feet of worry lines that etched her face.

' 'Ello, Edith, ah've 'eard that 'Is Master's Voice 'as been in.'

'Isabella! What a lovely surprise and, yes, Maurice was here.'

Mrs Isabella Wormley had been a dear friend of Edith's since they had attended Milltown Secondary School in the 1930s. In those far-off days United Dairies delivered their milk on a horse and cart and there were free gifts with their Fry's Breakfast Cocoa. Then on Saturday mornings in the queue for the cinema they would share a twopenny bar of Cadbury's Bournville chocolate.

'Don't worry, Edith. I'll sort 'im out. 'E won't know if 'e's comin' or goin' when ah've done with 'im.'

'Oh dear, Isabella. You've heard then. He was demanding we cancel our jumble sale.'

'Well . . . ah'm sick of 'is bring an' buy.'

'It's causing some concerns here.'

Isabella sighed and looked at her friend. 'Ah know what y'thinkin'. Why did ah marry 'im?'

Edith kept quiet. It was a question she had asked many times. It was also rhetorical. During those teenage years Isabella had made it clear she didn't want to be left on the shelf. Back then the youthful Maurice had seemed a good catch with his wavy black hair and job in the Co-op. It was only later that she learned he was an arrogant know-all with a bad temper and a liking for Tetley's Bitter.

'An' you never married.'

Edith gave an enigmatic smile. 'I had my reasons.'

'Then you were the one with some sense.'

'So you'll have a word with him. All we have to do is change the times so our event is in the morning and his in the afternoon.'

Isabella stood up. 'Yes, I'll tell 'im that's what we're doin' and I'll call in tomorrow.'

'Thank you, Isabella.'

' 'Usbands come and go, Edith . . . but our friendship lasts for ever.'

The door closed and Edith thought back to those giddy

days when the pair of them went dancing on a Saturday night in the local church hall. While Isabella danced with all the boys she had sought out a lovely girl named Yvonne.

They had shared a secret that could never be revealed and she smiled at the memory.

Isabella was true to her word and returned on Tuesday morning.

'It's sorted,' she said triumphantly.

'Wonderful,' said Edith.

'Ah gave 'im an earful and we've agreed you can have your jumble sale in the mornin' an' 'is bring an' buy will be in the afternoon.'

'Perfect,' said Edith. 'Thank you.'

'So 'e won't be comin' in. In fac' 'e 'ad a skinful las' night an' nodded off in t'chair,' and with a wave she was gone.

Edith left her office to tell Barbara the good news.

It was the end of school and the message had filtered through that the time of the jumble sale had changed.

I was with Connie and Penny in the school hall. 'So I can help at the jumble sale now,' I said. 'It clashed with my rugby game before but now it's in the morning I can be there.'

'That's good news, Jack,' said Connie. 'We need someone on the toy stall. Audrey's doing bric-a-brac, Travis is on men's clothing, Edith's doing the book stall and Barbara is selling footwear. Penny and I are on women's clothing, which is always the biggest stall.'

'What's Norman doing?'

'Nothing much probably,' said Penny, 'but he did say he would run the tombola if enough prizes came in.'

'And pigs might fly,' muttered Connie.

It was early on Wednesday morning and Barbara was in the car park talking to Donna Clayton.

'Thanks, Miss Clayton, I'm really grateful.'

Barbara had called in to the hairdresser's the previous evening. She was keen the revised time of the jumble sale would be advertised as soon as possible and Donna had offered to prepare posters.

'These are terrific,' said Barbara.

They looked impressive and the new time of ten o'clock was clearly displayed.

'Always happy to help,' said Donna. She looked at her watch. 'Anyway, must rush, my first wash and cut is in half an hour.' She waved to Sherri as she walked through the gate.

Penny was in the entrance hall when Barbara walked in.

'Morning, Barbara,' said Penny. 'What have you got there?'

'That lovely Miss Clayton has just called in. She's joined our PTA and has made a super new poster for the jumble sale.'

Barbara pinned it up. It read:

**HEATHER VIEW C. of E. PRIMARY SCHOOL**
**ANNUAL JUMBLE SALE**
**At the new time of 10.00 a.m.**
**SATURDAY 14th MARCH**
**Bargains Galore!**

Barbara stood back to admire it. 'She's really helpful,' she said, 'and very arty.'

'She's certainly made a good job,' said Penny and then looked thoughtful as Barbara set off for her classroom.

At morning break I was on playground duty. It was grey and cold but the children seemed oblivious and ran and skipped around me.

It was a surprise when Penny came out to join me. In her denim coat and leather boots she looked terrific.

'Hi. Nice surprise,' I said.

'It's difficult to talk in school.'

'What's on your mind?'

'Well, we all noticed Donna Clayton was in first thing talking to Barbara.'

'She's doing a lot to support the school.'

'It's just that Connie thinks she fancies you.' She stared at me, seeking a reaction.

'I don't know why.'

She grinned. 'Well, maybe it's your modest charm, Jack, or the fact you're a big hunky rugby player.'

'Don't think so. Otherwise I would appeal to you.'

There was a hint of a smile. 'Or maybe it's because you're single.'

A lock of her hair had fallen across her face and I longed to lift it gently and tuck it back into place. 'There's nothing to concern yourself about, Penny. I'm keen to help her become a teacher. She deserves a chance to fulfil her dream.'

'Maybe she thinks you're part of it.'

'If she does then I'll be cautious.'

'Make sure you are, Jack.'

I glanced at my watch and told Matthew Hesketh to ring the bell. He ran off and I turned back to Penny. 'Why are you telling me all this? You're with Seb. You've made that clear.'

She looked hurt for a moment and looked down at her coffee. 'That's different. It doesn't mean we don't care.'

'We? Has Connie put you up to this?'

'We've discussed it.'

'I see. What's her opinion?'

'That you should think of your future.'

The bell rang.

'I already have,' I said quietly and, as we walked back into school together in silence, a cold sadness filled my thoughts.

That evening I called in to The Weaver's Arms.

'Usual, Mr Sheffield?' She gave me a smile.

'Yes, please, and well done. The posters were excellent.'

'Thanks,' she said as she pulled me a pint of Chestnut.

'So how are you?'

She stared at the frothing pint. 'Mixed,' she said quietly. 'I should have remembered to look before you leap.'

I put a fifty-pence piece on the counter. 'What do you mean?'

She picked up the coin and looked at me. 'You and Miss Armitage. I heard it mentioned at the school gate. Mrs Pickles saw the two of you enjoying a tête-à-tête at morning break.'

I sipped my beer, reluctant to reply.

She leaned forward. 'Women notice things, Jack.'

I sighed. 'I didn't mean to hurt you, Donna.'

'You didn't. It was just a moment in time, a situation, something unexpected.'

I looked into her eyes. 'I do care . . . but it's complicated.'

She gave me an enigmatic smile. 'I understand, Jack. I always did.'

A group of local farmers walked in and, after she'd given me my change, she hurried to the far end of the bar.

I didn't stay long.

It was Friday lunchtime and Connie and I were in Travis's classroom helping him set up his art lesson. Travis was in a state of excitement. 'I'm launching it on Saturday night, Jack. So you're invited.'

Travis had started brewing his own beer. It was becoming the new trend. He had bought a brew-it-yourself beer kit from Boots.

'Sounds good,' I said. 'It would have to be after the rugby. It's the big game against Skipton.'

'Perfect. Let's say Saturday night will be my first beer festival.'

'Great. Who else is coming?'

'Usual crowd from school and a few friends from the Railway Society.'

'So what's the beer like?'

'It should be a seriously potent brew. I've followed the instructions and it promises to blow your socks off.'

I was interested. 'Can anybody do it?'

'I guess so but it can be frustrating.'

'Why? I thought you enjoyed it.'

'I do. It's just that the fermentation period takes up to three weeks.'

'I see what you mean.'

He smiled. 'But like a lot of things in life it's worth the wait.'

'I'm sure it is,' I said while wondering where this was leading.

At the end of school Elsie Pickles arrived with a large shopping bag. 'It's for y'jumble, Mrs Priestley.'

'Thank you, Mrs Pickles. All contributions are welcome.'

'Ah need t'get shut o' this lot. M'sister passed 'em on t'me in the fifties when 'er kids 'ad grown up.' She tipped out the contents on one of the hall tables. 'Y'can't move in our 'ouse f'books an' toys. Ah've not told the kids. They won't even notice.'

It was a motley collection including a broken Dan Dare Super-Sonic Gun, a Mr Potato Head Funny-Face Kit with some of the pieces missing, and a few moth-eaten annuals.

'I remember these,' said Barbara. She held up a Rupert Bear annual and a Noddy storybook. 'Happy memories.'

'Thanks, Mrs Priestley, no doubt some poor soul will buy 'em.'

It was almost ten o'clock on Saturday morning and the crowds were gathering outside school. We were ready behind our tables of jumble.

Barbara was always a reassuring presence at events such as this. 'Good luck, Jack. Your first jumble sale. It's one of the most important events in our PTA calendar and we use whatever we raise to replenish our stock of books. Without it we would struggle.'

The doors opened, parents flowed in and Mrs Atha

elbowed her way to the front and headed for the pile of boys' shoes. Reggie and Ronnie went through footwear like a dose of salts.

My stall of toys was busy immediately and children were crowding around the books on Edith's stall next to me. The boys and girls in my class were like bees round a honey pot. Keith Lumb bought a Doctor Who Dalek Gun, Janet Stubbs was delighted with her Flintstones annual, Charlie Dewhirst was thrilled with his Thunderbirds uniform and Terry Duff was undeterred by the fact that his Joe 90 doll had an arm missing.

I was impressed when Billy Woodcock bought *Roy Rogers and the Raiders of Sawtooth Ridge* and sat quietly in a corner of the hall reading it.

Lizzie Pickles bought *Noddy and the Magic Rubber* for a penny and her brother Harry spent twopence on a Dan Dare Super-Sonic Gun and a Rupert annual.

Penny and I were unaware that their mother had donated these items and Mrs Pickles was less than impressed that evening when she realized they had bought them back again.

Karen Swales bought a Rag, Tag and Bobtail jigsaw but returned it five minutes later, complaining there was a piece missing. I returned her money and she wandered off to purchase a snow globe from Audrey's stall.

By midday the crowds had dwindled and the jumble sale came to an end. In the school office Edith was busy. Coins were spread across the desk and she was putting them into neat piles.

Barbara put her head around the door. 'How's it going?'

Edith looked up with a smile. 'Excellent. As usual the

clothing stall raised by far the most. It's looking like we might have raised over forty pounds but I'll have to check.'

It had clearly been a successful morning.

Barbara hurried off to help with the big clear-up.

Norman walked into the office. He had spent the morning sitting in his own room. 'You get off,' he said abruptly.

Edith was surprised. 'It's no trouble, Mr Little.'

Norman had no intention of taking no for an answer. 'I'll finish this and take it to the bank.'

'Very well,' said Edith reluctantly and walked out to help put the tables away.

It was fifteen minutes later that she returned to her office. There was a slip of paper on her desk. On it was scrawled '£36.25'.

Edith was a little disappointed. At first glance it had appeared more.

A lady I didn't recognize walked into the hall and came up to me. 'Mr Sheffield. 'Scuse me. Ah'm Mrs Wormley. You'll recall my 'usband called in wanting y'jumble sale cancelled.'

'Yes, we had a brief word at the beginning of the week,' I replied guardedly. 'I heard what happened and wish you luck with your bring and buy this afternoon.'

She grinned. 'Ah won't be there. Ah'm going shopping wi' Edith.'

'Oh, I see. Well, enjoy your afternoon. So is Mr Wormley looking after the bring and buy?'

She smiled. 'Ah don't think so. 'E's still sleeping off last night's Tetley's.'

'Sleeping?'

'That's right. An' 'ow do ah know 'e's sleeping? 'E stops talkin'.'

'Really?'

She picked up her handbag and gave me a knowing look. 'In our 'ouse, Mr Sheffield, *silence is golden.*'

On Saturday afternoon there was a tense finish to the rugby game against Skipton. The score was 12–9 in favour of Upper Wharfedale when in the final minute Skipton's flying winger PC Phil Moxon made a desperate dash for the try line. He sidestepped our full back and looked sure to score in the corner. I was the last line of defence and tackled him with the force of an express train.

His knee crashed into my head as we both rolled into touch. The whistle blew. The game was over and we had won.

Phil was gasping for breath. 'Well done, Jack. Hell of a tackle.'

'Thanks, Phil. Well played.'

We stood up and shook hands while the crowd cheered.

'Hey, Jack, you've caught one. You're bleeding.'

My eye was closing and blood was pouring down my cheek.

We walked off together. 'Get it checked out, Jack, and see you later for a pint.'

Darkness had fallen before I returned home and, after changing into clean clothes, it was nearly eight o'clock before I arrived at Travis's house. It was clear the home brew was already having an effect. There was loud laughter from the kitchen where Arnie Crabtree was regaling

Jimmy Priestley with a story about one of his regulars who, according to Arnie, was dull as ditchwater.

I looked around Travis's home and was surprised at the neatness. Hundreds of books filled the shelves and railway journals were stacked in the magazine rack. In his kitchen there appeared to be a place for everything and the worktops were spotless. Pictures of railway engines hung in a neat row in the hallway and a globe was the main feature on his old oak desk in the corner of his study. I wondered how many times Travis had looked at it and thought of Australia.

Connie was sitting on a sofa in intense conversation with Penny while Travis roamed around topping up glasses with his home-made beer. The room was full of neighbours, fellow railway enthusiasts and colleagues from school. Norman was a notable absentee.

Piers Witherspoon was there in jeans, a black shirt and his clerical collar. He was full of *joie de vivre*. 'Hello, Jack. How did the game go? You look as though you've been through the wars.'

'Just a bump,' I replied. I could barely see now out of my left eye.

'But did you win?'

I grinned. 'Yes, we did . . . just.'

'That's good.' He patted me on the back. 'So maybe we're both in the business of winning.'

'How's that?'

'Proverbs eleven. "He who is wise wins souls".'

'Yes, perhaps we are.'

'Well, enjoy your evening, Jack. We all appreciate your good work at Heather View.'

I didn't like to tell him that Norman didn't share his view and that my days in Milltown were probably numbered. It was time to remain silent.

Piers had come well prepared: he had brought his own tankard. 'A present for my twenty-first birthday,' he said. He supped deeply on the dark frothy concoction and wandered off to talk to some of the model-railway aficionados.

One of them approached me, a curly-haired and bearded man who assumed I was one of Travis's railway disciples.

'I've just bought a Hornby Dublo Breakdown Crane 4620 with nylon spoked wheels. It's magnificent.'

'Sounds wonderful,' I said with false enthusiasm.

It was when he said it came with four free-running and well-lubricated screw jacks that I gave the excuse of seeking more of the home brew.

Meanwhile Travis's black-and-white television was burbling away in the corner of the lounge. Elvis Presley was the star of the Saturday night film *Roustabout*. Inevitably, as a jobbing handyman in a travelling carnival, he quickly became the star of the show.

The star of *our* show was undoubtedly Travis, who was full of bonhomie. Finally he came to stand next to me. He saw I was staring at Penny, who was still in conversation with Connie.

'Isn't she magnificent,' slurred Travis, raising his pint glass.

'Who, Penny?'

'No, Connie, of course. A force of nature. What a woman.'

I put my arm around his shoulder. 'Then why don't you go and tell her?'

He shook his head and quoted, '"The course of true love never did run smooth."'

'I know that one . . . *Midsummer Night's Dream.*'

'And it's true, Jack. I've no chance. Look at me. I'm just a short-arse.'

The beer was clearly having an effect and he swayed as he spoke.

'Travis, you're good-looking, intelligent and a great teacher. Connie will admire all of those things.'

He looked down at his beer. 'Maybe one day, but I think at the moment she's more into big rugby types like you.'

'I don't think so. You underestimate yourself.'

He looked up at me. 'Anyway, what about you and Penny?'

'She's with Seb.'

'Seb is just a self-opinionated upper-class twit.'

'Well, we're agreed on that one.'

'Jack, tell her how you feel.'

I breathed deeply. 'The time's not right and her life is complicated enough.'

So there we stood like two lost souls in the midst of a spinning world. I didn't want to reveal the strength of my feelings for Penny and decided to keep my thoughts to myself.

It was then I realized the most important parts of a conversation are the silences. They say so much. I recalled Mrs Wormley's words.

*Silence is golden,* she had said.

And she was right.

## Chapter Fourteen

# *Knock, Knock, Who's There?*

It had been a reluctant dawn but the season had changed. Outside Ivy Cottage the heady scent of wallflowers greeted me when I left for the last day of the spring term. Across the High Street swallows had returned to build their nests in the eaves of The Weaver's Arms. In the hedgerows the first daffodils were raising their yellow faces to the sky and the sticky buds on the horse chestnut trees were beginning to burst open. Primroses brightened up the grassy banks as I drove out of Lotherswicke village.

It was Friday, 20 March, the two-week Easter holiday beckoned and the journey to school was uplifting once again.

When I arrived I was surprised to see Seb's distinctive Citroën parked on the hill outside school. As I drove past, Penny emerged from the passenger seat. She picked up her shoulder bag, leaned in and kissed Seb. He waved and drove off at speed.

I tried to close my mind to what I had seen. There were

children to teach and I needed to immerse myself in a job I loved. Also, I had been trying to progress an idea that would benefit the older juniors. It would be an adventure for them and a chance to take them out of Milltown and breathe the clean air of the Yorkshire Dales. I had mentioned it to the rest of the staff and they were enthusiastic and keen to support me.

I hoped that our leader would approve.

The answer was waiting for me when I walked into the entrance hall.

Norman was there and he didn't look pleased. 'A word,' he said abruptly and beckoned me inside.

There was no offer of a seat as he knew I would refuse.

He fixed me with a stony stare. 'I've just had a call from the bursar at St John's College in York.'

'Yes, I called in last weekend. It was an idea I had.'

'He was on about you borrowing a load of camping gear for some sort of trip.'

'That was one of the things I was checking out. There's a campsite called Skythorns in the Dales. Terrific place. I thought we could take the top juniors who are leaving at the end of term. It would be during half-term in June. They wouldn't miss any school days and Connie, Travis and Penny have offered to come along.'

'You should have asked me first.'

'I was going to talk to you when I had got more information. These were just the preliminaries before discussing it with you.'

'It's a bit late for that. So what's it all about?'

'Well, I now know I can get a marquee from St John's – that's my old college in York – plus a cooking range and probably a few students to come along and help with the supervision and the cooking. I'm sorry if you were taken unawares by the bursar's call. I was going to talk to you about it later today. It's been difficult to catch you this week with you being out of school most days.'

'On school business.'

'Yes, so can I explain why he rang?'

'I didn't know what he was talking about.'

'I regret that but I wanted to ensure it was possible before approaching you.'

'You made me look a fool.'

I was determined not to give up. 'I'm sorry you feel that way but think about it, Mr Little. It would be a new experience for them.'

'You seem to forget: I run this school, not you.'

'It was simply meant to be something special for the top juniors. A camping trip. It would do them a world of good.'

'Camping! With these kids? You've got to be joking.'

'But it's just what they need. Many of them have never ventured from Milltown or even had a holiday.'

'They'll be running wild. Anyway, who's in charge . . . you?'

'Yes. I'm well qualified. I passed my Group Mountain Leadership Certificate on a course in the Brecon Beacons a couple of years ago.'

'Swanning around in Wales doesn't qualify you to take a load of delinquents to a place with no fences. Use your common sense.'

'I thought you would be pleased to support an initiative like this and I don't see these children in the same way as you. They're not delinquents.'

He stubbed out his cigarette and pointed a nicotine-stained finger towards the window and the crumbling terraced houses beyond. 'Listen to me. It's the scum of humanity on this estate. They need discipline and control. That's why I was appointed to take over from that arty-farty Miss Tipple.'

'I heard she was well respected and did a good job.'

'Well, you heard wrong.'

I took a deep breath. 'So are you saying we can't progress this initiative?'

He gave me a cold stare. 'The answer is a definite no. Is that clear enough for you? Forget your camping holiday and get on with the job I've asked you to do.'

I nodded slowly and walked to the door. It took a huge effort to control my anger. This was a man who crushed initiative. I paused and looked back. 'I'm glad we had this conversation, Mr Little. It's helped me come to a decision.'

Back in my classroom I looked around at all the eager faces. They would have benefited so much from a camping holiday in the Dales. Many of them had never been further than Leeds or Bradford and only around half had been to the seaside.

I recalled being surprised when I learned this but then realized the extreme poverty in this area meant holidays were a pipe dream for many of the families.

The Atha boys had once asked me what the sea looked like and Sandra Asquith had said, 'It's wonderful, sir. My mam and dad took me to Bridlington. The sea stretches out until it meets the sky and goes on forever.'

It seemed a perfect description.

After registration I took a deep breath. 'Right, girls and boys, tables practice time. Eleven times nine is . . .?' A flurry of hands shot up and another day had begun.

At morning break I was sipping my coffee in the staff-room deep in thought.

'Penny for them, Jack,' said Connie when she walked in.

I smiled. I wasn't thinking of currency.

'You look as if you're carrying the worries of the world on your shoulders.' She collected her coffee and sat down next to me. 'Come on then, what's wrong?' she asked quietly.

'Norman.'

'I should have guessed. What's he done this time?'

'He's spiked the camping idea. I thought I had done all the background work but I should have spoken to him first. He wasn't happy.'

'That's a shame. The top juniors would have loved it and we had plenty of supervision.'

'At my previous school the head would have jumped at the opportunity, particularly as it was during a school holiday.'

'Face it, Jack. You'll never get support from him. Plus you've stood up to him and he doesn't like to be challenged.'

'It's depressing, Connie. I just feel as though I've had enough.'

Penny and Travis walked in.

'Why the long face, Jack?' said Travis.

'The school camp has been squashed. Norman's not keen.'

'Never mind. Maybe there will be another opportunity,' said Penny.

We sat there drinking coffee, each with our own thoughts.

Suddenly Connie broke the silence. 'I know what will cheer us up.'

'Go on then,' said Travis.

'It's the Eurovision Song Contest tomorrow night. I always watch it. Let's have a Euro Party at my house. Just bring a bottle and I'll do the rest.'

'Brilliant,' said Travis.

'Great idea,' said Penny.

Even I managed the flicker of a smile.

Meanwhile, in Norman's office Eric Skinner was scanning the *Racing Post*.

'It's Uttoxeter this afternoon, Mr Little, and I've got some hot tips.'

Norman was interested even though many of Eric's *hot tips* were stone cold by the end of the race. 'Go on then.'

Eric put a scribbled note on the desk. 'Benny from the market gave me a couple of horses, one for the two fifteen Whiston Novices' Hurdle and another for the three forty-five March Novice Hunters' Chase.'

Norman was impressed. 'Benny's tips are usually reliable.'

'An' you'll never guess, boss. His tip for the two fifteen is called Jackie Little.'

'Great name for a horse,' said Norman. 'Let's put a fiver on the nose.'

'Are you sure?' said Eric, worried he had overplayed his hand.

'It's an omen,' said Norman. 'I can feel it in my bones.'

'An' for the three forty-five he's gone with Sicilian Lad at ten to one.'

Norman rummaged in his pocket. 'Come back at lunchtime. I'll give you the money then.'

Eric rushed out and walked swiftly down the drive. His *bad back* was forgotten.

At lunchtime everyone was in the staff-room with the exception of Norman.

'Are we all set for tomorrow night?' asked Connie. 'Come round at seven.'

'Looking forward to it,' said Audrey. 'Never miss it. I'll bring a cake.'

'And I'll bake some of my superior scones,' said Travis.

We all agreed the fifteenth annual Eurovision Song Contest was a good excuse for a party.

'I heard Mary Hopkin was the favourite,' said Penny.

'What's she singing?' asked Barbara.

'"Knock, Knock, Who's There?"' said Audrey.

'Ideal for Eurovision,' said Travis. 'Lively tune, catchy lyrics.'

'And we've even got a fifty-piece orchestra,' said Connie. 'No expense spared.'

'Well, we won last year,' said Barbara.

'Lulu's "Boom Bang-a-Bang",' added Audrey, our Eurovision expert. 'Tied for first place with Spain, the Netherlands and France.'

'I remember it,' said Travis. 'Pity they didn't have enough medals to go round. Bit embarrassing.'

'They've changed the voting rules this year,' said Audrey,

'so it won't happen again.' Audrey was very protective about her favourite song contest.

'I didn't know you were so keen, Audrey,' I said.

'Oh yes. I watch it every year and I was sad for Cliff in '68. He should have won with "Congratulations".'

'My favourite was Sandie Shaw in '67,' I said and smiled at Penny.

'"Puppet on a String",' said Penny with a grin.

The bell rang and we all got up to return to our classrooms. 'So see you all there,' said Connie. 'And bring a partner if you wish.'

*If only,* I thought.

It was during afternoon break that Barbara surprised us all. Penny was out on playground duty and the rest of us were chatting about Connie's party.

Barbara took her *Daily Mirror* out of her shopping bag and said, 'How about this?'

The chatter ceased and we all gave her our full attention.

She held up the newspaper and pointed to the headline 'LOVE LIFE QUIZ FOR NATION'. 'So, what's your love life like, everyone?'

Audrey blushed, Connie frowned, I shook my head and Travis said, 'Why do you want to know, Barbara?'

'Well, it says here that thousands of people throughout Britain are to be asked about their love life in a massive government family-planning survey.'

'Really?' said Connie. 'Why?'

Barbara looked back at the article. 'Well, apparently the aim is to improve family-planning advice and contraceptives.'

'Can't see many wanting to share private matters,' said Audrey firmly.

'I agree,' said Barbara.

Edith was washing cups in the sink. 'I think some things are too personal.'

'Well, they won't bother contacting me,' said Travis. 'My love life is non-existent.'

'Perhaps you need to make more effort,' said Connie.

The conversation ebbed and flowed while I simply stared out of the window. Penny was holding the end of a skipping rope and chanting out a skipping rhyme with a group of girls.

I dropped in to Travis's classroom at the end of school and it was difficult to determine which of us was the more discontented.

Seb's car arrived to collect Penny. She climbed in and they drove away.

'What does she see in him?' said Travis.

'Well, apart from being blessed with good looks he's training to be a doctor. He's got a lot going for him.'

Travis pursed his lips and shook his head. 'It's just that she's a great girl and he's a preening peacock . . . that is if peacocks do preen.'

'You'll have to check your encyclopedia.'

He grinned. 'Will do.'

'So, go on, where are you up to with the Australia idea?'

'Still keen. Just pondering if I should go. What about you?'

'After this morning with Norman I can't see me

staying here. He crushes initiative and even referred to the children here as scum. It's a disgrace he ever got this job.'

'I agree. Makes you realize the importance of good leadership.'

'So I'll be looking in the *Times Educational Supplement* to see if anything crops up.'

'I don't blame you, Jack, but it's been good working with you.'

'Likewise.'

'Anyway, we have a party to look forward to. It's always great at Connie's.'

Outside the rain began to beat against the windows and we sat there, each lost in our own thoughts.

It was shortly after seven o'clock when I walked out of Ivy Cottage across the road to The Weaver's Arms. They had begun to sell Guinness on draught and it seemed the perfect Friday-night drink.

Donna came to serve me. There was no one within earshot. 'Yes, Jack. What can I get you?'

'A pint of Guinness, please.'

There was surprise in her blue eyes. 'Not your usual Chestnut then?'

'No, I fancy a change.'

She selected a tankard from the shelf above her head and gave me an enigmatic smile. 'Don't we all,' she said quietly and began to pull the pint.

John Denver was singing 'Leaving on a Jet Plane' on the jukebox and I looked across the counter at this stunningly attractive woman.

She placed my pint on the bar. 'Three shillings, please.'

I gave her a fifty-pence piece and she turned to the till.

'Seven shillings,' she said as she placed the change in my hand.

I sipped my drink. It was perfect.

There was no one waiting to be served and she began to wipe the counter with a cloth.

'How are you, Donna?'

She gave me a level stare. 'I have news.'

'Yes?'

'I've got an interview at Bretton Hall.'

I put down my pint. 'That's great. When is it?'

'After the Easter holiday.'

'You'll be fine. It's a new opportunity for you.'

'I've thought a lot about *new opportunities* and where my life is going.'

'It's a fresh start for you, Donna . . . new hopes and dreams.'

She continued to stare at me in that familiar way. 'Jack . . . I had hopes for us.'

I remained silent.

'There's someone else, isn't there?'

'Yes, Donna.'

'She's lucky.'

I picked up my drink and walked to the end of the bar. Above my head the television was on. Richard Widmark and Sidney Poitier were starring in *The Long Ships*. Fortunately the sound had been turned down. I wasn't in the mood for a Viking odyssey epic. I had journeys closer to home on my mind.

*

It was early evening on Saturday and, after the rugby game, I arrived at Connie's with a family pack of Smith's crisps and two bottles of pale ale.

She was serving cranberry margaritas from a huge mixing bowl. 'Hi, Jack. Try this. It's my new concoction.'

Her home was heaving with friends and neighbours. We all settled down in front of her television to watch the Eurovision Song Contest. I was sitting on the floor next to Penny and Travis.

It turned out to be an eventful competition. The UK team were so sure of winning they had already organized a winner's party for after the show. With the lovely nineteen-year-old Mary Hopkin from Pontardawe in the Swansea valley singing 'Knock, Knock, Who's There?' they were sure of success.

In the end the only two countries in the running were the UK and Ireland with Germany a distant third while Luxembourg had the unfortunate distinction of scoring *nul points.*

Audrey fell in love with the singer from Spain, an unknown named Julio Iglesias. However, it was another unknown who took the prize. Dana, an eighteen-year-old schoolgirl from Derry, sang 'All Kinds of Everything' and won with thirty-two points. No one knew then that the song was destined to become a million-seller and make her an international star.

I was helping clear up in the kitchen when Penny came in, looking concerned.

'What is it?' I asked.

'Seb was supposed to pick me up. He must be working late.'

'Well, I could take you home.'

Penny glanced at the clock. 'Maybe we ought to give him another ten minutes.'

We spent the time washing a few glasses but there was still no sign of Seb.

She was not pleased. 'He does this too often. Come on, Jack, let's go.'

It was good to have Penny by my side as we drove through the darkness. A thought occurred to me. 'We could have a nightcap.'

'Not at mine, Jack. Sue is entertaining.'

'Entertaining?'

'Yes, Nerdy Neville the scientist boyfriend. I need to give them some space.'

'Well, let's stop at Ivy Cottage. I've got a jar of Nescafé in the kitchen cupboard.'

'You're such a romantic, Jack. Have you nothing livelier?'

'Drinking chocolate?'

'You'll be saying Horlicks next.'

'I've got Ribena.'

Penny smiled. 'With a drop of rum, I hope.'

I enjoyed the drive home and the chance to relax together. Lee Marvin was singing the record 'Wand'rin' Star' on the radio and we hummed along.

Back in my cottage I found a bottle of red wine while Penny scanned my bookshelves. She was skimming through my collection of Penguin paperbacks. 'Interesting, Jack. We have similar tastes.' She held up George Orwell's *Nineteen Eighty-Four* and John Braine's *Room at the Top*. 'Ah, now here's another three shillings and sixpence well spent.'

It was a Penguin Modern Poets edition entitled *The Mersey Sound* and featuring Adrian Henri, Roger McGough and Brian Patten. 'Please can I borrow this one?'

'Of course, help yourself.' She slipped it into her shoulder bag and I wanted to ask her to read 'Love Is' by Adrian Henri but didn't have the courage.

She saw my reaction. 'What is it?'

'Nothing. Just that some of my favourite modern poems are there.'

She sipped her wine. 'Tell me more.'

I sat beside her. 'Well, there's some lovely humour. Try Roger McGough's "Vinegar". Only seven lines. It will make you smile.'

She began to flick through the pages when there was a loud rat-a-tat-tat of the door knocker.

'Who on earth can that be?' said Penny, looking alarmed.

'No idea. Let me go and see.'

Now there was a fist banging on the door.

'Who's there?' I called out.

'Open up!'

I opened the door and Seb was standing there. 'I've come to collect my girlfriend.' He pushed past me and looked at Penny. 'You should have waited. I was held up. Anyway, get your coat.'

'But the party was over, Seb. Everyone was leaving and there was no sign of you.'

He gave me a withering look. 'I was told you had left with him. I guessed the rest.'

I stepped forward. 'It's my fault, Seb. I offered to take Penny home when you didn't show.'

'Take her home? So why is she here?'

Penny was collecting her coat from the hallway. 'Don't make a scene, Seb. We stopped here to give Sue some space.'

He frowned and opened the door. 'Come on. We're going.'

Penny walked out into the darkness. 'Sorry, Jack, and thanks for the lift.'

'Bye, Penny.'

As she climbed into the car a whisper of moonlight lit up her face.

I was annoyed by Seb's behaviour and tapped him on the shoulder. 'You need to calm down,' I said quietly. 'There was no need to upset Penny.'

He walked to his car and then turned back round. His face was a mask of anger. 'And you need to find your own bloody girlfriend. Just keep away from mine.'

This wasn't the moment to escalate the problem. I watched him as he slammed his car door and drove away and his tail lights disappeared into the gloom. From the trees beyond The Weaver's Arms a barn owl, like a spectre of the night, flew down to snatch a solitary mouse and flew off into the darkness. There was a cold clarity to my thoughts as I stood there in the sombre moonlight, silent as a shadow.

That night it was many hours before I surrendered to a sleep of broken dreams.

## Chapter Fifteen

# *New Life*

I had packed the final box.

All that was left was enough to get me through the day. Cardboard boxes filled the hallway, kitchen worktops and lounge. It was Friday morning, 3 April, the end of the Easter holiday, and a special weekend lay in store.

A day out in the Dales beckoned, followed by the move into my new home. A mortgage was in place, papers had been signed and a van had been hired. So it was with a sense of excitement that I opened the curtains on my penultimate morning in Ivy Cottage and looked out on a familiar view. Stretched out in the distance the vastness of the Pennine Hills towered over the silent land while the dawn light poured over the hills in a river of gold.

Shortly after nine o'clock Pete Murray was playing the current number-one record, Simon and Garfunkel's 'Bridge Over Troubled Water', on Radio 2 while I was finishing a bowl of Kellogg's Sugar Smacks. It had been Connie who had suggested a day out in the Dales towards the end of the Easter break. Travis and Penny were both keen to make up a foursome. Seb was in London on a week's training course so Penny was free to join us, which pleased me.

Penny had thought a picnic would be a good idea so I had put a few corned beef sandwiches, four apples and one of Jimmy Priestley's famous pork pies in a carrier bag. With a few cans of Pepsi it seemed a good contribution.

Then out of the kitchen window I saw Travis's car pull up behind my Morris Minor. He and Connie were laden with a couple of car rugs and a large wicker picnic basket. I slipped on my duffel coat, picked up my carrier bag and went out to greet them.

'Come on, Jack,' said Travis, 'let's load up.'

'This basket weighs a ton,' said Connie with a smile. 'I've packed enough to feed the five thousand.'

I opened the boot of my car and it was quickly filled. Everyone climbed in and we set off. 'Next stop Penny's,' I said.

As we drove to Cold Beck village I thought of her. Seb had been furious the last time we had spoken so I had been cautious and kept my distance. I wanted to avoid confrontation as I knew it would upset Penny. So, for the time being, my feelings were locked away.

'What a pretty village,' said Connie. 'The name doesn't do it justice.'

On the main street almond trees were in blossom and the heavy scent of wallflowers hung in the air. Outside Penny's cottage honeysuckle and variegated ivy clambered up the brickwork and a tub of yellow-orange tulips stood beside the front door.

Penny appeared in a roll-neck sweater, jeans and walking boots. 'Morning, everybody.' She was holding a canvas bag. 'I've got a quiche and salad and some of my mum's home-made lemonade.'

I opened the boot and she put it on top of the wicker basket along with her duffel coat and knitted bobble hat.

'Well, we certainly won't go hungry,' said Travis. 'You should see what Connie has packed.'

I saw Connie give Travis a tug to follow her on to the back seat. This meant Penny was sitting in the front next to me. I smiled. It felt as though we were two couples rather than simply four friends . . . even if it was only for one day.

As we drove through Grassington I turned on the car radio. It was 'Love Grows' by Edison Lighthouse but, of course, I already knew that.

When the news came on, inevitably it concerned the forthcoming election. The newsreader, in perfect Queen's English, said, 'The Tories will win if the nation accepts Ted Heath as a leader of national stature. However, Labour has a lead in the polls and will triumph if the nation approves of its time in power over the past six years.'

'Let's hope so,' muttered Connie from the back seat.

When Bobbie Gentry began to sing 'I'll Never Fall in Love Again' we all sang along although I guessed it had a different meaning for all of us.

The miles flew by as we sped through Wharfedale; beyond the hawthorn hedgerows, black-faced sheep were enjoying the new grass and I relaxed with a sense of freedom as I drove. It was a day for spending time together and being refreshed by the clean air that swept in from the high moors.

'Pull in here, Jack,' said Travis suddenly. We were passing Kilnsey Crag, an overhanging limestone cliff. 'Let's watch the climbers.'

A group was attempting to climb up the face of this remarkable crag shaped by glaciers thousands of years ago.

'Looks dangerous,' said Penny.

'I guess that's part of the thrill,' said Travis.

We watched in wonderment as each climber, supported by ropes, sought out clefts in the grey stone for handholds.

Soon we were back in the car and the Dales stretched out before us. We drove through the timeless village of Kettlewell and then on through Starbotton and Buckden on our way to Aysgarth.

We discovered Penny was a keen and knowledgeable naturalist and she pointed out some of the natural wonders as we drove along. She had spent her teenage years walking in the Dales with her parents from their home in Askrigg and she had learned so much. Around us life had returned to the hills and valleys after a brutal winter in the freezing Arctic winds. Now red squirrels in their treetop homes were foraging hard to sustain their young while in the far distance roe deer were moulting their winter coats to reveal russet fur.

'Look,' said Penny, 'the lapwings and curlews are flying to higher ground to lay claim to their territories.'

'They look frantic,' I said.

'Well, it's a short breeding season for them so there's no time to lose.'

'I know the feeling,' said Travis, only to receive a dig in the ribs from Connie.

Finally we parked at Aysgarth Falls, the famous triple flight of waterfalls that cascaded over the limestone steps and had attracted visitors for centuries.

It was a perfect setting for a picnic and we settled on a grassy bank under a copse of trees. In the woodland there were bright primroses and swathes of bluebells. Milltown seemed a world away at times like this.

'Just think,' said Travis as we laid out the picnic rugs, 'John Ruskin and William Wordsworth have sat on this very spot and admired the view.'

'Thank goodness it wasn't William Shakespeare,' said Connie, 'or you'll be treating us to another of your quotes.'

Travis put his hand on his heart in mock despair. '"Was ever woman in this humour woo'd?"'

'*Richard the Third*,' said Penny quickly. 'Did it for A-level.'

'Impressive,' said Travis with a smile.

'Hidden talents,' said Connie appreciatively.

I munched a ham sandwich and looked around me. 'I used to come camping around here as a boy,' I said. 'I loved it. That's why I wanted to bring my class here in June.'

'And Norman spiked it,' said Connie.

'It would have been a great experience for the children,' said Penny as she sliced up the quiche and the pork pie.

'And maybe for us as well,' said Connie with a smile.

'Fresh air and fun,' said Travis while serving up the lemonade.

'And freedom,' added Penny with a smile.

'Yes,' I said. 'A special memory for them before they move on to secondary school.'

'Maybe there will be another chance,' said Penny.

There was silence and I looked at Travis, who gave a resigned shrug of the shoulders and lay back on the grass and stared up at the trees.

We sat there for an hour enjoying a veritable feast.

'Hey,' said Connie, pointing. 'What a lovely bird.'

We all looked. It had red-brown plumage and bright yellow on its head.

'It's a yellowhammer,' said Penny. 'Bit bigger than a chaffinch. My mother spots them in the field next to their cottage. They seek out food in the stubble. She says it has a distinctive cry.'

'Yes,' said Travis, 'it's a mimic-mnemonic.'

'Oh dear,' said Connie dreamily and leaned back against a tree. 'He's been reading his encyclopedia again.'

Travis sat up. 'Actually, if you listen, it sounds like *a-little-bit-of-bread-and-no-cheese*. Short sharp sounds ending with a long note.'

We all listened. 'Well done, Travis, you're right,' said Penny.

It was a replete and contented group that packed up what was left of our picnic.

We took our time heading back for home. It was as if we were in no hurry and wanted the day to last for ever. Our meandering journey included many stops to enjoy our own private wilderness. The strong smell of wild garlic carpeted the woodland floor while a grey wagtail emerged to break the silence and skitter above the water.

In the shadow of Ingleborough, the second highest peak in Yorkshire, there were raven chicks waiting for food in their nests.

'They're scavengers,' said Penny. 'They feast on the creatures that haven't survived the cold.' This was a harsh existence where only the strong survive.

*Like life,* I thought.

Eventually, we returned to Lotherswicke and had a drink together in The Weaver's Arms. Donna was behind the bar when I bought a round of drinks.

'Had a good holiday, Jack?' she asked.

'Yes, thanks, Donna. What about you?'

'Fine. I took Sherri out for the day on Easter Saturday. We caught the train to Leeds and looked round the shops.'

'Sounds good.' I put a pound note on the bar.

There was a guarded look behind the shutters of her eyes. 'I know you're moving house.'

'Yes, tomorrow, to a flat up in Bradley village.'

'So you won't be in here again.'

'Not as often.'

'Well . . . I wish you luck in your new life.'

'Thanks, Donna.'

She passed over my change and looked at Travis, Connie and Penny, enjoying relaxed conversation. 'So . . . Miss Armitage . . . is she the one?'

'She has a boyfriend, Donna.'

She put a hand on mine as I lifted the tray of drinks. 'I'll always be grateful for the help you've given me.'

We exchanged a look of understanding before I walked away.

Mama Cass was singing 'It's Getting Better' on the

jukebox when we got up to leave. We stopped on the High Street to say our goodbyes.

'Thanks, everybody,' I said. 'A great day.'

'I've really enjoyed it, Jack,' said Connie.

'And we'll be back in the morning for the big move,' said Travis.

Penny stretched up and kissed me on the cheek. 'Goodnight, Jack.'

I watched them drive away and walked back into Ivy Cottage for my last night in Lotherswicke.

It was a fine sunny Saturday morning and Travis, Connie and Penny had all arrived early. Soon Connie and Penny were packing the last items while Travis and I drove into Skipton and waited for Bartlet & Bland Estate Agent to open its doors. At the stroke of nine o'clock a small man in a grey three-piece suit let us in and I signed on the dotted line.

'Here're your keys, Mr Sheffield.'

'Ah yes, Mr . . . er?'

'Bland,' he said. 'I'm Bland. It usually gets a smile.'

I could see why.

We shook hands. It was a special moment. After three years of saving for a mortgage I finally owned my own home. It was a new two-bedroom ground-floor flat in the pretty village of Bradley just south of Skipton.

'Thank you,' I said and stared at the key.

It marked the start of a new life.

We left quickly. There was much to do and we parked at the back of the High Street outside 'VERNON'S VANS'.

The youth behind the counter looked relaxed and was

supping tea from a huge mug with 'ACE DRIVER' printed on the side. His name badge read 'DENNY' and he didn't look old enough to have passed his driving test.

'Jack Sheffield,' I said. 'Booking for a Luton van.'

'Right you are, chief,' he said and scanned the typed sheet in front of him. A tea-stain ring at the bottom looked like a poor man's royal seal.

'It's t'big white 'un on t'end. Gorra dent front offside mudguard. 'Part from that it's a runner.'

'Thanks,' I said as I took the key from him. I had shown him my driving licence and he seemed unconcerned.

'Gorra full tank so bring it back full or yer'll gerrit where it 'urts.'

I got the message. 'Fine. No problem. I'm not going far and I only need it until lunchtime.'

'Dunt matter t'me. Same money if y'keep it 'til five.'

I signed on the triplicate form and hurried out with Travis.

I had enjoyed driving large vehicles ever since my time delivering Corona pop when I was a student, but this was different. The steering was dubious, the wheels spongy and the gearbox had a mind of its own.

'Not exactly in mint condition, Jack,' said Travis with a wry smile.

I managed to crunch it into third gear as we gathered pace down the road to Lotherswicke.

When we arrived outside Ivy Cottage we found most of my meagre belongings in boxes on the pavement. Penny was guarding them while Connie was inside sweeping the floor.

My furniture consisted of a sofa, a battered armchair,

an old bed, a kitchen table, a small fridge, two chairs, a bookcase and a television set. Travis and I loaded these first and Penny and Connie filled up the floor space with the boxes. It didn't take long and soon we had left in convoy. As we turned off the road to Skipton and up the long narrow road to Bradley village, I slowed to negotiate the wooden swing bridge over the Leeds–Liverpool canal. A colourful narrowboat was approaching on its way to the Skipton basin and the owner gave us a friendly wave.

The flat had a single garage and we parked the van on the driveway. The walls were of local Yorkshire stone, honey and amber in the morning light.

'It's lovely, Jack,' said Penny. 'I'm so pleased for you.'

'Well done,' said Travis. 'Looks a great choice.'

'And a good investment for the future,' said Connie, 'particularly if house prices rise.'

I unlocked the front door and walked inside. Everything was new. Magnolia walls, a shiny oven and empty floors.

Connie put a shopping bag on the worktop. 'How about a coffee before we start?' She took out my kettle, four mugs, a jar of coffee, a bottle of milk and a packet of digestive biscuits.

'You're an angel,' I said.

'Good thinking, Connie,' said Penny.

'Where's the sugar?' asked Travis and received a playful clip round the ear from Connie.

While Travis and I unloaded my limited collection of furniture Connie and Penny emptied the boxes and found a home for the contents, often on the floor.

'You could do with a wall cabinet,' shouted Penny from the bathroom.

'And a table for this television,' added Connie. She had propped it on one of the sturdiest boxes and plugged it in.

Soon the van was empty.

As usual, it was Connie taking charge. 'You two take the van back while we sort out here.' She had unpacked another of her shopping bags. 'I've got some bread and cheese and a bottle of wine here but something hot would have been good. We've certainly earned it.'

'We'll call in for fish and chips on the way back,' said Travis.

In Skipton we dropped off the van and returned the keys to Denny, who was still supping tea. Next door to the fish-and-chip shop was a bookmaker.

'Jack, I want to place a bet on the Grand National.' Travis looked at his watch. 'We've plenty of time before it starts and your telly is all set up.'

'What are you backing?'

'Miss Hunter. Saw the name in the paper yesterday and knew it was a sign from heaven.'

'Miss Hunter?'

'My first girlfriend, Jack, from secondary school. She loved my model railway.'

'I can see what the attraction was.'

We stood outside while he took out his wallet. 'Why don't we both put a bet on for the girls? It will make it more fun watching it this afternoon.'

I felt a little awkward. 'Sorry, Travis. I've never been a betting man. I'm not familiar with betting shops.'

'Come on, Jack. It's the National. Everyone has a bet.'

'OK, then.' I gave him two fifty-pence coins. 'Here, put a bet on for me and for Penny.'

He took the coins and marched in confidently.

The flat looked transformed by the time we returned and at three o'clock we were enjoying fish and chips, thick slices of bread and hot tea. Then it was time for the Grand National, the world's most famous horse race from Aintree near Liverpool.

'We've all got a horse,' said Travis. 'Should make it more fun.'

The horses were lining up for the start. 'Brilliant,' said Connie. 'What's mine?'

Travis took the betting slips out of his pocket. 'You've got Pride of Kentucky and Penny's got Gay Trip.'

'Distinctive names,' said Penny with a smile. 'What about you?'

'I've got Miss Hunter.'

'Miss Hunter?' queried Connie.

'Yes, just liked the name,' said Travis a little lamely. 'And Jack's got No Justice.'

'Very appropriate,' said Connie. 'Could have been picked for him by Norman.'

Everyone laughed as we settled to watch the race.

Remarkably only seven horses completed the course and Travis had selected three of them. My horse didn't get beyond the twenty-second fence, prompting groans from everyone. Connie's horse came sixth. Travis jumped for joy when Miss Hunter came in third at thirty-three to one whereas everyone was on their feet cheering as the jockey, Pat Taaffe, rode Gay Trip to finish first by twenty lengths.

'Amazing,' said Travis. 'Your horse, Penny, was carrying the top weight of well over eleven stones and it still won easily.'

'So what do we do with the winnings?' asked Penny.

'I suggest we have a house-warming party next week,' I said.

This was readily agreed and the four of us settled down to a cosy evening together. It was late when everyone finally took their leave and journeyed home.

It had been a hectic and happy weekend and I was alone at last . . . my first night in my new home.

Unknown to us, ten miles away, Norman was in despair. He had spent twenty pounds at the bookmaker's on Grand National horses recommended by Eric.

None of his horses finished the race and, sadly, one of his selections, Racoon, was a fatality at the third fence. Meanwhile, Perry Hill fell at the first and one of the favourites, Two Springs, fell at the third fence. However, the one that broke his heart was Villay, the one hundred to one outsider, who unseated his rider late in the race at the twenty-seventh fence.

He sought solace in a bottle of whisky.

## Chapter Sixteen

# *Mr Farthing's Railway*

It was Friday, 22 May, the last day before the Bank Holiday weekend, and as I left Bradley village the season had moved on. Rooks circled the tall elms and lambs were bleating in the fields. The swallows had returned to their nesting places in the eaves of The Eagle pub and the woods beyond were carpeted with bluebells. In the far distance, beyond the hawthorn hedgerows, cattle were grazing contentedly in the open pastureland.

When I arrived at school it was clear that Travis was excited. He gathered us in the staff-room shortly before nine o'clock to make an announcement.

'What is it, Travis?' asked Audrey. 'I've got to get ready for infant assembly.'

'I've got some news.'

'It must be important,' said Penny.

'Come on then,' said Barbara with a smile. 'Don't keep us hanging on.'

I had never seen him so animated. 'So what is it?' I asked.

'I'm going to be in a film,' he declared proudly.

'A film? That's brilliant, Travis,' said Connie.

'What sort of film?' asked Penny.

'It's on the railway where I help out and they've asked for volunteers during the May holiday.'

Suddenly we were hanging on every word.

Barbara pointed out of the window. 'You mean the Keighley and Worth Valley Railway?'

'The one that shakes my classroom windows every day?' I added.

Travis grinned. 'That very one, Jack, and most of the sequences involving train arrivals and departures are being filmed during the coming week. So I'm going to Oakworth Station in my guard's uniform.'

Travis had been a working member since 1968 and had recently qualified as a guard. We had all thought it was brilliant except for Audrey, who thought he was rather eccentric. Significantly he had avoided telling Norman.

'When are you filming?' asked Connie. 'Can we come and watch?'

'Next Monday, the Bank Holiday. It's perfect and yes I imagine there will be plenty of interest.'

'So who's in this railway film? Anyone we know?' asked Penny.

'The stars are Bernard Cribbins and Dinah Sheridan.'

'Oh, she was wonderful in *Genevieve*,' said Barbara.

'Anyone else?' I asked.

'There're three children that I've not heard of. The main one is somebody called Jenny Agutter.'

'When did all this begin?' asked Connie, clearly intrigued at the unexpected revelation.

'Well, it was back in the spring that the film crew suddenly descended on Oakworth Station.'

'What's the film about?' asked Penny.

Connie was eager to know more. 'Yes, what's the storyline?'

'I heard it was based on the Edith Nesbit novel,' said Travis. 'You know the one, *The Railway Children*, a lovely story.'

'One of my favourites,' said Barbara.

'There aren't many heritage railways in England,' said Travis, 'and we've got one on our doorstep that's perfect for the film.'

'That really is news, Travis,' said Connie. 'Well done.'

'I haven't told you the important bit yet.'

'Go on,' I said.

'I've got a *talking* part. I have to speak to one of the main actors, William Mervyn, who plays the part of an old gentleman and, best of all . . . I get paid.'

'How much?' we all chorused.

'Seven pounds and fifteen shillings. Not bad considering I only earn sixty pounds a month as a teacher. Maybe I should become an actor.'

Barbara glanced at the clock. 'Wonderful news, Travis, but it's time for the bell. You can tell us more later.'

As we all headed for the door Connie fell into step with Travis. 'So are you going to tell Norman?'

Travis merely shrugged. 'Thankfully . . . no need.'

Sadly, Mr Farthing's railway turned out to have a stop-start timetable.

I was on duty at morning break when a group of boys gathered round.

'Ah've gorra Action Man, sir,' said an excited Keith Lumb. He held it up for all to see.

'That's good, Keith. He looks terrific.'

' 'E's got fancy 'air,' said Keith.

'Looks real,' added Matthew Hesketh for good measure.

The revamped Action Man certainly looked impressive with his new fibre hair. Times were moving on.

'An' Charlie got a new Raleigh Chopper bike for 'is birthday, sir,' said Keith.

'It's great,' said Charlie Dewhirst. 'Cost Uncle Peter thirty-two pounds. Ah 'eard 'im tell m'mother.'

'Terry got a Space'opper for 'is birthday, sir,' said Charlie, keen his friend wasn't left out.

Terry Duff grinned. 'It's orange, sir, wi' a cartoon kangaroo face.'

I nodded. 'Yes, I've seen them. They're great.'

They ran off to make up games for Action Man. It was good to see them at play in their world where imagination knew no bounds.

After break Connie had offered to take both our classes for the weekly *Singing Together* radio broadcast. This left me free to support other staff. Today I was working with the infant classes.

When I walked into Penny's classroom she was doing some simple maths with a group of her children. She pointed at six-year-old Peter Brocklebank. 'If Peter has four sweets and he is given four more,' she said with an encouraging smile, 'how many will he have?'

'Four, Miss,' said Lizzie Pickles without hesitation.

'Four? Why only four, Lizzie?'

' 'Cause Peter eats 'em real quick, Miss.'

'That's right, Miss,' said Colin Phizackerley. 'Ah've seen 'im. Peter crunches aniseed balls. 'E dunt suck 'em.'

'Let's do this another way,' said Penny with a wry smile in my direction and reached for the box of number blocks. 'Thank you for calling in, Mr Sheffield. Please can you select a book from the book corner and share it with a group of children?'

She scanned the room and made a decision. 'Phoebe, Lizzie, Willy and David, please go into the book corner with Mr Sheffield.'

I settled down on a tiny chair and picked up a book that had become very popular since its publication last year. Soon I had read, in a quiet voice, the delightful story of *The Very Hungry Caterpillar*, written and beautifully illustrated by Eric Carle. It was a rare opportunity for me to work with such young children and it struck me just how hard the work was for teachers of the youngest children in school.

Seeing Penny at work was always a pleasure. She was immersed in supporting each child and moved effortlessly from one to another. All of them appeared to have immediate needs. I thought my work with the older juniors was challenging until I saw the demands on her. I glanced at my watch and realized it was time to move on.

She gave me a nod of appreciation as I left. I went and

tapped gently on Audrey's door. In Class 2 their 'Animals' project was in full swing.

'Now, boys and girls,' Audrey said. 'Can we make a list of ten animals?'

Two six-year-olds, Claire Lofthouse and Gary Stubbs, were the first to raise their hands.

'Yes, Claire.'

'A cat, Miss,' said the smiling little girl.

'Well done,' said Audrey and wrote the word 'cat' on the blackboard.

The eager Gary Stubbs was going red in the face. 'Miss, Miss!'

'Very well, Gary.'

'Ah know, Miss . . . ah know!'

'Yes?'

'Nine more cats, Miss!'

It was at moments like this that Audrey wondered if she had chosen the right profession. Perhaps working with Arnie on his market stall would be a better proposition.

She looked apologetically at me. 'Can you work with Claire's group, please?'

More often than not, although this divergent teaching increased my experience as a teacher, I found it a relief to get back to the ten- and eleven-year-olds in my class.

In the staff-room after lunch Connie was in full flow. 'They've finally ended the strike at Pilkington Glass in St Helens,' she said.

The three thousand workers wanted an extra one shilling and sixpence per hour and management had been given three weeks to 'deliver the goods'.

'Good luck to them,' said Barbara.

'I'd ban strikes,' said Norman.

Barbara frowned. 'But what's left to the workers when management won't give them a living wage?'

Everyone sat up. It wasn't like Barbara to challenge Norman, particularly in front of the rest of the staff.

Norman was shocked by her response. 'I would have thought you above all would have understood how the economy works. Pay the workers too much and you don't make a profit.'

'The latest opinion poll gives Labour a lead over the Tories,' said Travis.

Connie smiled and nodded.

Polling Day was coming up next month on 18 June and we had been informed by the local authority that Heather View would be used as a polling station.

'Don't count your chickens,' said Norman. 'Unemployment is down below six hundred thousand for the first time this year. That counts for a lot.'

There was no doubt the election war was hotting up over unemployment.

'It just seems that the rich get richer on the backs of the workers,' said Connie.

'Like Rupert Murdoch,' said Travis.

Last year Rupert Murdoch, the thirty-nine-year-old Australian, had gained control of the *News of the World* newspaper group after defeating a rival offer of £34 million from Robert Maxwell.

'You've got a lot to learn,' said Norman. He stood up and walked out.

'I think you've upset him,' said Connie.

'No change there then,' said Travis. He looked a little deflated.

It was moments like this when he thought of Australia.

During afternoon school in Class 6 we moved all the desks to create a central area where we could continue building our class robot. It had been an idea that had cropped up when we had a discussion about new technology.

Computers were emerging and we wondered how they might change our lives. It was Matthew Hesketh who said in his comic there was a robot that ruled the world. The idea gained momentum. So we split into groups to build a robot that we named Robbie. It was a huge construction made of sturdy cardboard boxes provided by Kathy at the Corner Shop. Matthew Hesketh's father was an electrician and he called in with a bag full of bulbs, wires and batteries. The local adviser had given the school a Grundig reel-to-reel tape recorder and one group was working on a story Robbie could recite to the infant classes. It was really satisfying to see them at work.

'We can make 'is eyes flash on and off, sir,' said an eager Charlie Dewhirst.

I had brought in my battered Olivetti typewriter and Sandra Asquith was typing out a script on foolscap paper while the Atha boys were mixing a bucket of wallpaper paste to stick on a covering of newsprint that could be painted in bright colours.

Reggie looked up as the paste spilled on to the sheets of newspaper spread over the woodblock floor. His ruddy face was wreathed in smiles. 'Me an' Ronnie could be decorators, sir, when we grow up.'

'An' earn a load o' money,' added Ronnie for good measure.

It was at this moment that Eric Skinner looked in horror through the open classroom door and hurried away.

At the end of school I called in to Class 4 where Travis was sitting at his desk talking to Connie.

'So, looking forward to Monday?'

He smiled. 'Can't wait.'

'The last I heard is we're all coming.'

'That's great, Jack. Thanks for the support but by all accounts there may be a lot of hanging about. The other extras I've spoken to say they can often wait in full costume for a couple of hours until they're called on to the set.'

'But worth it, Travis. A dream come true, I imagine.'

He nodded. 'I've always been interested in history and the railway is full of it. I had a train set when I was a boy.'

'We would never have guessed,' said Connie with the merest hint of irony.

'Anyway, must go,' said Travis. 'I've got a uniform to iron.'

'Tough life being a jobbing actor,' I said.

Connie stood up. 'How about I do it for you?'

Travis looked surprised. 'I've nothing in so I can't even give you a sandwich.'

Connie grabbed his hand. 'Come on, Clint Eastwood, a drink at The Cat & Kettle will suffice.'

Meanwhile, Edith had been to the Corner Shop on an errand for Norman.

'This should help. It's Sanatogen and Kathy in the shop

says it helps to calm nerves.' Edith was a kindly soul even though Norman treated her like a servant. 'Maybe you're not getting enough rest.'

Norman took the packet from her. 'It'll have to do,' he said ungraciously, then had second thoughts. He looked up at her. 'Thank you,' he muttered.

She glanced back at him as she left the office.

It was clear something was troubling Norman and she wondered what it could be.

I was in the stock cupboard at the end of the school day collecting a few maths exercise books when Eric Skinner sidled up beside me. He stank of sweat and cigarettes.

'Mr Little wants t'see you.'

'What about?'

'That mess in y'classroom.'

'There's no mess. We tidied up before the bell. My classroom is fine.'

'Well, 'e's not 'appy.'

'So you've been telling tales again, have you?'

He gave a sneer. 'Ah wouldn't keep 'im waitin' if I were you.'

I didn't hurry; instead I returned to my classroom, put the books for marking in my leather satchel and walked to Norman's office. I tapped on the door and walked in.

He was sitting in his chair and smoking a cigarette. 'I've had a complaint.'

I knew it irritated him if I said nothing.

'It's about your classroom. According to Eric it looked like a bomb had dropped. Desks scattered everywhere and those Atha boys spilling paste on the floor. It stops now.'

I remained silent.

'Well, have you an explanation?'

'Yes,' I said quietly.

'Go on then.'

'First of all, if you want to see my classroom for yourself you will see that I have left it tidy. Second, my class are involved in a project that encompasses English, maths, science and art. The children are writing scripts, measuring angles, learning about electric currents and designing a large construction. It's a positive learning experience for them all and they are loving it. Significantly there's no poor behaviour, which is why I've sent no one to you to be caned.'

He leaned forward in his seat. 'What about the three Rs?'

'We start every day with reading, writing and tables practice so you need not worry about what you call the *basics*. I believe I'm encouraging a love of learning and that counts for a lot.'

'Love of learning! You're here to *teach* them. I'm getting tired of having to call you in here. Conform or find another job.'

I stared at him, shook my head and walked out.

There was a *Times Educational Supplement* on the staffroom table. I picked it up. It was time to start looking for a new teaching post.

That evening in The Weaver's Arms Donna was serving behind the counter and the jukebox was on full volume. The England World Cup football squad were singing their number-one record 'Back Home'. Young men in scruffy work clothes were propping up the bar and singing along.

One of them smacked his tankard on the counter and yelled at Donna. 'Oy, blondie, another pint.'

Donna frowned. 'There's no need to shout.'

He stepped towards her. 'You'll be talkin' wi' a thick lip t'morrow, luv, so move yer arse an' get me a pint.'

Donna gave him a steely look. 'If you don't behave I won't serve you.'

'You'll do as yer told, y'cocky bitch.'

'Right, that's it,' said Donna firmly. 'You can leave.'

She leaned round the door to the kitchen. 'Gary, we've got a loudmouth who needs to be sent on his way.'

Gary played second row for Keighley and was built like a Canadian lumberjack. He only spoke in short sentences and they were always to the point. He walked up to the spotty teenager. 'Out . . . now!'

'Ah were only askin' for a pint,' he pleaded.

Gary's grizzled face was inches from the quaking youth's. He grabbed his shirt and almost lifted him off the ground. 'Ah said OUT!'

As the youth finished up on the pavement outside it was noticeable that everyone else in the pub carried on as if it were of no consequence. They all knew that if you misbehaved in Gary's pub you were kicked out as sure as night follows day.

'Thanks, Gary,' said Donna, appearing quite unperturbed. She looked at me. 'So, what's it to be, Mr Sheffield?' She gave me a hint of a conspiratorial smile.

'A pint, please, Donna, and maybe a sandwich.'

'Nothing hot, Mr Sheffield?'

I recognized a tease, particularly when it slapped me in the face. 'Not just now, thanks.'

'Maybe later?'

She pulled the pint with expert ease and sighed as she passed it over. 'Only joking, Jack,' she whispered.

I smiled. 'I know.'

It was as if we had called a truce.

A relationship with this attractive woman was an appealing thought but something held me back. Part of it was because she was a parent at my school, but deep down I knew the reason was that it simply wouldn't be real.

I cared for another.

Bank Holiday Monday dawned bright and fair and I was pleased for Travis. His day in the limelight had arrived and all the teaching staff had gathered at Oakworth Station to support our friend.

There seemed to be a lot of activity but no filming going on. Extras in costume were sitting on the grass and drinking tea. The main actors were seated outside the station surrounded by a camera crew and important-looking people carrying sheets of paper.

The director of the film, Lionel Jeffries, was talking to Bernard Cribbins. It was interesting to see them looking so relaxed when so much was going on. The railway was a five-mile-long stretch that ran from Keighley to Oxenhope and I could barely imagine the complexities of having all the trains in the right place at the right time and pointing in the right direction.

Travis looked resplendent in his guard's uniform complete with watch and chain and a small green flag. He came over to join us and share our picnic lunch. Over the past months he had grown a distinctive and luxuriant moustache that suited his character.

'My turn soon,' he said.

Suddenly he was called into position and we watched the actors move smoothly through their paces. It was fascinating for us all and even more so having Travis taking part.

Soon he was sitting beside us again. 'Brilliant!' he said and we all agreed.

It was the following morning before school when Edith summoned Travis to her office. 'Call for you, Travis,' she said, looking a little anxious. 'It sounds like someone important. Something about the railway film.'

Travis hurried in, picked up the receiver and listened intently. 'Yes, of course,' he said. 'I understand.' There was a pause while he wrote down a telephone number. 'Thank you. Let me arrange things here and I'll get back to you.'

Travis turned to Edith, beaming in excitement. 'Good news!' he said. 'They want me for another scene. I have to wave my flag and blow my whistle as a train leaves the station.'

Edith looked in her diary. 'Mr Little is in a meeting at County Hall this morning. He should be back at lunchtime.'

'Thanks, Edith. I'll speak to him then. It's only half a day away from school this week. I'm sure we can arrange it.'

He hurried out full of anticipation while Edith shook

her head and hoped Norman would be in a good mood when he returned.

But at one o'clock Norman was not in a good mood.

'The answer is no,' he said bluntly.

Travis looked stunned. 'But this is important.'

Norman leaned back in his chair and shook his head.

'Mr Little,' pleaded Travis, 'Connie and Jack have offered to provide cover for Class Four. They will organize a choir practice and a maths activity morning. So the children won't miss out. It's all arranged and you don't need a supply teacher.'

'The answer is still no.'

'But it's the film company who want me back and just for one short scene.'

Norman stood up, tired of the conversation. 'Your first responsibility is here in school, not poncing about pretending to be a film star.'

Edith heard the raised voices and called in to try to defuse the situation but it was too late. Travis was bitterly disappointed and told Barbara that he might take sick leave but Barbara persuaded him not to risk it.

He called in to my classroom before the start of afternoon school.

'I've had enough, Jack. It's impossible working for this guy. I've just had to ring the film company to say I can't be released.'

'I'm sorry, Travis. I'm not sure what to suggest.'

'No need, Jack. I know what to do.'

'What's that?'

'I'm going to follow up that advert for jobs in Australia.'

He stormed off to his classroom as the bell rang. I knew

how he felt and glanced at the *Times Educational Supplement* next to my satchel.

We both needed a fresh start.

It was early afternoon when Edith took the call and Norman was summoned to the telephone.

'Am I speaking with the headmaster, please?' said an official-sounding voice.

Norman was always pleased to be addressed as head*master* rather than head*teacher*. It massaged his ego.

'Speaking,' said Norman.

'This is Edward Fitzroy, assistant producer at the film company that has employed . . .' There was a riffling of papers. '. . . a Mr Travis Farthing who I understand is a member of staff at your school.'

'That's correct.'

'Mr Farthing has proved to be a most valuable extra for our railway film.'

'Has he?' Norman sounded surprised.

'However, we have to shoot a scene again owing to difficulties with the movement of rolling stock.'

'Oh yes.'

'So I'm trusting you will be able to release your colleague tomorrow. My understanding is your Chief Education Officer is lending us his full support.'

Norman was not happy. He would have to go back on his instruction to Travis. 'I didn't know the Education Office was involved. It means I have to supply a temporary teacher in his class.'

'I'm sure a man of your position can solve a difficulty of this nature.'

Norman ground his teeth. 'I suppose so,' he muttered reluctantly.

It was the end of school and Connie and I were in my classroom discussing the ever-deepening divisions with Norman.

'I'm looking for a new job, Connie.'

She looked sad for a moment. 'I'm not surprised. I think we all shall be by the end of term.'

I opened the *Times Educational Supplement* and spread it out on my desk. 'There're three jobs in the *TES*. I've circled them.'

'Where . . . local?'

'Yes.'

'Makes sense. So where are these jobs?'

'One in Barnoldswick over the border in Lancashire and another in Ilkley. They're both basic teaching posts.'

'What's the third?'

'Bit of a long shot. A deputy headship in Newbridge.'

'Well, why not? It's early in your career but you must have a decent chance. Nothing ventured and all that.' She sighed. 'I would be sorry to see you go. We've made a good team but working for Norman has become impossible.' She leaned forward and squeezed my hand. 'So good luck, Jack.'

It was at that moment an animated Travis burst into the classroom and sat down beside us. 'You'll never guess.'

I wondered why he was smiling. 'Go on then.'

'I'm back on the film set tomorrow morning. Apparently Norman got the hard word from the film company, or so Edith said. He's just told me he's changed his mind.'

I smiled. 'More like it was changed for him.'

'Hey! Great news, Travis,' said Connie.

He sat down and stroked his moustache thoughtfully. 'Mind you, some good has come from this.'

'What might that be?' asked Connie with a grin. 'Are you leaving us to become a full-time actor?'

'Not quite . . . but I am definitely leaving.'

Connie looked surprised. 'What, for another school in Yorkshire?'

He gave her a level stare. 'No, Connie . . . Australia.'

## Chapter Seventeen

# *Taken*

It was a perfect morning on Thursday, 18 June as I opened my bedroom window and looked out. A pink dawn had crested the distant hills and the sun was bathing the land with warmth and light. On the village high street butterflies hovered above the buddleia bushes and the scent of roses was in the air.

It was Election Day and Heather View Primary School was being used as a polling station. A busy day was in store for Travis and Edith. Travis had previous experience of working as the officer in charge and, once again, he was on duty. Edith was assisting him as polling clerk, a job she had done many times.

This was the first general election in which people could vote from the age of eighteen, following the passage of the Representation of the People Act. Voting commenced at seven o'clock and Travis and Edith had been in school from the crack of dawn to set up the voting booths and ensure all was ready in good time. The rest of the staff had agreed to call in to support them with sandwiches and coffee and I had arranged to collect Penny at eight o'clock.

She looked great in her summer dress when she walked out of her door but was strangely quiet as we drove away.

'I've just voted in our village hall. How about you?'

She gave a brief nod. 'Yes.'

'You OK?'

'Fine,' she said.

It continued like this for a few minutes. Her replies were monosyllabic.

Once again my mind was filled with confusion. She appeared to be in a diffident mood – her manner was uncharacteristically self-effacing.

'Sorry, Jack. Not quite myself this morning.' For a moment she clasped her hands as if in prayer.

I guessed there were problems with Seb once again so I switched on the car radio. The news was dominated by the anguish of England's World Cup defeat by West Germany earlier in the week and the fact that Labour were ahead in the opinion polls.

Meanwhile, Penny was silent. I glanced across at her. She kept her eyes averted as she twirled a strand of hair and stared at the road ahead.

The number-one record, Mungo Jerry's 'In the Summertime', began to play as we drove towards Milltown. Around us a morning mist caressed the land. The summer heat was building and the air was becoming heavy and oppressive.

Perhaps it was a portent of what lay ahead.

It was when we arrived at school that we realized something was wrong.

We drove past a large sign on the gate that read 'POLLING STATION' with an arrow pointing towards school. Next to the car park an anxious Norman was facing PC Moxon. Our local bobby was making notes. Alongside stood an ashen-faced Mrs Valerie Holmes, mother of eleven-year-old David in my class. Two other mothers were standing close by and seemed equally concerned.

After I parked my car, Barbara hurried towards us, looking anxious.

'What's going on?' I asked. I had never seen her looking so stressed.

'Oh Jack, Penny, it's dreadful. If only I had been a few minutes earlier.'

'What's wrong?' asked Penny.

I looked across at Norman and our local bobby. 'And why is Phil Moxon here?'

'It's David Holmes in your class, Jack.' Barbara shook her head. 'He's been taken.'

'*Taken?*' we both said at once.

'His father suddenly appeared and drove away with him.'

'His father?' said Penny. 'But he's not permitted to be anywhere near the family.'

I realized this was serious. 'There was a staff meeting back in January. It was just after he arrived. I remember it. You explained the outcome of the meeting with Social Services.'

Barbara frowned. 'I had to represent the school . . . Norman couldn't attend.'

'Poor Mrs Holmes,' said Penny. 'She looks in a dreadful state.'

We knew Mrs Valerie Holmes as a helpful and positive parent who always supported the school. She was rubbing tears from her eyes.

'You'll recall she split up from her husband last Christmas in really acrimonious circumstances,' said Barbara. 'He was a strange man . . . ordered to stay away from his wife and son.'

'So what's happened this morning?' I asked.

Barbara took a deep breath. 'Well, just before I arrived, Mrs Holmes had left David to play with his friends in the yard. She went into school to vote before going to work. Apparently it was then that Mr Holmes suddenly appeared. He must have been waiting for the opportunity. Norman had just arrived and they had a brief conversation. Mr Holmes told Norman he was taking David to a dental appointment.'

'Oh dear,' said Penny.

I shook my head. 'And Norman believed him?'

Barbara nodded. 'I'm afraid so. I guess he had forgotten the history of the family or maybe he was caught unawares. On the surface Mr Holmes appears quite lucid. I arrived just as he was driving away with David. Mrs Holmes was frantic. That's when I called the police.'

Barbara bowed her head and Penny put her arm around her shoulders. 'Don't worry.'

I looked across at Norman. He was in trouble and it showed. 'Barbara, I'm sure Phil Moxon will sort it out and find him.'

'I do hope so,' she said.

I was thinking hard as we walked into school. 'I'll see if there's anything we can do to help.'

Meanwhile, our local bobby was trying his best to collect as much relevant information as possible. He had picked up some of the background from his sergeant but he was aware time was of the essence. It was possible a young boy's life was at stake.

He had begun to question David's mother. 'Mrs Holmes . . .' He glanced at his notebook. 'Your husband's name is Richard Holmes?'

'Yes . . . answers t'Ricky.'

'Did you give your husband permission to collect David from school?'

'No, definitely not. I wouldn't let 'im near my son.'

'Mr Little mentioned a dentist appointment?'

'No, Ricky were lying when 'e spoke to Mr Little.' She glared at Norman. 'My 'usband can be very persuasive.'

Our headteacher shifted from side to side and was looking more uncomfortable with every revelation.

PC Moxon persisted: 'According to Mr Little it would appear that David went willingly with his father.'

'Yes, 'e's a trusting boy.'

'So if his father told him there was an appointment would he have believed him even if you hadn't mentioned it?'

'Yes, because 'e would accept t'word of an adult.'

'I need to ask this, Mrs Holmes.' Phil Moxon paused and spoke quietly. 'What can you tell me about the violence in the home?'

Mrs Holmes spoke defiantly. 'David saw none of it. Ricky only ever 'it me where bruises wouldn't show.'

Phil Moxon gave a brief nod. 'And what car does Mr Holmes drive?'

'An 'Illman ah think . . . an' it's red.'

'Finally, Mrs Holmes, is there anywhere that you think your husband may have gone . . . friends, relations, favourite places?'

'Maybe 'is mother in Leeds but ah doubt it.'

'The address would be helpful.'

'Of course . . . but she 'ates him as well.'

Phil Moxon nodded. 'I see.'

'Thing is, Ricky used t'be difficult but 'e became . . . well, *disturbed*.'

Phil Moxon closed his notebook. 'That's all for now, Mrs Holmes. Thank you for being so helpful. We'll do our best to make sure David is safe. I suggest you go back home and wait for news. Have you got friends who would sit with you?'

She gestured towards Dorothy Nuttall and Peggy Stubbs, who had been waiting out of earshot. They stepped forward and walked slowly away with a distressed Valerie Holmes.

Ricky Holmes was driving north towards Skipton. Unshaven, with shoulder-length hair, and wearing dirty jeans and T-shirt, he did not cut an inspiring figure.

'Where are we goin', Dad?'

He lit a cigarette and pressed hard on the accelerator. 'On an adventure, son.'

'Adventure?'

'Somewhere special.'

'What about t'dentist, Dad, like y'sed t'Mr Little?'

Ricky Holmes grinned. 'Do y'want t'go to t'dentist?'

'No, Dad.'

'Then we won't go.'

'What about m'mam? Is she comin'?'

'No, it's jus' us. Like it used t'be.'

He was a skinny, pale, nervous man, but at that moment his sunken, pockmarked cheeks were flushed with excitement. As they neared the outskirts of Skipton his mind was racing.

I approached PC Moxon. 'Phil, is there anything we can do?'

He glanced at his notebook. 'We think he's driving a red Hillman.'

I knew the car. It had been Hillman's answer to the Mini. 'I saw a red Hillman Imp going like the clappers down the hill as I arrived at school.'

'Thanks, Jack. I'll put out a check on that. Any ideas where he might be going?'

I shook my head. 'If I think of anything I'll let you know.'

'Let me contact the station.' He walked towards his motorbike. 'Ring me there if you think of anything.'

Norman was back in his office when Barbara walked in. She was furious. 'What on earth were you thinking?'

Norman stubbed out his cigarette angrily. 'Don't you start. I've had enough from that jumped-up constable.'

'But you must have known that Mr Holmes should be nowhere near school. I went through it with you.'

'That was long ago and he seemed decent enough when

I spoke to him. Bit scruffy but they're all like that round here. Anyway, school's closed today. It was just by chance I called in to pick up some papers. He could have taken his son at any time.'

Barbara was red in the face. 'You should have stopped him, Norman.'

He clenched his teeth. 'Your job isn't to tell me what to do.'

'Well, someone needs to,' said Barbara as she walked out.

Connie had arrived in her car and Audrey had been dropped off outside school by Arnie in his greengrocer's van. The school closure meant they could catch up on work in their classrooms and they were chatting happily as they walked towards us. Suddenly they recognized the concern on our faces.

We gathered on the entrance steps while a distressed Barbara told the newcomers what had happened. 'It was awful,' she said. 'David Holmes had just arrived with his mother. She was on the early shift at Hunter's Mill and was intending to drop David off at her friend's house. The boy was on the playground when his mother went inside to vote. That was when his father appeared.'

'Ricky Holmes is a bad lot,' said Connie.

Barbara shook her head in despair. 'If only I had been here sooner.'

'So what's happened to David?' asked Audrey.

'Apparently his father had a quick word with Norman before collecting him from the playground and they drove away.'

'Why didn't Norman stop him?' said Connie. 'We all know what David's dad is like.'

'Norman didn't recall,' said Barbara. She glanced back towards the entrance door. 'We've just had words.'

It was clear that our deputy headteacher was in a withering mood, completely at odds with her usual sunny disposition.

With a deep sigh we walked into school.

Ricky Holmes was driving north-west out of Skipton through Gargrave.

It was when he took a right turn at Coniston Cold towards Malham that he turned to his son and smiled. 'We were 'appy 'ere, son . . . once.'

'When were that, Dad?'

Ricky ground his teeth. 'Before y'mam started sayin' things.'

'What d'you mean, Dad?'

'She weren't kind. Said stuff. Deliberate.'

'She's allus kind t'me, Dad. I 'ad a birthday cake wi' choc'late flakes on top. It were m'favourite.'

Ricky gripped the wheel tighter. *No more cakes,* he thought.

He stared ahead at the limestone walls and the criss-cross pattern of endless fields. His mind whirled but at its core there was a grain of certainty. He knew why he was here. When you've nothing left to live for this was the best place to be.

In the middle of the school hall a series of wooden voting booths had been erected but no one was using them when we walked in.

Travis and Edith were sitting behind a table. Travis had a long list of voters in front of him along with a ruler and a red biro while Edith was in charge of the special hole-punch that validated each voting slip. A large black metal box stood on another table beside them.

'Two coffees, please,' said Travis cheerfully and then realized something was wrong.

Connie turned to us. 'Audrey, why don't you take Barbara into the staff-room for a cup of tea?'

'What's happened?' asked Edith.

'You explain, Connie, and I'll go to my classroom,' I said. 'There might be a clue in something David's written.'

'I'll come as well,' said Penny.

Connie leaned over the table and spoke quietly: 'It's about David Holmes.'

'Lovely boy,' said Edith. 'Always cheerful and polite.'

'There's been an incident with his dad.'

'A nutter,' said Travis bluntly.

Our footsteps echoed as we walked into my empty classroom. I lifted the lid of David's desk and took out a collection of his English notebooks. Penny picked up a folder of his artwork. It was interesting going through the many stories and poems he had written. I knew he enjoyed writing and that his mother gave him constant support.

As I skimmed through the pages I came across a story he had written about a day out he had enjoyed. It described a visit a year ago before he came to Milltown. His father had taken him to Malham in the Yorkshire Dales and David had written: 'It was great. My dad said it was special. Just me and him.'

'Look at this,' said Penny.

It was one of David's drawings in wax crayon. He had

written at the top 'Me and My Dad'. A tall figure and a shorter figure were standing side by side and holding hands.

They were on top of a cliff.

Penny stared at the drawing. 'Jack, it looks like Malham Cove.'

Moments later I walked into Edith's office, picked up the telephone and rang the local police station. 'Phil, this is a long shot but David and his father went to Malham last year. It sounds as if it was a significant place.'

'That's interesting. If he's going north I've already been in touch with the Skipton police.'

'Phil, I'm free, so I could drive up there. It's only twenty miles. Better than waiting around here.'

There was a pause. 'OK, Jack, let me know if you spot anything . . . and don't do anything hasty.'

'There it is, son. Told you we were comin' somewhere special.'

David stopped and looked up. 'It's great, Dad.'

After they had parked the car it was a two-mile walk to the limestone crag that was Malham Cove. Formed in the Ice Age, it was a spectacular tourist attraction and a miracle of nature.

It was also three hundred feet high.

'So come on, Dave. We're off right to t'top.'

'Ah'm a bit 'ungry, Dad.'

'Ah've got some sweets.'

'OK, Dad.'

As they trudged steadily up the side of the valley the heat was building and dark clouds were coming in from the west.

*

Traffic was slow approaching the market town of Skipton but beyond it, twenty minutes later, Penny and I reached the old bridge over Malham Beck and parked by the grassy verge outside The Lister Arms.

'Penny, look what's there.' It was a Hillman Imp. Bright red.

'It's got to be them,' she said.

I nodded. 'Distinctive car.'

Penny gave a strained smile. 'I remember looking at one with my dad. Bit quirky. Engine in the back, boot in the front. Rear window lifts so you can put shopping bags on the back seat.'

I squeezed her hand. I could see she was nervous. 'You wait here, Penny. I'll check inside the pub.'

They weren't there, only walkers in sturdy boots, rucksacks scattered by their table. I spoke to the barman and explained what had happened.

He jerked a thumb towards a telephone behind the bar. 'Use this,' he said.

The desk sergeant put me straight through to PC Moxon.

'Phil, I'm in Malham in The Lister Arms. There's a red Hillman parked outside. It's got to be them. They may have gone up the cove.'

'I'm on it, Jack. I'll get the Skipton police out there and I'll be with you as soon as I can. Pray the guy doesn't do anything stupid.'

'I'm with Penny so I'll get her to wait by this phone.'

'OK, Jack, we'll deal with it from now.'

Outside Penny was standing by my car and staring at the brooding clouds in the distance. The air was stifling. A storm was coming . . . a big storm.

'Penny, I've spoken to Phil and he's alerting the local police. When they arrive say I've gone up to the cove to see if David and his dad are there.'

'No, Jack, it might be dangerous.'

I put my hands on her shoulders. 'Penny, this is important. I want you to wait in the pub. There may be a message on the phone. The barman is helpful. So please stay there. I'll be fine. Don't worry.'

I set off and Penny watched me leave. When she was out of sight I began to jog along the valley bottom and prayed all would be well.

In the distance there was a flash of lightning followed ten seconds later by a crashing roll of thunder. The storm was two miles away.

'Ah'm scared, Dad.'

'No need, son. We're 'ere now. Where we're s'pposed t'be.'

'It's all rocky up 'ere.' David pointed towards the crazy paving of limestone.

'They're clints an' grikes. Funny names. The clints are t'blocks an' t'grikes are t'gaps in between.'

'The clouds are dark, Dad. Looks like rain's comin'.'

Ricky stood up and walked towards the edge of the cliff and spread his arms wide. He felt invincible. King of the world. Soon it would be time to fly.

It was a strenuous route up the narrow track that led up the side of the valley to the top of the cove. Beneath me a few walkers were hurrying back towards Malham and the haven of shelter.

I was fifty yards away when I saw them.

David was crouching on a rock and his father was standing near the edge of the cliff and staring out at the valley beyond.

I approached carefully until I was ten yards away.

'Mr Holmes,' I called out.

He spun around. 'Who are you?'

'I'm Jack, one of the teachers at Heather View. David is in my class.'

Ricky Holmes eyed me suspiciously. 'What y'doin' 'ere?'

I took a step sideways towards the edge of the cliff and stretched out my arm. 'This is one of my favourite places. My father brought me here as a boy. He said it was the best view in Yorkshire.'

Ricky walked back to David and put his arm around his shoulder. ' 'E were right.'

I walked closer. 'Hello, David, good to see you.'

David smiled. ' 'Ello, sir.'

I took a step nearer and pointed towards the onrushing clouds. 'There's a storm on its way, Mr Holmes.'

He shrugged. 'Meks no diff'rence.'

'I was just thinking about getting David down into Malham. We could have a drink and a sandwich in the tea rooms.'

He took a step nearer the edge. 'No need.'

There were now only five yards between us.

I had to prolong the conversation.

In the distance there was another boom of thunder and the sky had grown even darker. The first spots of rain began to fall.

It was then I saw movement behind him. Four men in

police uniform were crouched low and moving slowly towards us.

I stepped once again to my right and almost stumbled.

'Be careful, sir,' shouted David.

'Don't worry, I'm fine.'

I knelt down. It was important to look less threatening.

'What y'doin'?' asked Ricky.

'I think I've twisted my ankle. Maybe you could help me get back to Malham.'

Ricky shook his head. 'We're not goin' back there.' He gripped David's shirt a little tighter and moved closer to the edge.

'Ah'm scared, Dad.' David looked pleadingly up at his father.

'No need, son. We'll never be scared again.' He took another step towards the final rim of blocks.

'I've got something to show you, Mr Holmes.'

'What?'

'It's in my pocket.'

'Show me.'

I took out David's drawing of the two of them here at the top of Malham Cove. I stretched out my hand, offering him the folded sheet.

'What is it?'

'It's special, Mr Holmes. David drew it.' I unfolded the page.

David's eyes were wide. 'It's my drawing, Dad.'

I stepped closer to the boy and his father. The smell that clung to Ricky's stained shirt was putrid. He viewed me with a manic stare.

I had his full attention now. The four policemen were

almost behind them. 'Can I give it to David?' I held it out and David stretched out his hand to receive it.

At that moment lightning flashed and thunder boomed. The storm was overhead and rain sheeted down, soaking us instantly.

I knew this was the opportunity. As David took the drawing I grabbed his wrist and held on. The police moved instantly and dragged Ricky back from the edge.

David screamed and I held him tight.

Two of the policemen marched Ricky back to their van on the narrow high road behind the cove. Another carried the distressed David in his arms while I stumbled through the rain with the other policeman.

Suddenly I felt exhausted.

Back in Malham village Phil Moxon was standing by his motorbike, oblivious to the torrential rain. 'Well done, Jack,' he said. 'Although I did say don't get involved.'

'Good to see you, Phil. The police did well.'

He grinned. 'They're a good lot in the Skipton station. Anyway, everything is in hand. They've got the message at school and Mrs Holmes should know the good news by now.' He looked at his watch. 'I need to get back.'

We shook hands. 'Thanks, Phil. I just hope the boy recovers. It was scary up there.'

'Time's a great healer, Jack.' Rain was streaming off the peak of his cap. 'In the meantime I suggest you dry off in the pub.' He nodded towards The Lister Arms. Penny was at the window.

She was waving.

*

We picked up a fish-and-chips supper in Skipton and drove on to Bradley. It was a relief to relax in our private space.

While I changed into dry clothes Penny prepared the meal. She set the table and found a bottle of wine. She had been like a coiled spring for most of the day but now slowly she unwound. We finished our meal and sipped wine in silence.

Finally, she looked across the table at me and gave a sad smile.

'I'm glad you're here,' I said.

She sighed. 'It's been a difficult week.'

'Seb?'

'Yes.'

'How are you?'

She sighed again, even more heavily. 'Broken.'

I leaned over the table and rested my hand on hers. 'I'm so sorry.'

'No need, Jack. It's over.'

'Really?'

For a moment her eyes were soft with sorrow. 'Yes, Jack . . . at last.'

She stood up. 'Let's clear these plates.'

We stood side by side in my tiny kitchen. She washed. I dried.

When we had finished we sat together on the sofa and finished the bottle of wine. The tensions of the day eased.

At ten o'clock I switched on the television. David Frost and Alastair Burnet were introducing *The Nation Decides* and discussing the general election.

Penny's head was resting on my shoulder. 'Decisions,' she murmured and stood up.

'Shall I take you home?'

She moved closer. 'Jack, it's been quite a day.'

I traced a finger down her cheek. 'It has . . . So, are we going?'

She rested her head on my shoulder. 'It's time to move on.'

I held her in my arms. 'Finally?'

'Yes, Jack.'

We kissed as the rain pattered against the window and held hands as we walked to my bedroom.

It was a new dawn and golden light shimmered in the eastern sky.

I crept out of bed and looked out of the window. The marching army of storm clouds had gone, leaving behind moist vapours of mist over the fields. Early-morning sun was spreading its light over the sleeping land.

It had been a perfect night and I smiled at the memory.

Penny was still asleep. Her naked body was stretched out on my bed, relaxed in her slumber. Making love with this beautiful woman had been a journey of exploration, a fusion of ice and fire. It had begun with a gentle caress followed by an insistence, an urgency . . . a *need*. Two hours later we had drifted into a welcome sleep while the storm outside raged.

It was a night I would never forget.

I went into the kitchen to make a pot of tea. I filled the kettle and turned on the radio. It was full of news about the election. There had been a surprise victory for Ted

Heath. The Conservative Party had defeated Harold Wilson's Labour Party. Meanwhile, the Liberal Party, under its new leader, Jeremy Thorpe, had lost half its seats.

It was later than usual when Penny and I pulled up in the school car park. Connie was in the entrance hall when we walked in.

She smiled. 'Well done, Jack. We've all heard what happened.'

I guessed she was talking about Malham but my mind was elsewhere. 'Thanks, Connie. Yes, it's been eventful.' I glanced at Penny and she grinned.

'I'll catch up with you later.'

When I was in my classroom I took an envelope out of my pocket. I had picked it up in haste as we left home. I opened it with interest. It was an invitation to attend County Hall on Thursday, 2 July for an interview for the post of deputy headteacher of Newbridge Primary School.

# Chapter Eighteen

## *Decision Day*

I looked around. It was a case of déjà vu except this time there were only four of us: two women and another man. The room was familiar and it still felt like a funeral parlour. However, today there was more at stake: the deputy headship of Newbridge Primary School. It was Thursday, 2 July . . . decision day and one that would change my life in more ways than one.

Speaking of *life* . . . yesterday Norman had made it hell. He had been furious when he heard I had an interview. His last words to me were 'Get out!' However, he was clearly in a dilemma. As far as he was concerned I wasn't wanted at Heather View but it was difficult to replace me in the short term. Everyone else on the staff had been supportive and wished me luck.

That was all behind me now and I was determined to do my best as I drove out of Bradley village. I had left early for County Hall when the first soft kiss of sunlight had crested the distant hills. It was a perfect summer morning. In the hedgerows the drone of bees could be heard in their search for pollen while cuckoo spit sparkled in the tall grasses . . . a good day to be alive.

I felt well prepared. Yesterday Connie and Travis had given me a mock interview in my classroom during the lunch break and it went well. Also last weekend Penny had taken me shopping in Leeds and selected a smart grey three-piece suit and pair of black shoes with shiny toecaps. I felt like a BBC newsreader when a new white shirt and a tie had been added to the ensemble. On Saturday evening Penny had persuaded me to try it all on for an impromptu fashion show before leaving it in an untidy pile on the bedroom floor and making love.

I was still smiling at the memory when I arrived at County Hall.

Minutes later, after checking in at the reception desk, all happy thoughts had dissipated.

I sat down and we introduced ourselves. The two women interviewees were a contrasting pair. In her late thirties, Mrs Phyllis Bloom was already a deputy headteacher of a primary school in Halifax. She was short and plump with a surprising frizz of ginger hair, and wore a severe tweed suit. 'I'm ready for a fresh challenge,' she declared.

Mrs Jane Dalton was tall, slim and beautifully dressed. Her high heels emphasized her height and her long blonde hair hung in an exquisite ponytail. She was head of an infant department in the Cotswolds and exuded confidence. 'I need a post in Yorkshire,' she said. 'My husband has just got a job in Leeds.'

Mr Oliver Peterson was a friendly, engaging man who

had applied for several promotions in his native Lancashire and was now exploring opportunities in Yorkshire. He was six feet three inches tall and athletic – apparently he was a keen badminton player; he was also blessed with a ready humour. 'Well, sixth time lucky,' he declared with a grin.

The atmosphere was friendly but guarded during the preamble in the waiting room. Mrs Bloom seemed a little on edge when talking to us but the other two were composed and engaged confidently in conversation.

In accordance with convention we were seen in alphabetical order, which meant I was last in. It was over an hour and a half before it was my turn and the others had returned to their seats looking relaxed and assured. No one revealed what they had been asked but all confirmed the members of the interviewing panel were fair in their questioning and perceptive in their responses.

Finally the door opened and a female secretary appeared. 'Mr Sheffield, please.'

I followed her to the inner sanctum. My impression of the room was better than last time. There was a chair for the candidates and the interviewing panel looked both smartly dressed and serious. I realized immediately this was very different to my last interview.

The chairman was a tall, imposing man in a pinstriped suit with a colourful handkerchief in his top pocket. He stood up to welcome me and we shook hands.

'Good morning, Mr Sheffield, I'm John Nightingale, Chief Education Officer. Welcome to this interview for the post of deputy headteacher of Newbridge Primary School. Please take a seat.'

'Thank you, Mr Nightingale.'

He glanced to his left and right. 'My colleagues are here to ask you some questions and you will have the opportunity to respond as you wish and also at the end of the interview to clarify any queries you may have.'

'Thank you.'

Then he studied the document on the desk in front of him thoughtfully. 'Now, Mr Sheffield, we need to start with the obvious question.'

'Yes?' I wondered what was coming.

'You don't appear to stay very long in your posts to date.'

*This was it. Time to show what I was made of. Speak clearly.*

'Well, my first school in Leeds was closed by the local authority so I had no choice.'

'What about your present post? It seems early to want to leave – before you've given a year's service.'

'That may be so but I do feel I've given a lot to both the schools in which I've worked.'

'Really? It doesn't appear so from your curriculum vitae. So why this job and why now?'

'I believe I have had a considerable range of experiences in my time in teaching so far. I should also mention I'm keen to stay in the locality. I've just purchased my first home near Skipton so this post at Newbridge Primary is an excellent opportunity for me to stay in the area and progress my career. Also, I play rugby for a Yorkshire team so I've no wish to move.'

'Yes, we've heard about your rugby prowess.' He turned to his left. 'Miss Featherstone?'

'Thank you.' She gave a gentle smile. 'Mr Sheffield, I

can see why you wish to stay in the area. Your sporting achievements are well known and congratulations on securing a new home – a positive sign in one so young.'

She looked down at the notes in front of her. 'Which brings me on to my main question. It concerns *credibility*.' She paused to assess my response but I remained stoic and still. 'You would have to show *leadership* with colleagues who are more experienced than you. Do you see this as a problem?'

Travis had said in my mock interview to make sure I addressed the person who had asked the question directly but also to embrace the rest of the panel with my answers.

'I don't see this as a problem, Miss Featherstone. I believe I have leadership qualities that would overcome the issue you describe. My teaching has developed in recent years and my experiences have been varied.' I noticed an almost imperceptible nod at this point. 'I know I have an empathy for the children in this area, many of whom are from severely deprived backgrounds. I believe my teaching encourages a love of learning rather than merely following an outdated one-way pedagogy of chalk and talk. My teaching would show colleagues my level of dedication to the profession. I feel confident I could lead a team while being sympathetic to the views of others.'

She paused, scribbled on a sheet of typed notes before her. 'Thank you.'

The chairman looked to his right. 'Mr Wright, our local adviser.'

'Good morning, Mr Sheffield.'

'Good morning, Mr Wright.'

He picked up his fountain pen and circled a heading on the page in front of him. 'You will be aware there have been significant changes in education in recent years and many challenges await us in the seventies. I see you have attended several of our local authority in-service courses. Could you tell me if they have been beneficial and, if so, why?'

'The honest answer is a mixed response, I'm afraid.'

He raised his eyebrows in surprise. 'Perhaps you could explain.'

'The best courses for me concerned the impact of the Plowden Report. I took the main messages on board and integrated them into my teaching and the children in my care benefited.'

He leaned forward. 'Yes, go on.'

'On the other hand, there have been courses where there has been no input from the leader of the course and we have merely been put into groups to discuss a current issue. I'm not saying there isn't value in that. It's good to be made aware of how other schools tackle the problems we all share. So it could be said the leader is actually a *facilitator*, who provides opportunities for interaction with colleagues. Unfortunately on the last two teacher-training courses I've been put in a group with secondary staff with whom I've not a great deal in common.'

'I see,' he said and there was a long pause while he scribbled notes with a frown and pursed lips. I recalled Connie had said, 'Be honest, Jack,' but perhaps I had been *too* honest.

The chairman nodded towards the man on his far left. 'Mr Patterson, Headteacher of Newbridge.'

'Pleased to meet you, Mr Sheffield.'

'Likewise, Mr Patterson.'

I viewed him carefully. I could be working with this man next academic year. His assessment would be crucial. He was a tall, dark-haired, athletic man in his mid-forties with a square jaw and large hands. He clasped them together, leaned forward and studied me carefully.

He spoke in measured tones. 'I'm aware you are a young man but it is clear you seem to have integrated much into your career. I can understand my colleagues questioning your level of experience but I have visited many schools where members of staff boast twenty years' experience when in fact they have had one year's experience twenty times.' He paused to let the message sink in.

I remained passive and waited for the sting in the tail.

'Nevertheless, Mr Sheffield, you are asking us to take a significant leap of faith when considering you for this post. It's a large school in a demanding area. Tell me, and please be frank, why should we consider you for this post?'

I recalled Connie had said, 'Remember to *engage*, Jack. When responding, make eye contact with the other members of the panel and refer to them by name.'

'Mr Patterson, I believe I can offer a great deal not just to Newbridge but also the local community. In my first school I was in at seven thirty supervising a breakfast club and staying on until five thirty running football, cricket and athletics teams along with a chess club.'

I paused to assess the response. 'Miss Featherstone asked me about *credibility*. If I may I should like to offer an example . . . during morning break I began a reading workshop which was well received by fellow members of staff. I encouraged parents and grandparents to come in and hear children read and report back to the teachers via notes in a reading-record book. At my present school I also work hard to improve communication with parents by standing at the school gate most mornings to welcome pupils and exchange a brief word and assess any parental concern. It may seem almost trivial in the set of skills you require for this post but I believe it is important.'

I surveyed the intense faces before me. 'Mr Wright was interested in my response to the various courses run in this authority and I tried to give an honest reaction. I've taken much on board and work hard through my teaching to celebrate the work of every child regardless of ability. To this end I have developed a process of *individual* learning that encourages each child to progress at their own rate. I've done this through developing my maths and English lessons by adding personalized workcards to supplement the core schemes. I've spent countless hours making workcards to this end.'

The headteacher nodded. 'Thank you.'

They were all scribbling furiously until the chairman looked up. 'Mr Sheffield, Newbridge is a challenging area with some tough parents and considerable teenage problems. Would you be prepared to cope with these demands?'

I thought for a moment and said quietly, 'Could I be permitted to tell you a story about goalposts?'

There was a smile from Miss Featherstone. 'Go on, I can't wait.'

Mr Patterson gave me a wide-eyed stare. 'Neither can I.'

The local adviser, Mr Wright, leaned back in his chair.

'Actually, I know of this story – if it's the one I'm thinking of. It did the rounds in my office. Does it concern tree-planting, Mr Sheffield?'

'As a matter of fact, it does.'

John Nightingale put down his pen and folded his arms. 'Well, Mr Sheffield, it would appear you have our full attention.'

There were smiles and knowing glances as I related the tale. Suddenly I felt relaxed, as if I had revealed my true self and an understanding had emerged between us.

Questions and answers ebbed and flowed. I was asked about strategies for mixed-ability teaching, the use of corporal punishment and the emergence of multi-cultural education. However, when the interview came to an end it seemed almost too soon. I was asked if I had any questions. My only concern related to the notice required to leave one post within the authority and commence another. I was told this could be accommodated.

After that, the chairman asked the final question that had been put to all candidates: 'Mr Sheffield, if you are successful and offered the post would you be prepared to accept?'

'Yes, I would.'

'In that case, thank you and please return to the waiting room while we make our decision.'

So it was that the four of us sat there waiting and I wondered what my future would be.

I glanced up at the wall clock as it ticked away the heartbeats of our lives.

It was high noon.

*

Back in Heather View the bell rang for school dinner and the children filed into the dining room for their boiled beef, potatoes and cabbage.

After lunch Connie joined Travis in his classroom. 'Well,' she said, 'I've just been speaking to Penny. What do you think?'

'I think Jack's got a good chance. He'll be a head one day. This is just another step on his journey.'

Connie shook her head. 'Sorry, I wasn't speaking about his interview and, yes, I'm sure he could do well at Newbridge. They would be lucky to get him. I meant Jack and Penny.'

Realization dawned. 'Ah, I see. I knew she had moved in with him.'

'Just weekends at present.'

'So, where's the problem? They both look happy enough.'

Connie sighed. 'It's Jack I'm concerned about. Penny's clearly on the rebound from Seb. It was all a bit sudden.'

'Surely Seb's off the scene.'

'I wouldn't be too sure.'

'Really?'

There were footsteps in the corridor. Connie spoke quietly: 'Just something I heard.'

Barbara popped her head round the door. 'Edith has brought a cake just in case Jack gets the job. We reckon he should be back by afternoon break.'

'I'm on duty,' said Travis.

'I'll do it for you – then you can be there to celebrate or commiserate.'

'Thanks, Barbara, that's really kind.'

She hurried away and Travis turned back to Connie. 'So, what aren't you sure about?'

'Whether she's over the dashing young doctor.'

'Oh.'

She folded her arms in a determined manner and sat back in her chair. 'Exactly.'

Suddenly the lumbering form of Billy Woodcock tapped on the door. Keith Lumb and Terry Duff were in close attendance.

'Yes, boys,' said Connie, slightly irritated at being interrupted. 'What is it?'

'Sorry, Miss, but we're wond'rin' what t'do.'

'And why is that?' asked Travis with a smile. He had taught these boys and knew them well.

'Dinner lady sent us t'see Mr Little, sir,' said Billy, 'but Miss Verity said 'e's not 'ere and t'find Mrs Priestley or you.'

Connie faced the boys. 'I see. So why has Mrs Duckworth sent you in? Have you misbehaved?'

'Sort of, Miss,' said Keith.

'But we were only practisin',' pleaded Terry.

'Practising?'

'Yes, Miss,' said Billy. 'For t'competition.'

'An' we only do it on t'grass,' said Keith.

'Not on t'playground,' added Terry.

Travis had heard enough. 'Boys, what were you practising?'

'Spittin', sir,' said Billy. He was an honest boy.

'Spitting!' said Connie and Travis at once.

'Yes, t'see who can spit farthest,' explained Terry. 'Billy reckons 'e's t'best but me an' Keith reckon we're better.'

Connie stood up. 'I'll deal with this if you like, Mr

Farthing. Come with me, boys.' She gave Travis a wink as she marched out.

It was twelve forty-five when Edith walked into Penny's classroom. She was busy sorting a collection of flashcards.

'Penny, there's a call for you.'

'Really? Who is it?'

'It's Sebastian. He wants a quick word. Says it's important.'

Penny blushed profusely. 'I'm so sorry, Edith. You shouldn't have been troubled.'

'Well, he sounded anxious so I came to find you as quickly as I could.'

'Thank you. I had better see what he wants,' and she hurried out.

Edith looked at the cards covered in sticky-backed plastic. They read: 'tree', 'little', 'milk', 'egg', 'book', but it was the two on the teacher's desk that caught her eye. They read 'lost' and 'cost', and Edith sighed as she walked slowly to the staff-room. As she passed her office the door was closed but she could hear the high-pitched murmuring of Penny's voice.

The County Hall secretary finally reappeared at one o'clock. There was a pause as she looked at her list and the underlined name. Then she looked at me. 'Mr Sheffield, would you come with me, please?'

I knew it was either to be offered the job or to be told my attendance had been appreciated but my application had been unsuccessful.

The murmur of voices died as I entered the room.

'Please, take a seat, Mr Sheffield,' said John Nightingale.

He looked to his left and right and there were discreet nods indicating a mutual decision. 'I'm sorry to have kept you waiting,' he said, 'but this has been a very difficult decision.' He looked down at the list of names before him. 'We have been blessed with a number of very strong candidates for this particular post and our discussions have been wide-ranging. Your evident lack of longevity in the teaching profession was clearly an issue we had to consider. However, after great deliberation we believe you have made positive strides in your career and could offer much to the authority. Therefore, we should like to offer you the post of deputy headteacher of Newbridge Primary School.'

He looked at me and smiled. 'Do you accept?'

I took a deep breath and said simply, 'Yes.'

The drive back to school was a strange experience. I felt elated. The Newbridge headteacher, Jim Patterson, had been welcoming and shaken my hand. We had met for twenty minutes after the interview and arranged several meetings as a form of induction. He was a positive man and I felt comfortable when discussing the future with him.

'It's a tough area, Jack,' he'd said, 'but if you can cope up at Milltown you'll do fine.'

It occurred to me he was a world away from Norman Little.

It was two o'clock when I reached the school. The supply teacher, Mrs Cope, a lady approaching her sixtieth birthday and an old colleague of Norman's, looked relieved when I walked back into my classroom. She was clearly in a hurry to leave and was walking to the school gate within minutes.

I sensed the mood in the class. They looked utterly bored. They needed to let off steam so I took them into the school hall to do some lively educational gymnastics including energetic rolls, leaps and balances.

When the bell rang for afternoon playtime I was immediately surrounded by the rest of the staff.

'Well?' said Connie. 'How did it go?'

'I got the job.'

'Wow! Brilliant!' said Travis.

'So mixed feelings leaving you all . . . but I'm pleased to have this opportunity.'

Barbara came up and gave me a hug. 'Congratulations, Jack. I'm delighted for you but sad you're leaving us.'

I looked at Penny. She was simply staring at me. 'Sorry, Jack,' she said. 'I'm still taking it all in.'

'Come on then,' said Audrey. 'Edith has made a cake. Let's celebrate.'

I looked towards the school entrance hall. 'I'll need to speak to Norman first.'

'He's not here, Jack,' said Barbara, 'but he'll be back at the end of school . . . at least that's what he said. Anyway, must rush as I'm on duty. Save me some cake,' and she bustled out to the playground.

We all set off for the staff-room.

'Come on, tell us all about it,' said Connie.

'We want a blow-by-blow account,' said Travis.

Penny squeezed my arm. 'I'm pleased for you, Jack. It's the next step.' She smiled but looked a little subdued.

It was a lively afternoon break. Edith served up a

delicious fruit cake and mugs of tea while I was peppered with questions. It seemed all too soon that the bell rang and we all returned to our classrooms.

When I looked at all the children in my class it occurred to me we were all moving on in three weeks' time.

At the end of school Norman had indeed returned and I went to see him in his office. He lit up, sat back in his chair and shook his head.

'This puts me in a difficult situation. I've no time to find a permanent replacement for you. It may be I'll have to employ Mrs Cope for anything up to a term. At least she'll do as she's told,' he added pointedly.

I decided to remain silent. It was clear he wasn't going to congratulate me.

'County Hall have been in touch to say leaving here and moving to Newbridge will not be a problem . . . except for me.'

Now it was time to respond. 'Yes, the transfer was confirmed at the interview.'

'It was a pity the old Chief Education Officer left a year ago. I don't know this new boy Nightingale although I've seen him once or twice at meetings.'

It struck me that Norman might not have got the job had John Nightingale been in post a little earlier.

Again, I merely nodded. I had no wish to prolong any conversation.

He looked up at me. 'So I won't mince my words, Sheffield. I'll be glad to see the back of you.'

*Likewise,* I thought but said nothing as I walked out.

*

I called in to Penny's classroom at the end of school.

'Barbara has invited us into the staff-room for more tea and cake before we go home,' I said.

She glanced out of the window. 'Sorry, I can't, Jack. Something has cropped up. I have to rush off.'

I was disappointed. 'Well, Connie suggested meeting up later in The Cat & Kettle for a drink.'

'Not possible, Jack.'

'That's a pity. I was hoping we could go out to celebrate.'

'Sorry, it will have to be another time.' There was a pause while she seemed to gather her thoughts. 'It's my mother. I've promised to see her tonight.'

'So what is it? Not serious, I hope?'

'No, nothing like that.'

'Well, another time then and best wishes to your mum.'

That evening as I drove home under a velvet sky I felt content. I only wished Penny could have shared the night with me. It was good to have a partner in my life. There was something special about her.

In that moment I realized she had seared my soul.

## Chapter Nineteen

# *A Walking Shadow*

It was Friday, 17 July, the end of the penultimate week of the school year and PC Moxon was talking to Barbara at the school gate when I arrived.

I wound down my window and called, 'Morning, Phil,' and he gave me a cheery wave as I drove into the car park.

'So, how can I help?' asked Barbara. Her husband Big Jimmy had just dropped her off before setting off to make some deliveries. On this perfect summer morning Barbara was wearing a straw hat to protect her fair skin from the sun.

'Can we arrange some dates for the autumn term, Mrs Priestley? The sergeant wants me to do some safety talks in the local schools.'

'Yes, of course.'

'I could call by later if it suits.'

'That's fine. Around ten fifteen is best and we can talk during morning break. The school diary is on Edith's desk so we can meet in there. It would be good to get it organized.'

'Fine – see you later.' He wheeled his motorbike out of the school gate.

In his office Norman was about to receive an unwelcome telephone call.

'Yes?' Norman was never forthcoming on the telephone.

'Is that Mr Little?'

'Yes, who's speaking?'

'It's John Nightingale here, Chief Education Officer.'

Norman sat up in his chair. 'Oh, I see.'

'I'm ringing to let you know we have a replacement for Mr Sheffield.'

'Not necessary, Mr Nightingale. I've asked Mrs Cope, our supply teacher, to commence in September.'

There was a pause. 'No, that won't be happening. We have a transfer already organized.'

'What do you mean?'

'Owing to the closure of Grantley Junior School, Miss Elizabeth Bywater will be moving to Heather View. Miss Bywater is an excellent top junior teacher and comes highly recommended. It will be an ideal appointment.'

'But I've no idea who Miss Bywater is.'

'Of course, I fully understand, but time is tight and circumstances have thrown up this situation. You will have the opportunity to meet Miss Bywater next week.'

'I can't say I'm happy about this.'

'I am aware that such arrangements are not always ideal with regard to timing but this decision is final.' John Nightingale had received a few damning reports about the professional conduct of Norman Little and had no intention of wavering. 'Have you any questions?'

'Er, no, I haven't.'

'Very well, my secretary will be sending you a letter today. Goodbye.'

The phone went dead and then buzzed like an angry wasp. He reached for his cigarettes and muttered, 'Damn, damn, damn.'

As I walked towards the school entrance a young mother with a voice like a foghorn was shouting across the playground, 'Stop lickin' them winders!'

Mrs Drew was delivering her son, Tommy, to Penny's class. It was an induction morning when next term's new starters could come into school, meet their teacher and discover where their coat peg would be.

Tommy's two-year-old sister, Daisy, had run off. The classroom windows were particularly dirty and splashed with bird droppings. For some reason this had appealed to the little girl and she had begun to lick them with gusto. It occurred to me the taste was not exactly fine dining.

'AH SED, STOP LICKIN' THEM WINDERS!'

Daisy turned and stared defiantly at her mother. She was not to be denied. Instead, she turned her attention to the next window frame, which was even dirtier, and began to lick that.

I could still hear Mrs Drew's voice as I entered the entrance hall where Eric Skinner suddenly appeared and gave me a shifty look. I returned his look without saying anything and walked on into the main hall where Penny was arranging a line of chairs.

'Morning, Penny.'

She was wearing a bright summer dress. Her arms were tanned and her hair had become bleached in the sun. 'Hello, Jack.'

'Need a hand?'

'Yes, please.'

I collected a few more dining chairs and added them to the row at the front of the hall. 'Penny, I was thinking about this weekend. There's a summer fête on the cricket ground in my village.'

'Sorry, Jack. I've promised to go to a friend's wedding.'

'Oh, I see.' I was disappointed and it must have shown.

'It's up in North Yorkshire. An old girlfriend.'

'Shall I come with you? I could give you a lift.'

There was a slight pause. 'No, thanks. I'll be driving myself up there. It's all sorted.' She picked up a pile of paintings from the table and started to put one on each chair.

'Never mind,' I said. 'Catch you later.'

In Norman's office Eric Skinner looked excited. 'Ah've gorra good tip from Solly in t'market. Looks a winner.'

Norman gave Eric his full attention after he heard the word 'winner'. He needed a lucky break after a long series of losses. He also needed some good news after John Nightingale's telephone call. 'Go on.'

Eric held up that morning's copy of his *Racing Mirror*. 'Hunter's Treasure at Chester, boss. Ten to one in t'Apprentice 'Andicap. Good odds.'

Norman made a quick decision. 'Come back at lunchtime.'

Eric hurried out and Norman stood up and paced the

room. Then he stared at the door that linked his office to Edith's. It was locked as usual and the key was on his side.

At the end of morning assembly Barbara stood up to thank Penny's class for their contribution. The children had held up their paintings of flowers and read out some of their writing. I noticed that Penny looked preoccupied. Her thoughts seemed to be elsewhere.

Through the double doors I saw Edith in the entrance hall. She was going into the staff-room to prepare morning coffee while, out of the window, PC Moxon was parking his bike in the car park. The children hurried out to play in the sunshine and I saw Phil Moxon smile at them as they played hopscotch, skipping and leapfrog.

Barbara went to meet him on the entrance steps. 'Thanks for coming. Perfect timing. Have you time for a coffee?'

'Sorry, Mrs Priestley, lots to do. Better just sort these dates out then I'll be on my way.'

Barbara popped her head round the staff-room door. 'Edith, we're just going into your room to put some dates in the diary for next term.'

'Hello, PC Moxon,' said Edith. 'I'll come with you.'

I followed Penny back to her classroom.

'What is it?' I asked. 'You don't seem quite yourself.'

She folded her arms, walked to the window and stared out. 'Sometimes I get a bit fed up with this profession.'

'But you're good at it. I've seen you with the children.'

'I know . . . but that's not it.' She rubbed her eyes with the heels of her hands. 'It's the parents. Most are fine but some are abusive and never satisfied. I've had that Mrs Drew in this morning giving me a hard time.'

It was then I thought back to previous conversations and realized this concern of Penny's was becoming a recurring theme.

'I would like to help.'

'Thanks, Jack, but this isn't a good time. Let's get a coffee,' and she strode out of the classroom with me in her wake.

Edith opened the door to her office and walked in with PC Moxon and Barbara close behind. To her surprise the connecting door between the secretary's office and the headteacher's was open. It was always closed and locked from the other side. This was a relief for Edith as it stopped the smell of Norman's cigarettes invading her space.

Norman was standing with his back to them and staring down at Edith's desk. He spun round in surprise. Edith always spent morning break in the staff-room. Her sudden appearance was unexpected. Next to him the metal money box was open.

It seemed clear to Barbara what was happening and she was angry. 'Mr Little,' she said abruptly. 'What are you doing?'

Norman glared at her. 'Just checking something.' He looked at the money box. His face was suddenly flushed. 'It was, er, open when I walked in.'

Barbara noticed Norman's right hand was clenched. 'What are you holding?'

'What's it to do with you?'

'It's a simple question.'

'How dare you speak to me like that?' He glanced nervously at PC Moxon. 'And in front of a visitor.'

'If you've nothing to hide you can show us.'

PC Moxon began to take an interest. He had seen enough guilty expressions in his career to last a lifetime. He decided to intervene. 'Mr Little, it's a reasonable request.'

'Well, it's fifty pence if you must know.' He held it up. '*My* fifty pence.'

Barbara and Edith shared a knowing look. 'Could you show it to PC Moxon, please?'

'Whatever for?'

'That isn't a problem, is it?'

He handed it over. 'I'll have it back when you've finished.'

Barbara turned to Edith. 'Shall we ask PC Moxon to examine the coin?'

Edith nodded. 'Could you please look and see if there's a black dot in the nought next to the five?'

PC Moxon studied the coin carefully. 'Yes, there is. What does this mean?'

Edith had been reluctant to share her problem concerning the missing money and hesitant to speak of it, but now she was glad that she had confided in Barbara. It looked as though Barbara's scheme had produced a result.

'It was Mrs Priestley's idea,' said Edith. 'We wanted to try to catch the culprit who has been taking money from the box. It's been fifty pence short on many occasions and we realized someone was taking it.'

PC Moxon turned to Norman. 'Mr Little, could you explain how this coin came into your possession?'

'I don't recall. Probably someone gave it to me.'

Phil Moxon stepped forward. 'It would appear at this moment that there is a strong suspicion you are guilty of theft – unless you can explain otherwise.'

Norman leaned back against the desk and hung his head.

'This is a serious matter, Mr Little,' persisted PC Moxon.

Norman rocked forward then stopped, completely still, sphinx-like and staring at the wall. He seemed too shocked to move. His breathing was shallow and his face was grey. It was as if he were surrounded by his own shroud of silence and no words were needed.

It was clear to all that he was guilty.

He stood up and walked through the connecting door to his room.

Barbara touched Phil Moxon's sleeve. 'Philip, I need to deal with this internally. Perhaps you might come back later if you have time?'

It was unusual for Barbara to call him by his first name when he was in uniform but these were unusual circumstances. Pandora's box had been opened and there would be consequences. 'I understand. That's fine. I'll call back at the end of school.'

He walked out and Barbara turned to her friend. 'Say nothing, please, Edith, and leave this to me.'

She closed the connecting door and walked into Norman's office.

He was sitting in his chair and clinging to the last vestige of bravado. 'All this rubbish about marked coins. This is kids' detective stuff.'

Barbara folded her arms and stared stonily at him.

'Norman, listen to me carefully. PC Moxon will be back at the end of school. This will be a police matter if I so wish. County Hall will then be informed and disciplinary proceedings will follow.'

'You wouldn't dare.'

'Are you willing to take that chance?'

It was at that moment Norman realized the day of judgement and retribution had arrived. He was a shell of his former self.

Only the husk of hatred remained.

There was silence while Barbara paced the room. 'Norman, listen very carefully to me. Your behaviour has been sickening. There's no excuse for it.'

He spoke as if he had brimstone in his throat. 'It's the gambling. Got out of hand.'

'We've known about the gambling for some time. Eric Skinner has always been one for telling tales after a few drinks. It's a common problem. You could have shared it with us and we would have helped. That's what a good team will do . . . help those in greatest need. You chose to keep this secret.'

Norman twisted in his chair. The sickly odour of sweat and cigarettes clung to him like vile perfume. 'I couldn't speak of it.'

'But it's not just the odd fifty pence from the dinner-money box is it, Norman?'

There was fear in his eyes. 'What do you mean?'

'The jumble-sale money was probably five pounds short.' This was a guess on Barbara's part but Norman's reaction showed that it was true.

Suddenly, she was furious and saw Norman for what he

was. She gripped the edge of his desk and spoke with quiet authority. 'There's no excuse for stealing from your colleagues. For months now you have caused great anxiety for Edith. She has always been a wonderful supporter of this school and takes a pride in her work and you have treated her with contempt. You are a thief, Norman, and this school needs rid of you once and for all.'

He tried to speak but no words came.

'And I haven't mentioned the struggle we have had with our school allowance budget and the secrecy that surrounds it. That will need to be investigated further.'

Suddenly there was fear in his eyes.

'I'm giving you a chance. Go now, Norman . . . jump before you are pushed. If you resign now, then – for the good name of the school and what we want to achieve in the future for these children – I won't take it further.'

He put his head in his hands and his shoulders began to shake.

He was no longer a headmaster . . . merely a master of melancholy.

It was Saturday morning and I had some shopping to do. As I drove out of Bradley village and over the canal bridge sunlight caressed the distant hills and the air was humid and warm. A breathless promise hung over the land and the trees stirred in the gentle breeze with a sibilant whisper. It seemed to be a perfect morning and my mind wandered as I turned on to the main road.

Tender images of Penny flitted through my mind in a mist of memories. I couldn't decide if my thoughts of love were simply personal to me or part of a universal scepticism. Either way I felt uncertain which way to turn. I knew I was at a crossroads in my life and it was time to choose a new path.

I parked in one of the side streets and walked back to the centre of the town where Skipton market was in full swing. At the top of the High Street stood the magnificent war memorial, a twenty-foot column on top of which the dramatic sculpture of Winged Victory looked down on Arnie Crabtree's market stall. He was doing a roaring trade and looked content in his world.

I decided to start with some refreshment and headed for the Gateway Café. I chose a table on the cobbles in the sunshine and sat down. Suddenly there was a tap on my shoulder.

'Hello, Jack. An unexpected pleasure.'

It was Peter Armitage, looking tanned and healthy in a short-sleeved shirt and old flannel trousers. He was jingling a set of car keys.

'Hello, Peter. Fancy a coffee?'

'Sorry, no time. On my way to the car park to meet Viv. She's been shopping for new shoes.' He glanced at his watch and smiled. 'Only been two hours to select the right pair.'

I grinned back. 'No comment.'

'Well said, Jack. These women certainly keep us in check.'

'Hope Penny got off in time.'

'Oh, you mean for that posh wedding up in Richmond. Yes, she was talking dresses last night with Viv. Not my scene, Jack. Upmarket horsey friends. They own stables, apparently. Seb will blend in well.'

'Seb?'

'Yes, she went with Seb in his car.'

'Oh, I didn't realize.'

'Quite a big event, so I'm told. She'll be back late tomorrow night according to Viv.' He glanced at his watch. 'Anyway, must rush. See you later, Jack.'

He shook my hand and hurried away.

I sat there for a long time sipping my coffee.

The sun beat down from a cloudless sky but I felt cold.

On Monday morning school was a hive of activity and it was clear there were issues of great import. Barbara was in Norman's office and Edith was answering a constant stream of telephone calls.

'Something significant is going on, Jack,' said Connie. 'I've never seen Barbara looking so intense.'

Penny only gave me the merest glance when she emerged from the stock cupboard with an armful of sugar paper. I knew there was much to discuss but that was for later.

Travis introduced morning assembly but was then called away by Barbara, and Connie took over the story of Oscar Wilde's *The Selfish Giant* and Audrey played the piano.

After lunch Barbara called the staff together for a meeting. We sat there sipping tea until silence settled like a comfort blanket and we waited for her to speak. 'I have some important news for you all.'

She had our full attention.

'Norman has decided to take early retirement and will be leaving at the end of term. He has informed County Hall by letter and they have confirmed they will accept his resignation.'

There was a stunned silence.

'I have been asked by the Chief Education Officer to take the post of acting headteacher during the autumn term until a permanent appointment can be found.' She looked around at our stunned expressions. 'I have accepted and will be securing the services of a part-time supply teacher to teach my class as I wish to continue teaching.'

Connie was the first to respond. 'That's wonderful news, Barbara. I'm so pleased for you. Well deserved after all your work . . . and you know my feelings about Norman.'

There were tears in Barbara's eyes. It had clearly been an emotional morning for her. 'And Travis has some news as well.'

We all turned to him in surprise.

'Well, I've been asked to be acting deputy next term,' he said. 'I was unsure but Barbara persuaded me.'

'That would be perfect,' said Audrey. 'What do you think, Connie?'

'I'll tell you what I think,' she said firmly and stood up and gave him a hug.

'Well done, Travis,' I said. 'Looks like I'm moving on just at the wrong time.'

'Never mind, Jack,' said Travis with a whimsical smile. 'Even as a deputy I doubt I'll be able to control Connie.'

'Too true,' said Connie.

'Congratulations, Barbara, and well done, Travis,' said Penny. 'I'm so pleased for you.' She looked across at me and then lowered her gaze.

*

At afternoon break Penny was on duty and I walked out to join her in the sunshine. We leaned against the school wall and watched the children at play.

'So . . . how was your weekend?'

She stared straight ahead. 'Fine, Jack, a lovely wedding.'

'When did you get back?'

'Last night, really late. That's why I'm tired today.'

'What was it, an old girlfriend?'

'Something like that.'

'Anyone I know? I would have liked to have driven you.'

'My car was fine. It was a good drive.'

There was silence between us while I struggled with the lie.

'Penny, I met your dad. He told me you had gone with Seb in his car.'

She froze and the colour drained from her face. 'I didn't want you to know.'

'But why not tell me the truth? I could have understood if you had explained.'

'I suppose I knew how you would react. Seb will always be a friend. He's part of my life.'

'I guess that's also part of the problem.'

'Well, I don't regret it,' she said defiantly.

I shook my head. 'It was the lie that hurt, Penny,' and I walked back into school.

When the bell rang for the end of the school day and the children had left I sat at my desk and considered my future.

I realized Penny was not the woman I'd thought she

was. It was a strange feeling, almost an atavistic fear and difficult to comprehend. I tried to engage reason, to think clearly and understand how I felt. I had come to see that infatuation could be an unwelcome companion. It blurred the senses, crushed logic, denied common sense.

Even if her actions had been born out of innocence she had felt the need to lie.

I stayed in my classroom thinking until almost five o'clock when I joined Connie and Travis and watched Penny walk across the playground to the car park. Norman was standing next to his car.

'It's finally over for him,' said Connie. 'Good riddance.'

We watched Norman climb into his car. He looked diminished, smaller; his power had gone.

Travis spoke quietly:

> *'Life's but a walking shadow, a poor player*
> *That struts and frets his hour upon the stage*
> *And then is heard no more.'*

Connie nodded. 'Even I know that one . . . *Macbeth*.'

'His time is up,' said Travis. 'End of an era. The door hasn't just closed on him . . . it's slammed shut.'

As I watched Penny's car follow Norman out of the school gate it occurred to me it wasn't the only door that had closed that day.

## Chapter Twenty

# *Back to School*

It was a perfect morning when I awoke to a new dawn. The first soft kiss of sunlight caressed the world as I lay on my bed and thought of Penny. There had been tensions in our recent, brief conversations. She had changed and I knew I had to be wary. My feelings for her had become an unwelcome paradox. It was hard to be torn between loving her and disliking her behaviour. The division between pain and joy was paper-thin. Suddenly my life had become uncertain, a conundrum in a crucible.

It was Friday, 24 July. My last day at Heather View beckoned and there were decisions to be made.

After a hasty breakfast I drove out of Bradley village. The fields shimmered in the early-morning heat haze and the air was humid and warm. Everything was still. It was as if we were waiting for a welcome breeze and a wind of change. I switched on the radio. Peter, Paul and Mary were singing 'Leaving on a Jet Plane' and I hummed along. The familiar journey sped by and, on the way into Milltown, I decided to call in to the Corner Shop. Peggy Stubbs was being served and her children, Janet and Gary, were staring at the sweets on display.

Kathy was in her usual positive mood. 'Morning, Peggy, what's it t'be?'

''Ello, Kathy.' Peggy Stubbs looked up at the stacked shelves of cigarettes. 'Ah'll 'ave twenty Consulate.'

'Posh ciggies,' said Kathy. 'That's five shillings an' fivepence.'

'Ah know they're dear but you 'ave to 'ave some treats in life.' Peggy held up the packet. '"Cool as a mountain stream",' she said, repeating the familiar advertisement.

'Don't know about a mountain stream,' muttered Kathy, 'more like my Ernie's socks. Anyway, talkin' of treats, 'ere's a couple o' liq'rice sticks.' She passed them over the counter to the two children.

'Thanks, Kathy.' Peggy spotted Ernie up a stepladder stacking bottles of Corona pop. 'An' ah'll tek a Dandelion an' Burdock an' one o' them 'Merican Cream Sodas.'

Kathy's voice boomed out: 'ERNIE, SHEK Y'SELF!'

Ernie responded as if he had been shot.

Kathy glanced at me. ' 'E's improvin', Mr Sheffield.' I gave a non-committal nod. 'Did 'is deliveries in two shakes of a cow's tail.'

*Lamb's tail,* I thought but said nothing.

'That's another 'alf-crown for y'pop, Peggy, and threepence back on t'bottles.'

'Thanks, Kathy.' She smiled at me. 'Mornin', Mr Sheffield. Ah'm sorry y'leavin' but thanks for all you've done f'my Janet.'

'Thank you, Mrs Stubbs. It's been a pleasure teaching her. She's a hard worker.'

'Teks after me then,' she said with a grin. 'Anyway, good luck at y'new school.'

She left with her children, their teeth blackened as they chewed contentedly. The bell above the door rang as they walked out.

'Can I have a cake, please, Kathy. It's for the staff.'

'Yer in luck. Got t'perfec' one 'ere. Jam sponge wi' plenty o' cream. Fresh in this mornin'.'

'Thanks. I'll take it.'

'An' no charge, Mr Sheffield. You've been a good customer.'

'That's very kind, Kathy.'

She put the cake in a box and handed it over. 'An' don't f'get. If you've any problems, come t'Kathy.'

As I climbed back in my car it occurred to me there was one problem Kathy couldn't solve.

When I drove into school I was surprised to see Donna Clayton standing next to the car park. It was only when I got out of my car that I realized she was waiting for me.

She looked left and right and then spoke softly. 'Good morning, Jack. Hope you don't mind me hanging around here but I wanted to catch you before I go to work.'

'Morning, Donna. Good to see you. Can I help?'

She shook her head and smiled. 'No, not this time. I simply wanted to say thank you for all you've done for me and to give you this.' She handed over a small envelope. 'You can open it if you wish.'

It was a photograph of Donna in a smart two-piece business suit standing outside Bretton Hall College.

'Well done, Donna. You made it to Bretton.'

'Yes. My mother took the photograph. It was the day of my interview and it went really well. A letter of acceptance came in the post so I start my teacher-training course there in September.'

'I'm so pleased for you. Congratulations. You've worked hard to achieve this.'

She gave me that familiar firm handshake and it lasted a little longer than last time. 'I won't forget you, Jack.'

I watched her walk away until she turned suddenly and gave me a wave and a winsome smile. Her new journey had begun whereas mine was almost over.

I turned the photograph over. There was a message on the back. It read, 'Thank you, Jack, for changing my life. Love, Donna x'.

As I was reading it Seb's Citroën pulled up with a screech of brakes outside school and Penny got out. We reached the entrance hall together.

'Morning, Penny.'

We had barely spoken during the past few days.

She gave a hesitant glance in my direction. 'Morning, Jack,' and she set off for her classroom.

Travis and Connie were standing outside Edith's office and studying their school registers. Each hoped their attendance figures were better than the other's. They had seen Penny hurry away.

'Cold shoulder, Jack,' said Travis.

'Never mind,' said Connie. 'Penny's got a lot on her mind.'

Travis saw the box under my arm. 'I hope that's a cake.'

I grinned. 'Might be.'

'I'll take it, Jack,' said Connie. 'You've got enough to carry.'

She was right. In my satchel I had a card and a small gift for each child in my class.

The weight of doubt was also a heavy burden.

The bell for morning assembly rang earlier than usual. There had been no sign of Norman all week and it was Barbara who made the announcements after we had sung 'One More Step Along The World I Go'.

'Good morning, boys and girls.'

The children chanted their usual response: 'Good morning, Mrs Priestley. Good morning, everybody.'

Two hundred children sat there, cross-legged on the wood block floor. Most of the six- and seven-year-olds were missing their front teeth while the ten-year-olds looked behind them, thinking they would be the top juniors when they returned after the holiday. I noticed Ronnie and Reggie Atha whispering to each other. They should have known better. Barbara didn't miss a thing.

'Ronnie and Reggie, see me after assembly,' said Barbara sternly.

The boys looked up in amazement, wondering how her hearing could possibly be better than Butch's, their lively bulldog who would have given the Kray twins a run for their money.

'Boys and girls, we're having an earlier assembly today in order to say goodbye to Mr Sheffield.' All eyes turned towards me and I looked back at the expectant and curious faces . . . so many children, so many stories. I knew them all.

'I know that our Chair of Governors, Mr Witherspoon, would like to say a few words.'

Piers, in a smart grey suit and clerical collar, walked to the front. 'Good morning, boys and girls. I first met Mr Sheffield just before the first day of the school year way back in September and I know we both remember it well.' He looked at me and raised his eyebrows. Images of washing lines and undergarments crossed my mind. This was a vicar with a sense of humour. 'Even though he has not been with us very long at Heather View, Mr Sheffield has worked very hard to support your work. We are all the better for his time here on the Milltown estate. On behalf of the governing body, the staff and parents and all of you pupils, I should like to thank him for his hard work and support for all we try to achieve in our school.' He paused and smiled. 'With this in mind we have a small gift for him that we hope he will remember us by.'

He beckoned to two children sitting at the side of the hall.

Sandra Asquith and Terry Duff came out to the front each holding a small parcel. I opened them and held up a leather-bound notebook and a Platignum pen.

Piers continued, 'So, Mr Sheffield, we know you enjoy writing and have often seen you making notes. We trust you can make good use of this small gesture of our appreciation.'

I was deeply moved and said a few words of thanks before being rescued by Barbara, who began a round of applause. It was good to retreat to the staff-room and enjoy one of Edith's piping-hot milky coffees.

Penny was on duty and the rest of us settled, content

with our drinks and generous slices of cake. It wasn't long before the conversation returned to normal. Barbara was telling Connie she had read that long skirts designed by Pierre Cardin were now in fashion. 'So it's midi and not mini,' she said.

Travis was telling me he had heard on the news that an advertisement asking for black people to audition for the hit musical *Hair* had been scrapped because in the eyes of the Race Relations Board it discriminated against white people. 'But you've not heard the best of it, Jack. It's been rephrased, requesting *people with a special knowledge of African music.*'

'You ought to tell Connie,' I said. 'She might be interested.'

'I did but it didn't go down well. She said it was just me wanting to see her on stage in her birthday suit.'

'Oh well, you can live in hope.'

On the other side of the staff-room Connie had brought in her newspaper and was frowning at the headline: 'BOMBS DRAMA IN COMMONS'.

'Look at this, everybody. A man threw two gas bombs from the People's Gallery. He was shouting "Belfast". It says here MPs were running for their lives.'

'They need to check who's getting in,' muttered Barbara.

'Worrying security,' said Connie.

'Another problem for Ted Heath,' said Travis. 'We're already in a state of emergency with the dock strike. Our overseas trade is grinding to a halt. The country's in a mess.'

'It's a baptism of fire for the Prime Minister,' said Barbara.

'And maybe for you as well, Barbara,' said Audrey. 'Except everyone will be supporting you.'

'Well said,' said Edith as she served up more slices of cake.

When we walked back to our classrooms Barbara caught up with me. 'The new Class Six teacher will be calling in at lunchtime, Jack. So if you could show her around your classroom that would be helpful.'

'Yes. I'm looking forward to meeting her.'

'I've heard she's really good, which is encouraging.'

It was at times like this I appreciated Barbara's constant support for the school. Teachers came and went but she simply pressed on, holding the fort in changing times.

I was soon to learn that Elizabeth Bywater was better than good. She was exceptional. A slim redhead in her mid-thirties, she engaged wonderfully with the children during school lunch.

Harry Pickles was sitting at our table. 'Will you be my teacher nex' term, Miss?' he asked plaintively.

'What's your name?'

' 'Arry, Miss. What's yours?'

Elizabeth smiled. 'I'm Miss Bywater.'

'That's a funny name, Miss. Mebbe y'dad lived near a stream.'

'Perhaps he did. Or maybe *his* father,' added Elizabeth. 'So, how old are you, Harry?'

'Nine, Miss.'

'One day you will probably be in my class.'

'Will you be as good as Miss Brooksbank?'

'I shall try.'

'An' ah'll promise not to talk.'

'Why? Are you noisy?'

'It's 'cause of m'mouth, Miss. It won't keep quiet.'

'I see.' Elizabeth turned to me and raised her eyebrows. Nine-year-old logic clearly didn't surprise her any more.

After lunch we looked at the resources in my classroom while Elizabeth made copious notes. She was keen to see the mathematics scheme I had developed with individual workcards supplementing the basic textbook. I had encouraged lots of practical weighing and measuring. We had recently made clinometers and used protractors to measure angles to discover the height of the brick wall on the playground.

'I see you're incorporating lots of first-hand experience,' said Elizabeth approvingly. 'That's what I try to bring into my teaching.'

She looked at my attempt at a reading corner. 'The school looks to be struggling for books, Jack. I'll do my best to progress this.'

She was being polite and this wasn't the time to complain about Norman. All would be revealed in good time. Most of the second-hand books had been purchased by me in Skipton market. 'I'm sure Barbara will assist in increasing your book stock,' I said.

'These heavy, old-fashioned desks are a bit inhibiting,' she said.

'I agree but I've heard there's a new primary adviser so maybe you can work on him.'

She gave me a playful smile while appreciating the subliminal message. Meanwhile, I was encouraged that I was leaving Class 6 in good hands.

'Let me get you a cup of tea and we can go outside and enjoy the sunshine.'

I left her looking at the meagre collection of paint and bristle brushes next to the sink.

In the staff-room Audrey was in conversation with Penny while Travis and Connie were looking through a school-equipment catalogue.

'What was the wedding like, Penny?' asked Audrey.

'Really good,' said Penny. 'The bride turned up in a horse and carriage. All very grand.'

'Who was she?' asked Audrey.

'Anastasia, a friend from school. Her dad inherited a lot of money and they now live in a stately home up in North Yorkshire.'

'Did you go, Jack?' asked Audrey. I was busy pouring tea from our huge teapot.

'No,' said Penny quickly. 'It was just relations, their society set and girlfriends from school.'

I looked across the staff-room at her but Penny showed not a flicker of emotion.

'What was her wedding dress like?' asked Barbara.

'Spectacular. The train must have been ten yards long. There were six bridesmaids carrying it.'

'Well, when I get married it will be a budget wedding,' said Connie and she got up. 'Excuse me, everybody, things to do.'

Travis and I followed her out. It was clear they were not interested in society weddings whereas I was tired of half-truths.

For the final twenty minutes of the lunch break we

walked out on to the playground. Around us the eleven-year-olds were sitting in a group on their final day at Heather View and talking about what lay ahead. A long summer holiday awaited them before moving on to the Ridge Comprehensive School. It would be so different for them there, in blazer, collar and tie, with lessons that lasted forty minutes and public examinations on the far horizon.

When the bell rang at one o'clock I shook hands with Elizabeth and wished her luck. I watched her walk to the school gate and wondered what the future held in store for her.

It was an enjoyable afternoon in Class 6 and we made cardboard folders so that the children could take home their paintings and exercise books in safety and as a souvenir of all their hard work.

I had volunteered to do the final playground duty and, after collecting a cup of tea, I went outside. I stood there in the sunshine and reflected on the past year. The familiar faces of the children played around me, happy in their world.

It had already been an eventful year. The first jumbo jet had landed at Heathrow, Brazil had won the World Cup, Ted Heath was Prime Minister, Apollo 13 had told Houston they had a problem and the Beatles had split up. I wondered what the seventies would bring for all these children. This was their decade, one they would remember as adults in years to come. Such was the cycle of life.

Each one of them had their own story to tell. Terry

Speight was pleased that his pet mouse, Brian, had a cage in which to enjoy his solitary life. A knowledgeable neighbour had confirmed that the mouse was in fact female but Terry was sure the name wouldn't concern his rodent friend and he continued to read bedtime stories to Brian. It was peaceful again at home now that his father, Mad Micky, was in Leeds jail and his brother, Kenny, had got a job delivering coal.

Mary Capstick had fully recovered from her dreadful accident and she and her friend Lizzie Pickles were playing with her rag doll outside the boiler-house door. They were engaged in a world of make-believe. Meanwhile, Margery Duckworth and Susan Bell were twirling a skipping rope and chanting out their skipping rhyme:

*'Little fat doctor*
*How's your wife?*
*Very well thank you*
*That's all right*
*Eat a bit o' fish*
*An' a stick o' liquorice*
*O-U-T spells OUT!'*

Terry Duff and Keith Lumb came over to speak to me. They had enjoyed their recent induction visit to the comprehensive school.

'They've got proper woodwork benches, sir,' said Terry.

'An' a big gym wi' ropes an' wall bars,' said Keith.

'It's brilliant, sir, and they 'ave a proper field,' said Terry.

'Wi' grass,' added Keith with emphasis.

I smiled to hear how the wonders of the big school had

dawned on them. A new world of activities, adolescence and acne awaited them.

David Holmes was sitting with Matthew Hesketh reading Matthew's *Shoot* football magazine. David was pleased his father was no longer a threat. Ricky Holmes, according to his mother, was now in a place where he couldn't interfere with their lives.

The memory of his experience on top of Malham Cove would never leave him but, although he didn't know it then, a university career was in store for this hardworking boy.

When the bell rang my last playground duty at Heather View was over. I walked back to the entrance hall and smiled as Ronnie Atha kicked a football between our two silver birch trees and Reggie yelled, 'Goal!'

It turned out to be a quiet end to the day. After I had said goodbye to all the children in my class the staff gathered in the entrance hall. There were hugs and handshakes and Travis and Connie helped me load up my car. Penny had left quickly and Barbara and Edith were hard at work in the office. Audrey had tidied her classroom and was looking forward to a short break in Bridlington with Arnie.

'Let's meet up for a drink over the weekend,' said Connie.

'Sounds good to me,' said Travis.

'Cat & Kettle?' I said.

'Yes, Jack,' said Connie. 'You can buy me a pint.'

'Or maybe two halves.'

She gave me a dig in the ribs and then a kiss on the cheek.

Travis smiled up at her. 'You never kiss me like that.'

'You've never asked,' said Connie with a smile.

They both waved me off as I drove out of the gate.

It was after my evening meal that I spotted Penny's toothbrush in the bathroom. I stood there staring at it and made a decision. I found a clean cardboard box and began to fill it. There was evidence of Penny in every room: a hairbrush in my bedroom, a dress in the wardrobe, a discarded T-shirt hanging over a kitchen chair. I wandered through the flat collecting the assorted items, each one bringing back a memory of a day with no cares or a night of tender passion. Everything comes to an end and I knew this was such a time.

I looked down at the box's contents and reflected that love is more powerful than logic; it bends life to its will. I had walked its path until I had reached a crossroads and there were decisions to be made. So it was with a sense of sadness that I locked my front door and carried my box of memories out to the car.

I put it next to me on the passenger seat as I drove through Skipton and on to Cold Beck. There were open spaces here with scattered farmhouses and rich agricultural land. Beyond the hedgerow, fields of barley swayed with a sinuous rhythm in the gentle breeze and I wound down my window to enjoy the evening air. On the car radio Ray Stevens was singing 'Everything Is Beautiful', which seemed apt as the colours of the countryside swept by. It was getting late and, as I drove towards Penny's cottage, the sun was setting. It lit up the far horizon where the sky met the earth with a rim of golden fire.

Finally I parked in the main street and carried the box to Penny's door and placed it at my feet. On the walls of the cottage the last of the evening sun had gilded the petals of the climbing roses. I stood there in the silence of the deserted narrow lane until, finally, I knocked on the door and heard footsteps.

Suddenly Penny was standing before me in jeans and a cheesecloth shirt. 'Jack, this is a surprise.'

'I needed to speak to you.'

'Why, what's the matter?' She showed a hint of concern. 'Do you want to come in?'

'No, thanks. It's just a quick visit.'

'So what is it?'

There was a pause as we stood facing each other.

'I've given this a lot of thought. It was the fact you went to the wedding with Seb. I know you were with him over the weekend.'

She was quick to respond. 'It wasn't your scene, Jack. Anastasia is one of the country set. It's all horses and fast cars. A different world.'

'So you chose Seb instead.'

'Is that a problem for you?' Suddenly her voice was strident. 'You didn't even know the girl who was getting married.'

'Did Seb?'

'Well, no, but that's not the point.'

That moment confirmed to me she was not the woman I thought she was or hoped she would be. 'I was concerned that you felt the need to lie to me.'

Her face was suddenly ashen. 'I see.'

'You should have been open and told me the truth.'

'I suppose I knew you would react like this.'

'Perhaps I could have accepted it if you had been honest. You know how I felt about you.' I sighed and stepped back. 'So I've brought back your belongings.'

She looked down at the box. 'This seems very *final*.'

'It won't work, Penny. Seb will always be there between us. The time is right now for us to move on . . . not only in my job. It's a good thing that I'm leaving.'

'Is it?'

'We both deserve to be happy . . . but sadly it won't be together.'

'I'm sorry, Jack.'

'So am I.' I stepped back from the doorway. 'Goodnight, Penny.'

As I drove away I knew the right woman was out there somewhere. I just hadn't found her yet. I was beginning to understand the journey I was on and the man I would become.

And in a heartbeat I had moved on with my life.

# *Epilogue*

Connie Brooksbank and Travis Farthing were married in Durham in the autumn of 1972 and the following year they emigrated to Australia. Both gained teaching posts at Castle Hill High School in the northern region of Sydney. It had a headteacher that believed in high expectations, academic excellence and an emphasis on the creative and performing arts . . . very different to Norman Little at Heather View. They live there still, happily married and members of a local railway society.

Penny Armitage moved to London with Dr Sebastian Courtney in the summer of 1971. They married in the autumn and their child, Henry Peter, arrived in 1972. Sebastian had a series of affairs and they were divorced in 1975. Penny continued to live in London as a single parent and worked in a number of primary schools. She had many partners but never married again.

Barbara Priestley became acting headteacher on the departure of Norman. She was appointed as full-time head a year later and transformed the school into one of the best in Yorkshire with pastoral care second to none. New staff were appointed and benefited under her positive leadership. Barbara was matron of honour at the wedding of Audrey Clegg and Arnie Crabtree in St Peter and All Angels. The service was conducted by Piers Witherspoon.

Norman Little took early retirement with a reduced pension. He bought a property in Ireland on the east coast near Carnfunnock in County Antrim where he was a regular in the local pubs and betting shops until his premature death from lung cancer.

Eric Skinner was dismissed from his post in 1971 following the theft of cleaning materials.

Jack Sheffield thrived as deputy headteacher of Newbridge Primary School and enjoyed his new life.

He was hoping one day to meet the girl of his dreams.

**If you loved *Back to School* don't miss Jack Sheffield's wonderful new novel . . .**

## SCHOOL DAYS

**The year is 1976 and Jack Sheffield never wants to leave his job.**

Having been assistant head at Newbridge primary school for eight years now, Jack likes where he is – even if it feels like there are a few things missing from his life. After all, the kids keep him busy and there's always a game of rugby to play.

However, it's a time of change and Jack's life is no different. New and old faces appear in Jack's life and while a romance blossoms it exposes a buried secret and hidden threat. Soon, Jack must make a decision as to where his future is heading, and prepare to face whatever change is yet to come . . .

**A classic Jack Sheffield tale, ready to transport you back to a much simpler time . . .**

*Available in September 2021 . . .*

**Or see where it all began with . . .**

**TEACHER, TEACHER!**

It's 1977 and Jack Sheffield is appointed headmaster of a small village primary school in North Yorkshire. So begins Jack's eventful journey through the school year and his attempts to overcome the many problems that face him as a young and inexperienced headmaster.

The many colourful chapters include Ruby the 20-stone caretaker with an acute spelling problem, a secretary who worships Margaret Thatcher, a villager who grows giant carrots, a barmaid/parent who requests sex lessons, and a five-year-old boy whose language is colourful in the extreme. And then there's also beautiful, bright Beth Henderson, who is irresistibly attractive to the young headmaster . . .

**Or discover a fan favourite in . . .**

## PLEASE SIR!

It's 1981, the time of Adam and the Ants, Rubik's Cube, the Sony Walkman and the Falklands War, as headteacher Jack Sheffield returns to Ragley-on-the-Forest School for another rollercoaster year.

Vera, the ever-efficient school secretary, has to grapple with a new-fangled computer – and enjoys a royal occasion – while Ruby the caretaker rediscovers romance with a Butlin's Redcoat. And for Jack, wedding bells are in the air. But the unexpected is just round the corner . . .

**Or venture further back in time with . . .**

## STARTING OVER
## Ragley, 1952.

Lily has just arrived, ready to begin her first year as a teacher at the village school. There to welcome her is John Pruett, who, after his years in the war, has settled into the role of headmaster. Tom, the local bobby, is also on hand to make her feel at home up north. But Lily has a secret lurking in her past that threatens the new life she's trying to build.

**Can she move forward and begin to love again?**

In this novel, Jack Sheffield invites you to travel back in time. Back to the days when owning a television made you the envy of the neighbours, Woolworth's still had pride of place on the high street and the village panto was the height of entertainment.

*Available now . . .*